Honey Creek Treasure Hunt
By Dana Mentink

Copyright © 2021 Dana Mentink
Published by: Winged Publications

This book is a work of fiction. Names, characters, places, and incidents are the product of the author's imagination and are used fictitiously. Any resemblance to actual events, locales, or persons, living or dead, is coincidental.

No part of this book may be copied or distributed without the author's consent.

All rights reserved.

ISBN: 979-8-8690-3652-0

"One road leads home and a thousand roads lead into the wilderness."- C.S Lewis

Chapter One

A five-letter word for country living.

Alexi Quinn could normally come up with a dozen possibilities without taxing a neural synapse, but at the present moment, the only word he could come up with was c-r-a-z-y. There could be no other plausible explanation as to why he was driving down a country road in Honey Creek in the heart of California's Gold Country. It was 1979 for goodness sake, but he wouldn't have been surprised to see a covered wagon creaking by. Sizzling temperatures, roads that barely qualified as paved, and deafening quiet. He turned on the radio but the only static-free station played songs exclusively from a group called The Bee Gees. He did not see how it was possible for grown men to sing at such an octave. The only other choice was the news, but he had already endured six-plus hours of commentary about the Ayatollah Khomeini's trouncing of the Shah and his tidy assumption of power three months before. Alexi did not, in fact, care much, except that the men at the last two diners he'd visited were certain that the Ayatollah was directly responsible for the price of their recently pumped gas.

Mopping his brow with a folded handkerchief, he scanned the sleepy hamlet that unrolled before him in excruciating slow motion.

Acres of brittle, golden grasses edged the town, licking at an August sky so blue it hurt to look at it. It did not seem possible that it was the same sky that framed New York City.

A horse, cropping grass through a split rail fence, flicked his tail as Alexi motored on, probably curious as to why someone was entering the town instead of exiting.

He could not fully explain it himself, but there he was, driving into Honey Creek in a Sherman Tank of a station wagon with no shocks to speak of, that sucked down the precious gas to the tune of eighty-six cents a gallon. His driving skills were rusty which might factor into the roughness of the ride.

Sweating, thanks to a malfunctioning air conditioner, he waited precisely twelve minutes for a flock of wild turkeys to clear the road. Their feathers seemed to him to be in disarray, fleshy wattles slinging grotesquely. The turkeys were hostile like all fowl. One had pecked his driver's side door and more than likely left a scratch.

C-r-a-z-y.

Alexi wished he could straighten out his six-foot-three frame, but a dent in the vehicle's roof necessitated a slouch. He took in the surroundings as best he could, ignoring the kink in his neck.

It was as if he'd stepped from the nineteen seventies, a land of noise, convenience, progress, back a couple of decades into an era where people, he tried hard not to outright stare, actually sat on bona fide porch swings. Though there was no visible basket of peas in the swinging lady's hands as he passed her white-painted house, he felt certain there must be a supply in the kitchen waiting for shucking. Or was it husking? Shelling? He made a mental note to research the proper terminology. The porch swinger nodded at him, a smile livening up her tanned face.

He nodded back. Through his open window, he could hear the tinny music from her radio. The squeak of her porch swing melded with the staccato rhythm of a gospel tune as he drove on.

Honey Creek unfurled in all its dubious historic splendor, a blur of red brick and bleached wood, bits of some cottony plant billowing through the air on puffs of wind. It might have been the scalded gold grass that made his eyes water, or perhaps he was allergic to the smell of aging wood and mildewing brick of the buildings that seemed to have a decided lean. He sneezed twice and idled at the sun-drenched corner of Main Street and Nugget Road, reading from the flaking sign.

Welcome to Honey Creek, Population 432. Germ of the southern mines.

It took him a few moments to process the added 'r' in the word gem, probably courtesy of some bored teenager. Boredom must be a constant threat in this forgotten corner of the world. Old buildings flanked the intersection on either side, casting long shadows across the cracked asphalt. At this particular intersection, the offerings were slim: Al's Mercantile, a gas station with two pumps, The Gold Pan Cafe which looked to be some sort of eatery circa 1950, and a hardware store offering up a mannequin dressed as a forty-niner, panning in a river made of rolls of blue painter's tape. Two men stood watching an afternoon program on the hardware store TV which flashed back to a tired-looking President Jimmy Carter. Alexi figured Mr. Carter might be more at home in a town like Honey Creek than Washington, taking into consideration his roots as a peanut farmer.

His stomach grumbled since it was used to being filled at precisely eleven-thirty and it was now close to one o'clock. Should he stop somewhere and collect rations for his stay? How badly did he need groceries? There had to be something in the cupboards where he was headed. A thin, bird-like woman with her black hair caught tight in a bun, stepped out the front door of the Gold Pan clutching a broom. She offered a wave, the kind he figured meant 'hello and welcome' instead of 'lookout you're going to back into a trash can.' It had taken him a while to discern that there are many types of waves. People in New York City used a wide arsenal of hand gestures, but waving was not high on the list.

Since his window was down, there was not even a thin barrier of glass to prevent her from strolling over and striking up a conversation. The fingers of his good hand tightened on the wheel and he gulped. With a quick nod and a forced smile, since he was not an accomplished waver, he rumbled on down the road.

"What is a ten-letter way to describe someone unwilling or unable to associate in an amicable way with other people?" his conscience inquired.

Antisocial.
Unfriendly.
Alexi Quinn.

The thought made him squirm. He tried to remember when he'd willingly last done something in the company of others. Well, perhaps playing for thousands of people wasn't the normal method of social interaction but it involved being in the same room with a crowd didn't it? And long ago he'd spoken right into the microphone, looking out over the heads of the audience, but still speaking more or less in their general direction. It was not chatting, but it was social.

So why was it a chore to say hello to one friendly Honey Creeker? His social muscles had atrophied along with those of his hand, aged beyond his twenty-nine years. Discomfort licked at his insides.

"I will go back tomorrow," he promised himself. "And eat something in the cafe. And speak. To people."

His damp shirt stuck to the seat back as the lady and her friendly wave vanished in the rear-view mirror.

The next wave he encountered was more of a frantic 'stop the vehicle' kind of gesture. It happened just after he coaxed his grumbly car up a sloped road that shimmered in the heat and rounded a blind bend with a sign that said, "Slow horse crossing." He could believe in Honey Creek even the horses were slow, along with everything else.

Smiling at his little joke, he jerked as a slender woman with a short crown of hair the same color as the burnished hillside stepped directly into the road, blue-jeaned legs churning to a stop right in front of his left front fender. He hit the brakes. Hard.

"What are you doing?" he called out the window. "I might have run you down."

She flipped the bangs from her green eyes with a bob of her head. "You might?"

"No...yes." He pushed a hand through his dark thatch of damp hair. "Well, I meant I might have struck you by accident."

Her smile was impish. "It would have been pretty unneighborly to do it on purpose."

Two facts simultaneously juggled for attention in his mind. First off, her face was exquisite, even in its slightly sweaty state with a streak of dirt smeared across her left cheek. The streak vanished under the messy chop of hair which a dangling silver barrette failed to hold in place. The spangle of freckles, a dimple on one side of the mouth, green eyes framed in thick lashes. Her appearance triggered the second fact in his gut, there was something undeniably familiar about her.

"I would not have..." He trailed off when her eyes rounded at something on the side of the road.

"There he is. Come on." She tore off across the road and

down the grassy hill on the other side, leaving him staring, eyes still watering.

The situation was unexpected and impractical. He did not know her, except for the odd sensation that he'd seen her before. He did not wish to know her, nor anyone else in Honey Creek. The landscape caught in his windshield was right out of a Western, the kind where people encountered rattlesnakes and hillbillies with shotguns.

Not practical.

Worse, the scenario would result in social interaction. Again, not optimal.

"I am not...I mean, it is not a good idea for me to participate, ma'am, um, madam," he called out the window.

He counted a full thirty seconds, hearing nothing but the rustle of grass and some sort of insectoid trilling.

A fellow Honey Creeker would be off like a shot to assist, he figured. Country people were like that, he'd heard from his friend Denny, not like big city dwellers who might possibly use a person as a leg up if they happen to drop unconscious on the subway platform. He looked around for any passersby. Nothing came his way except a bird dipping along under the tree line. Not one helpful resident sauntering along this country lane? The place was rank with quiet.

"I will not be coming," he called again. "I am not acclimated to rural conditions. And I'm from New York City, so there is that."

Sweat slicked his face now and his insides twisted. What if the lady with the golden hair was chasing a lost child who would fall into an unused well and die of fright before she got him out? And all because Alexi had not gone to help, whipping off his belt to haul the kid out. How would he live with that?

But the potential for insects, snakes and... talking.

After a moment more of paralyzed indecision, he pulled

the station wagon to the side of the road and got out.

It did not occur to him until precisely forty-six steps later that he was not even wearing a belt.

***

Alexi imagined the army of blood-sucking ticks that were salivating at the sight of his ankles plowing through the grass. There had been no choice but to strip off his socks earlier that morning when a child in the Frosty Fill in some town or another lost his grip on the 65-ounce electric blue fizzy drink and dropped it within six inches from Alexi's leather loafers.

The boy cried. The mom looked like she would like to cry, and Quinn had resisted the urge to howl, instead, backing away with polite assurances that, blue socks notwithstanding, the whole mess was merely a slight inconvenience.

Because he abhorred the thought of putting his soiled ankles into his neatly packed second set of socks and loafers, his feet were now sliding around in his shower shoes. A grown man with blue ankles and shower shoes chasing a stranger deep into no man's land.

The golden-haired lady made good speed, and he hopped awkwardly over tall mounds of grass as they headed into the wild country. Dry stalks scratched at his shins. Ticks, members of the order Parasitiformes, he remembered, had an affinity for tall grass.

"Down here," she called, breaking into a sprint and disappearing over a rocky ridge.

"Should we stay alert for rattlesnakes?"

She did not appear concerned about reptilian ambush. Comforting. Surely Honey Creekians knew more about local reptiles than he did, though he had created a crossword puzzle solely about tetrapods three weeks prior as a sort of audition for the role he'd taken with the Mountain Holler newspaper. Pushing the nerves aside, he scrambled down a slope and found himself at the edge of a creek, no more than a trickle of water coursing along a rocky bed.

She'd skidded to a stop. "You're absolutely the naughtiest thing ever."

Was she speaking to him? He watched in confusion as she leaned forward and snatched a goodish-sized white duck out of the water and tucked it under her arm. None of it made sense to Alexi.

Unexpected? Check. Ridiculous? Check. Yet there she was, the exquisite woman, smoothing the white feathers as the duck gabbled his or her disgruntlement. "You are...chasing a duck?"

She grinned. "Of course. What did you think I was chasing?"

He decided not to tell her about his boy-in-the-well theory. "Might have been anything."

"Just Lovely." She patted the fowl.

"Lovely? That is an unusual name for a duck."

"Named after Jim Lovell..."

"Commander of the Apollo 13 mission, yes," he finished.

She smiled. "Lovely flew into our yard eight years ago, just as the Apollo 13 blasted off, so what else could we possibly name him?" Her eyes twinkled as they locked on his.

Why was he talking about naming ducks in sweltering heat with a woman in the middle of nowhere?

Unable to find an answer, he closed his mouth and stared.

Chapter Two

Lucy looked him over carefully, this newcomer. There was something disconnected about him, though it took her a second look to decide what was odd. The top of him looked very well put together with a neat button-up short-sleeved shirt in a shade of blue that tried to coax some color from his serious grey eyes. Formal for a town like Honey Creek, unless he was a salesman, or running for office or something. The pants were formal too, khakis with sharp creases all the way down to the knee. It was somewhere around the patellas when things started to go wrong. The khakis were bunched at the bottom.

"Your pants have blue splotches on them," she said. "Your ankles, too."

"Yes."

It was probably rude of her to point this out, but Lucy did not often slow the things that tumbled from her mouth. Her older brother Kelby would have elbowed her at such a moment.

"It was a Super Gulp accident," Alexi said.

"Oh." That brought her up short. "Do you drink Super Gulps?"

"No."

"I love them. Especially the red kind that turns your teeth pink."

He remained silent, a trickle of sweat ribboning down his

temple.

That seemed to be the end of things. The duck wriggled his behind in vigorous disapproval, loosing a white feather into the air, but she clamped him tight. "I'm Lucy Winston. You've met Lovely. He's taken to escaping."

"From your yard?"

"No. The hotel."

"You keep ducks in the hotel?"

"Only this one. I think he's been upset by the earthquakes. We've had a mess of them lately, earthquakes, not ducks. Nice to meet you, by the way."

She reached out for a shake but got only the tip of his left-hand when he jerked his palm away from hers at the last minute. His fingers were twisted up, clenched, like coiled rope.

He withdrew them and clasped his hands behind his back. "I'm Alexi Quinn. I am new. I am a new resident. Temporary resident."

She thought he stopped and restarted like the old lawn mower her brother used to keep the weeds down at the hotel.

He continued. "I am staying in a trailer. It is my friend's. A colleague, to be more precise. Just for a while. I mean, I will live there just for a while."

Lovely flapped peevishly. "Hold your flippered feet still, duck," she said.

"Palmate."

"Come again?"

"Palmate, an eight-letter word meaning the three toes are completely webbed, enabling efficient propulsion through the water."

"Do you know a lot about ducks?"

"No, but I know a lot about words." He sighed and shook his head. "I see that you have secured your duck so I will be going."

"How about a ride?"

He started. "In my car?"

She laughed. "Yes, unless you've got a jet plane around here somewhere."

He stared, eyes shifting in thought from the duck to the patch on the knee of her jeans and back to Lovely.

"It's okay if you don't want to," she said, though she didn't, in fact, think it would be okay in the slightest. Lovely would take off for the creek again the moment she put him down, and he would in no way cooperate if she tried to hold onto him for the mile walk back into town.

He was stopping and starting again. "I... I suppose it would be neighborly to give you a lift."

"Yes, it would. The Lady Quail is only a mile from here. It would be..." She thought a minute and smiled. "What's an eight-letter word for someone who is friendly and cooperative?"

"Obliging," he said, without hesitation.

"Yes." She giggled and patted him on the shoulder, finding his muscles taut and unyielding like the rest of him appeared to be. "I like words, too. Obliging wasn't as good as palmate, though. I promise I won't let him poop in your car." She thought Alexi blanched a bit.

"Ah. Well, that is important, the no pooping clause," he said. One more moment of thought. "Yes. I will drive you back to the Lady Quail."

"Thank you." They swished their way back through the tall grass, him hopping along as though he was trying to avoid land mines. He stepped in front and wrenched opened the passenger side door for her. It let loose with a metallic groan.

"How polite," she said as she scooted in.

"I have good manners."

It was more a statement of fact than a boast. He took his

seat behind the wheel and she gave him directions back to the Lady Quail. He drove tentatively as if he expected someone to dart out in front of him at any moment like she had done.

She waved to Ida as they passed her small cottage with the row of garden gnomes standing guard in the flower bed. The dented watering can splashed out a stream as she waved back.

"She loves her garden gnomes."

"Gnomes were created in the mid-1800s by a sculptor in Germany."

"I doubt Ida knows that." Lucy would have rolled down the window to chat, but Alexi wasn't slowing enough and Lovely might take it as an invitation to flap his way out the window.

"No peas." Alex's brow furrowed as he peered into the rear-view mirror.

"What?" she said.

"I thought there might be people shucking peas here."

"Ida's more into flowers than vegetables. She's won the county fair blue ribbon twice for her peonies. They're practically the size of dinner plates." She glanced at Alexi.

"Not everyone sits on their porches and shells peas in Honey Creek, you know. Where are you from?"

"New York City."

An odd expression drifted over her face. "No front porch pea shellers there."

"I have never seen any."

"I didn't either, though they've got neighborhoods with stoops which are kinda the same thing. Front porches are one of the big blessings in life. I left Honey Creek for a while and I missed them like crazy. Why don't you come over and sit on mine? I'm not a big pea sheller, but we can drink lemonade."

He shot her a worried look and then cemented his gaze out the windshield again. The muscles in his throat convulsed as he struggled to answer.

"Of course," he finally said weakly, though his face screamed, "*not on your life*."

Had he thought she'd intended something more than a simple friendly chat? What a puzzle, was Alexi Quinn.

When they pulled up at the curb of The Lady Quail, she gathered Lovely, who was doing his best to slink down onto the floor and grub for nonexistent crumbs. Alexi came around and opened the door for her.

"You do have good manners," she said.

His cheeks reddened. "Thank you."

She struggled to both hold the duck and open the gate that surrounded the overgrown gardens of the historic hotel. Alexi pushed the gate ajar with his foot.

Shower shoes, she thought, smothering a smile.

Alexi shaded his eyes to get a look at the once stately three-story building with the peeling paint and the roof which was in sore need of repair. The corner window on the lower level was open to allow in the summer breeze, all the others shuttered and dark. His nose wrinkled with distaste or confusion. She did not know which.

"The Lady Quail's been in the family for generations," she said, doing her best tour guide impression. "It was originally built in 1851 by my great great grandparents. They made a killing off the gold miners and never even stuck a pan in the creek. Smart, huh? Entrepreneurism at its finest."

He continued to stare. "Is the hotel in operation?"

"Sort of. There's only two rooms in use at this very moment."

"One is for the duck?"

She laughed. "Good one."

He did not appear to know he had been funny.

"No," she added. "The duck lives outside, mostly, unless he manages to scoot into the kitchen when we're not looking or escape the yard." She finally opened the gate and let Lovely into the overgrown space. He promptly waddled by the mounds of climbing shrubbery, past the rusted garden sculpture, to the edge of the greenish pond, and launched himself into the water.

"Hellllllpp," a voice shouted. Alexi froze.

"That's Uncle Paul," Lucy cried. Clanging the gate closed behind them, she darted across the narrow street and burst through the front door into the Angel of Hope Church. A pair of feet in white sneakers scrabbled above her from the rafters, the denim-clad legs bicycling in the air.

"Lucy?" her Uncle Paul called out. "Thank God. I've lost the ladder." He gripped the rough beam with wiry arms.

"Hold on." She ran for the fallen ladder, struggling against the heavy weight of it. Alexi, whom she hadn't seen follow her in, grabbed the other end with his good hand and pincered it against his body. Together they hoisted the ladder until the wriggling feet found purchase and Paul climbed down.

She grabbed the barrel of a man into a hug, straining on tiptoes to brush away the cobwebs that stuck to his head, bald except for a fringe of red hair.

"That was close, Uncle Paul."

He wiped a hand across his eyes. "I'll say. I was trying to check on our angel, what with all these earthquakes, she's begun to creak a bit. I kicked the ladder clean over."

He extended a palm to Alexi. "Paul Winston. I claim the title of Lucy's uncle, though actually, I'm her second cousin or some such relation. I'm the pastor here. Don't usually greet guests while dangling from the ceiling. Thank you for your help. You really came through in the clutch."

Alexi waved awkwardly instead of taking the pastor's

hand. "You are welcome. I mean for the help." He frowned, looking at the angel statue perched on the apex of the ceiling above the tiny wooden podium. "That is an angel?"

"I know she doesn't look like your typical heavenly messenger," Paul said, "but she's been in Honey Creek since before anyone can remember. I'm told the miners used to come and touch her elbow to bless their efforts at finding gold, but that may be more tall tale than fact."

Lucy did not agree. The angel's left elbow was the only spot of shine anywhere on the old plaster figure, the rest having been discolored over time to the tint of weak tea. She tried to look at the statue with fresh eyes. Hope, as they called her, was in a sitting position with one hand tucked contemplatively under her chin. Her expression was perhaps a shade more mournful than serene, the staining on her face giving her the appearance of tears. Lucy respected an angel who had a couple of miles on her, not some perfect marble entity who hadn't got up close and personal with the dirt. Life was messy. Oh, how well she knew it.

"Can I get you a cup of coffee at least and ask you to sit a spell?" Paul asked Alexi. "You look all in."

Alexi did, too, Uncle Paul was right. Alexi's face was pale.

"I uh, no, no thank you. Perhaps I will return when I am properly dressed for church." He waved vaguely at his blue ankles.

"Don't hafta worry about that, son. God put you on this earth naked as a jaybird. He doesn't care how you're suited up." Paul's thick eyebrows drew together. "Only thing we can't stomach here is a Dodger fan. You aren't one of those, are you?"

"Uncle Paul," Lucy chided.

Alexi was now completely befuddled.

"He's joking, of course," Lucy said quickly. "Mostly.

Uncle Paul was a minor league pitcher for San Francisco back in the day."

Paul sighed. "Had to give up watching baseball, on account of I turn into a sinner of the worst kind when I tune in, but I allow myself to read the coverage in the Mountain Holler. You a baseball guy, Alexi?"

"No."

Her uncle's face registered surprise as it always did at the possibility that any human being anywhere could conceivably not be a baseball fanatic. Typically, within the first few minutes of meeting someone, Paul had sniffed out their sports affiliation like a bloodhound tracking a fugitive.

Lucy repressed a smile at the look of distress that crossed Alexi's face. "He's staying in Denny's trailer for a while," she said.

Alexi started. "How did you know?"

"It's the only trailer around here empty and fit for habitation," Paul said with a hearty chuckle, "and in Honey Creek, everyone knows everything. We heard Denny was expecting a houseguest, so to speak."

Fran Trawler swept in holding a limp robe draped over her arm. Lucy noted Uncle Paul's long-suffering exhalation as Fran waved the robe. "Do you see this?" Her brown hair clung in swirls around her thin face, the polyester skirt and blouse glaringly unwrinkled compared to Paul and Lucy's mild dishevelment. "We can't expect the choir to stand up in the house of the Lord and wear robes that look like this."

Uncle Paul peered dutifully over the top of his glasses at the limp garment. "It's...eye-catching."

"It's the color of old rubber erasers and now we are not only trying to pass off secondhand graduation robes as choir robes, but we'll look like a row of gums without teeth. We need to purchase some respectable robes, Pastor Paul, and I mean it. No more putting it off."

Lucy clamped her teeth together to keep her words inside where they would not "set gasoline to the kindling" as Uncle Paul would have said. Fran reminded Lucy of a keen-eyed bird, always picking, pecking, squawking.

Paul sighed and punched one hand into the palm of the other. "It isn't as though I wouldn't like you all to have the robes, Fran, but there just isn't enough in the offering basket to go around. Had to gas up the church van to take Percy to visit his mum and man, well, at near eighty-six cents a gallon, you know…"

"And the Angel," Lucy pitched in helpfully. "She desperately needs repair."

Fran snorted. "She always needs repair. There's no amount of spackle and rebar that's going to save that sad sack angel." Fran finally noticed Alexi. "What do you think?" she asked, thrusting out the robe for his examination. "Aren't these the most horrible-looking things you've ever seen?"

Alexi opened his mouth to respond when the floor began to shudder. The candlesticks chattered on the altar and toppled over. A single sheet of music from atop the organ took flight.

"Take cover," Paul shouted. "Earthquake."

Lucy scrambled under the nearest pew, listening to the creaking of the little wooden church as it flexed and groaned with the movement of the earth. The floor under her palms rolled and rippled as if it were made of rubber instead of old tile. An ominous rumbling started up and filled the tiny space. Another tremblor, she told herself, nothing more than the lower end of the Richter Scale. Just when she began to feel the first swell of true panic, that maybe the "big one" all Californians feared had come at last, the shuddering ebbed away, and the rumbled turned into a whisper. When the shaking stopped completely, she climbed out to find Fran in the doorway, still clutching the robe, and Uncle Paul unfolding himself from under the communion table.

"Well, that wasn't such a bad one," he said as he bent to brush himself free of dust. "Don't you worry about these little quakes, Alexi. Last year we had a shaker that knocked over the folding table where the pies were all laid out for the Thanksgiving dinner. Pumpkin and whipped cream everywhere. Kids hope for a replay of that every year. Really there's nothing to..."

She realized her uncle had stopped talking because Alexi was gone. They went to the door in time to see him speeding away in his beat-up station wagon.

"How about that?" Fran said. "He didn't even say goodbye."

"Maybe the earthquake upset him," Lucy said. Or the duck in his car, or the festering robes. It seemed as though anything at all might have upset the odd Mr. Quinn.

"That probably didn't even make a 4.0," Fran said. "What's the big deal?"

From behind them came a groan of nails ripping free from wood as the Hope Angel tore loose from the ceiling and fell to the floor with a shuddering crash. Her head snapped loose and rolled until it came to rest under the first-row pew.

HONEY CREEK TREASURE HUNT

Chapter Three

Trooper picked at the mosquito bite under the brim of his battered straw hat, watching the kid sitting behind the wheel of Denny's old station wagon. Maybe he wasn't a kid exactly, but once Trooper hit fifty-five years and change, he began to think of everyone as a kid. He'd gotten a glimpse of the station wagon from his perch on his treehouse and strolled over to offer the promised assistance. Denny was mostly absent and since they were fishing buddies and sworn to secrecy about the location of the best fishing hole in the entire region, Trooper lent a hand when he could. Trooper's dog, Gummy, an eighty-pound Labrador something or other mix, had settled himself to laze in the shade of the rusted trailer, one paw twitching idly.

This stranger was staring at the trailer as if it had just crash-landed from another planet. He was tall, dark-haired, slightly hunched over where his head skimmed the car roof. He didn't seem to be in a hurry to unload himself from the vehicle. Normally Trooper was content with inactivity, but he had laundry simmering on his camp stove and he didn't want to leave it too long. Time or two ago he'd set off a wildfire with a kettle of fish stew and what a hullaballoo that had caused, a sensation to rival when Stevie Raymond won a free Disneyland ticket on the radio. He couldn't imagine paying $7.00 for a ticket to any newfangled park unless it came with a dozen hot dogs and a few bottles of cold pop.

Bunch of babies in Honey Creek, the smallest thing could tangle them right up.

He gave it another two minutes and then he sauntered to the station wagon, rapping once on the driver's side window. Entertaining, the way the kid jumped and thwacked his head on the sun visor. The guy stared at him through the window which was open a few inches.

"Hiya. Name's Trooper. Denny's my friend. He told me he was gonna loan out his trailer for a while."

The man did some more staring, wide eyed, and Trooper now saw that he was probably in his very late twenties and likely not an English speaker. His look was more glazed than a donut from Steffie's, the twenty-five-cent variety that she sold as 'day old treasures.' He thought about flashing a smile to comfort the guy, but Fran had once remarked that his smile was more terrifying than his scowl, a sure sign that she was warming to him, he figured.

He went with a brief nod and tried again, louder. Slowly. Pointing to his chest he spoke into the crack, "Folks call me Trooper. Denny is my friend. He said to look out for you." He tapped a calloused finger to the glass on the last word for emphasis.

Incrementally, the stranger's look changed from bewilderment to the barest hint of understanding.

"I am Alexi Quinn," he said through the crack in the glass.

Huh. Guy was an English speaker after all. "Yeah, I figured. Denny said you were fixin' to come stay in his trailer."

Silence unrolled between them like a stretch of bad road. Trooper, picturing his simmering laundry, broke the silence a second time.

"You gonna get out and let me tell you the particulars or what? I got things to do."

Alexi seemed to consider that.

To speed things along, Trooper fished a key from his pocket. "Normally Denny don't lock it, but he figured you'd want a key, being as how you're from New York City."

Key. New York City. Some words must have penetrated because Alexi stepped out of the car, a good foot taller than Trooper, a posture West Point would espouse.

"You're a tall glass of water."

Alexi frowned. "I am...tall, yes."

Gummy looked up and barked twice, which sent the kid to jumping again.

"That's Gummy. He don't hurt anyone ever except Pearl and Bee's cats in which he sees demons that need exorcising. For some reason, Gummy can't stomach them."

Alexi's grey eyes scanned the portly dog. "Why do you call him Gummy?"

"Missing some bottom teeth. Busted them out eating Meg Piper's siding when she tried to keep him after some family dumped him in the woods on their way through town."

Alexi looked aghast. "Siding?"

"Aww, it's okay. He lives with me now in the woods so's there's no trouble with him eating anything of importance. Sticks and rubber tires if he can get hold of them, once a construction cone, but nothing major."

Alexi stared, mouth open a slice, seemingly struck dumb.

Trooper figured further conversation was going to be a waste of time. He marched to the door and flung it open. Alexi hauled a small box from the back seat of the station wagon and followed. "Small enough place you don't need a tour. Bedroom, bathroom, kitchenette, living room. Propane and electrical's all hooked up..." Trooper stopped as he took in the upright piano occupying the entire side of the living room where the two easy chairs had been. "What in the green goodness did Denny go and jam a piano in here for?" He glanced at Alexi who looked stricken.

"You play, Quinn?"

"I..." There was a mountain of yearning in that expression, yearning for something long ago lost. Trooper had seen that look in his own mirror when he forced himself to look. Now he had no mirror at his current digs which was fine and dandy.

"No," Alexi said, clamping his lips together. "I do not play." It was then that Trooper noticed the shriveled hand.

Something lost indeed, Trooper thought. "Huh. Well, I guess you can set your stuff on it. Anyway, if something important comes up, just ask around for Trooper."

"Can I have your phone number in case anything requires maintenance?"

"First, I don't have a phone and second, it's not my job to fix things around here."

"Oh."

"If you need something, I'll make sure Denny gets the message. You're his tenant, not mine."

Alexi and Trooper did an awkward dance as Trooper squeezed around him in a hurry to get back out the front door. How could anyone live in such tight quarters, with a piano thrown in to top it all off? Trooper wiped sweat from his brow. As he barreled by, he noticed the titles of the books that Alexi had deposited on the kitchen table.

Essentials of Music Theory

Post Injury Rehabilitation

The Physiology of the Hand

Alexi still stood there, gaze flicking between the piano, the box he was carrying, the tiny kitchen.

Alexi was definitely a guy who needed some relaxing. He should be stretched out long and lean and left outside to bake all the tension out of him, like he'd seen the snakes do while they let the sun bring them back to life. *Not your business, Trooper. What do you know about bringing people back to life?* With that thought stinging his insides, he pushed out onto the porch.

Alexi offered another stammered thank you, shut and locked the door behind Trooper.

Trooper wondered if there could ever be enough sunshine in Honey Creek to untwist all the tangles in Alexi Quinn.

***

Alexi would have been content to hole up in his trailer for several days, sneaking out only when there was no further fear of earthquakes, or running into Trooper, or the woman with the choir robes, or any species of duck. Unfortunately, Denny's cupboards contained only a box of matches and a container of peanut butter which Alexi abhorred. He'd met his deadline for the Mountain Holler twelve hours prior instead of sleeping, clacking away without a single mistake on the typewriter he'd brought, and now, at eight thirty-two a.m. he was ravenous. Easing by the piano, careful not to touch it, he loaded the papers into his briefcase, fired the station wagon to life, and drove to town.

The door of the Gold Pan Cafe was open to catch the cool morning breeze. Alexi braced himself for social interaction, straightened his spine, and stepped in. His senses were dizzied in a wash of white paneling, black and white checkerboard floor, red booths, and stools snuggled up to an old-fashioned counter. He should have foregone the sports jacket, judging from the casual attire of the diners,

The dark-haired lady he'd avoided earlier greeted him with a smile. Her nametag read 'Meg' undoubtedly the Meg Piper of the Gummy and the siding story.

"Morning. You must be the newcomer to town. Welcome to Honey Creek."

He was relieved she did not try to shake his hand. "Thank you."

"I hear you're working for the Mountain Holler. Are you a new reporter?"

"No." He cleared his throat, cheeks hot. For the hundredth time, he wished he was able to lie convincingly. "I write the crossword puzzles."

Her black eyes widened to saucers. "Really? Well, that's my favorite part of the whole darn newspaper. Trudy," she called to a tall, skinny teen in bunchy overalls, shoving napkins into a dispenser. "This gentleman writes the crossword puzzles in the paper."

The teen lifted a shoulder and offered a lukewarm smile.

Meg shook her head. "Kids aren't impressed by much these days, especially seventeen-year-olds."

Alexi didn't reply. He knew less about teen girls than he did about lying. "I have come for breakfast."

"That right?" She laughed, showing a chipped front tooth. "Then you've chosen the perfect place." She ushered him to a booth, and he passed several men in baseball hats with their hands wrapped around thick mugs. They nodded. He bobbed his head in response, finding himself liking this Honey Creek method of silent greeting. Another booth held a quartet of spotty-faced boys with bushy heads of long hair, shooting each other with straw wrappers.

She put a plastic-coated menu in front of him before bustling off. While she wasn't looking, he skimmed the tabletop with a stray napkin, rubbing at a spot that turned out to be indelibly tattooed into the Formica surface.

"Coffee?" Trudy said, sliding up to the table.

He pulled his cup from his pocket and set it on the table. "Yes, please."

She cocked her head, dark hair held back by an assortment of mismatched barrettes and elastics. Her thick fringe of eyelashes was enhanced by mascara that clumped a bit on the lower lids and a smear of something glossy on her lips that smelled of cherries. "You brought your own mug?"

He nodded.

"And your own silverware, too?" she asked, pointing to the utensils protruding from his breast pocket.

"Yes."

"Ummm, okay," she said, filling his cup.

"I would like two eggs, scrambled, and a bowl of oatmeal without any raisins."

She raised a delicate eyebrow. "Coffee, eggs, and oatmeal."

"No raisins," he repeated. He did not trust anything that started out as one thing and morphed into something completely different.

"I don't like raisins either. They look like rabbit poops."

He did not know what to say to that, so he said nothing.

"You don't even want to look at the menu?"

"No, thank you."

He heard the boys snickering, darting glances in their direction.

Blocking their view with her back, she reached over and slid the utensils from his pocket, setting them on a clean napkin on the table.

"Eggs and oatmeal, coming right up," she said, brightly, and he noticed she was wearing several strings of plastic beads. *So many baubles on one small frame,* but he suspected she had done him a kindness, giving the boys less to stare at.

They'll always stare, he wanted to say, *they always have.* Something about her made him think she already knew that.

Trudy headed towards the kitchen.

He busied himself thinking about a crossword puzzle theme, perhaps breakfast foods.

Five letters. A breakfast meat product prepared from pork and typically cured.

Bacon.

Eight letters. A state of extreme hunger.

Famished.

Ten letters. Food or drink regarded as a source of nourishment.

Sustenance.

But, his brain insisted, there was the adjectival form of the verb sustain, to strengthen or support physically or mentally, which had nothing to do with eating. Music had been that type of sustenance for him once, the withdrawal of it leaving him undernourished, starving, endlessly hungering for food that he could never eat again. Oh, but he could see and hear and crave it, which was the torture of the thing. Like Tantalus, forever reaching for fruit he could not pick and water that would recede before his parched tongue.

Meg interrupted his thoughts when she delivered his eggs and oatmeal and refilled his coffee. "Trudy had to catch the bus to summer school. I'm short a helper today so sorry for the wait. Say," she said, fixing wide eyes on his. "How would you like to do me a favor, Mr. Quinn?"

How? Perhaps the question was rhetorical. He stalled. "Uh, you may call me Alexi, if you wish."

"Alexi?"

She seemed to be waiting for a reply. He gulped some coffee and stared at her.

"I need to deliver breakfast to the Lady Quail, and I don't have any hands to spare. Would you be able to drop it over when you're done?"

"Drop what?"

"Breakfast."

"Isn't it a hotel?"

"Yes."

"And they do not give the guests breakfast?"
"Well, um, it's not your typical hotel."
Mysterious.
"Hey, Meg," one of the men called. "Can I settle up? We're pouring concrete today and I can't be late."
"Be right there," she called back. Alexi hoped she'd forget about her favor, but the black eyes skewered him once again.
"So, about that favor. Can you do it for me? Your breakfast will be on me. Alexi, didn't you say?"
"Yes."
The crow's feet under her eyes deepened when she smiled. "Great."
By the time he'd rallied a response, she was tending to the concrete man, so he ate, enjoying the perfectly cooked scrambled eggs and oatmeal which, although a bit too runny, was adequate. Eating gave him time to consider the oddity of a hotel that did not provide food for the guests. He'd finished his meal when she brought him a foil-wrapped plate.
"Only one breakfast?" he said.
"There's only one official guest."
He stared. Lucy had told him as much, but he assumed more would be checking in. "How can a hotel only have one guest?"
Her eyes rolled in thought as if no one had ever asked her the question before. "Ummm, it's complicated. I've got to scoot. Thank you, Mr. Quinn."
"Alexi," he said again. He wiped his utensils, dried his coffee cup with a napkin, and scooped up the foil pan.
One breakfast for a single guest.
He hoped he might spot Lucy Winston at the hotel because it was driving him mad as to why she looked so familiar. But maybe the crazy town of Honey Creek was tricking his senses, toying with his mind.

Head down to avoid any eye contact with the diners, he marched silently out the door.

Chapter Four

"It will run you a thousand dollars, easy," Kelby said, hooking his thumbs through the belt loops of his jeans, peering at the angel lying like a concrete corpse on the church floor.

Lucy stared at her younger brother. "You have to be joking. A thousand dollars just to fix the angel?"

Uncle Paul scrubbed a hand over his bald head as if he was rubbing up a new baseball. "I was afraid it'd be something like that."

"The angel's not the problem." Kelby rolled a shoulder, a clue that his rotator cuff was acting up again and confirmation that he persisted in his stubborn refusal to see a doctor. Vietnam left him with a damaged shoulder and partial hearing loss, and a myriad of invisible wounds. The unspoken horror of what he'd endured had dulled the snap of his spirit and left shadows deep in his eyes that never quite retreated.

"It's what holds her up that's the real issue," Kelby said. "Wood's rotted through. We'll need to rebuild the bracing and rip out that whole section of ceiling to repair the dry rot."

"But what about Hope? Her head's snapped clean off," Lucy said, gazing at the stump of a neck. A surgeon could not have removed it any neater. "Actually, I never realized there was a seam there like she and her head are two different pieces. Odd."

Kelby crinkled his nose at the broken statue, unwrapped a starlight mint, and popped it in his mouth. Since he'd quit smoking, he was the Sweets and Treat's best customer. Sometimes he was there waiting for the doors to open. She'd see him, slouched against the door in the early morning, quiet and still in the shadows and the stark look on his face cut at her heart. Was his missing Webber? Was it pain for the daughter he'd only seen in a picture before she'd been snatched away from him? She feared his insatiable need for candy was an ache for sweetness that could not be assuaged.

Kelby rubbed his shoulder absently. "The angel's the easy part. Got a guy who can do magic with rebar and plaster. He can slap her together again."

Lucy didn't feel her brother was giving the angel the proper respect and she was about to say so when her attention was caught by the angel's body. She looked closer. There was something there, inside the severed neck, something dark against the white, she'd got a glimpse of it stuffed down in the plaster. Picking her way past bits of grit and broken wood she knelt next to the fallen angel and peered inside.

"Look," she said. Uncle Paul and Kelby crowded near. "There's a little compartment inside the neck." Heart pounding, she drew out a leather packet, tied with a strap so brittle it broke away under her fingers.

"What'cha got there?" Uncle Paul asked.

She laid it out on the floor and carefully opened the packet to reveal a cylinder of rolled papers, fastened with another thong. "Old papers," she whispered. "Really old." She unfurled them enough to get a glimpse.

Uncle Paul huffed. "Too bad. I thought it might be a stack of bearer bonds or a pouch of gold coins. That's what we really need if we're going to get this church put back together and reunite Hope with her head."

"But it's a mystery, isn't it?" Lucy said, stomach

fluttering with excitement. "Who put the papers in here and why?" She held the moldering papers almost to her nose. "The writing is faint and some of it looks almost faded away. I'll need to use Mum's magnifying glass and maybe gloves so I don't damage the papers."

Kelby unwrapped another starlight mint for his other cheek, sucking thoughtfully as he looked around the sanctuary. "So where is it?"

"What?" Uncle Paul said.

"Hope's head. Where did it go?"

Lucy could not tear her eyes away from the brittle paper.

"It rolled under the first pew after the earthquake," she said. Excitement beat a quick tempo in her veins. Whatever the papers could tell her, she was sure it was something important, important enough to change everything. It was the same feeling she'd gotten when she entered that contest and later discovered that envelope in the mail, an innocent sheet of paper that had indeed completely changed her life. Of course, that venture had taken her to New York and brought her face to face with ruin, but those were memories to revisit another day.

"Yeah, well, the head's not there now," Kelby said.

This time she let her brother's words sink in. "Sure, it is." Lucy got up, cradling the packet under her arm. "It's right here." Only it wasn't. Neither was it under any of the other pews. The three of them began a search for the escaped head, but it was not to be found underneath the pews, the altar, behind the wastebasket, the box of eraser-colored robes or anywhere else in the tiny church.

Uncle Paul swirled a hand around his bald dome, stirring the fringe of red hair into prickly disarray. "Well, I'm jiggered."

"Did you put it somewhere for safekeeping, Uncle Paul?"

He fixed a bewildered look on her. "No, I figured it was best to leave it there and get everyone out of the church in case there were more earthquakes coming. I locked the door last night so's no one coming in to pray would get beaned if anything else fell down."

That was a shocker. Uncle Paul never locked the door of the church. As a small child, she'd often sneaked into the old building on Mondays to do her homework curled up at Hope's feet. Monday was the quietest day and there might also be a bowl of hard candies left out from Sunday service for her to pinch, or a partial can of pineapples leftover from the pineapple chicken served at Sunday fellowship night. "If you didn't move her head, then where is it?" she asked.

All three looked at each other.

Kelby crunched both his mints simultaneously. "Looks like you got two mysteries to solve now, sis."

***

Lucy desperately wanted to examine the bundle of papers or continue looking for the missing head, but the time was drawing close to nine-thirty a.m. She walked across the street and entered the historic Lady Quail hotel, breathing in the scent of age and old wood. As always, she noted the elegant tapestry drapes and the fine marble fronted fireplace, allowing her imagination to inform the view. How grand and regal was this relic from the 1800s when carriages deposited their occupants at the door of the Lady. She could imagine them, those well-to-do individuals who came from all around the world to dip a toe into the river of gold seekers. Honey Creek had been a festive spot then, with a theater, saloon, and plenty of locals willing to take the well-heeled visitors to the mining camps for a day of diversion.

Inevitably reality punched through and reduced her to seeing the room as it was, the drapes faded beyond salvage, the fireplace boarded up, the parlor rug thin to bare in spots.

But the aroma of dust and leather-bound books and aged oak was the perfume of generations of Honey Creek residents, and somehow it comforted Lucy. "Someday, we'll have the Lady back in action." She refused to allow her mind to contemplate exactly how much money that resurrection would cost.

With a sigh, she left the precious bundle on the oak roll top desk, pulled her hair back behind a velvet headband, and tied a crisp white apron around her waist. When she changed from her Keds into a pair of leather mules, she wished once again that their only resident did not equate the wearing of heels with feminine virtue. It was the seventies, after all. A woman was more than her footwear. Sneakers would be the best choice for tramping up and down the steep stairs, in fact.

Manny appeared, dark face shining with sweat and frizz of hair finally grown out of the buzzcut from his time as a Vietnam Army medic. The work belt around his skinny waist had been adapted so he could easily access the tools with his only remaining hand, the other having been lost to a nasty infection acquired in the jungle, the same jungle where Lucy's brother Webber lost his life and her other brother Kelby had fought. Manny's other wounds ran deep and invisible, like Kelby's.

On Manny's second day as the Lady Quail's gardener and handyman, he had encountered a gopher snake near the pond. His reaction was explosive, the screaming deafening. It was her brother Kelby and Trooper who finally found him cowering in the woods, talking to himself. She did not know what Kelby said to Manny to calm him, since Kelby and Trooper refused to discuss it. From that day, Manny acted strictly as a handyman, and Kelby helped with the gardening. The incident was never spoken about again.

Working soothed Manny, he'd told her once, and there was plenty to do at the Lady, though she wished they could pay him more than his meagre wages. At the moment, he had a tape measure clamped under his armpit and a nail in his mouth. He mumbled something.

"Huh?"

He took out the nail with the hand that already held a hammer. "Got the upstairs window unstuck but the wood frame's shot. Should I scrounge around for some scrap to fix it or do you want me to install a new window?"

"Manny, when was the last time we bought anything new for the Lady Quail?"

He screwed up his face, considering.

"It was a rhetorical question," she said with a smile.

He nodded.

She set to work arranging the silver tray and added a richly scented pink rose from the garden.

"Doorbell's new," Manny said.

She started, not realizing he'd persisted in coming up with an answer. "You're right. We did spring for a new doorbell last month, didn't we?"

"Yes, ma'am."

"You've got to stop calling me ma'am. Go ahead with the repairs, but since we still have precisely zero paying guests, you'd better scrounge whatever you can to fix the window."

"Yes, ma'am," he said as he left.

A peal of chimes from the mint condition doorbell surprised her. Why in the world would Meg bother to ring it? Flinging the door open, she gaped at Alexi Quinn, holding a white bag and gaping right back at her, grey eyes rounded, framed by impossibly thick lashes.

"Hi, Alexi. What are you doing here?" she finally managed.

"I was told to bring this," he said, thrusting the bag at her. "It is breakfast for your guests, er, guest. Is there only one, then?"

The earnest squint made her understand that the man had probably been puzzling over that very question all the way to the door of the Lady.

"Well..." she thought over her answer while Alexi kept glancing at her apron, the silver tray, and looking up at the ceiling until his eyes traveled back down to take in the velvet headband and heels. She sighed. "It's kind of hard to explain. Maybe you should just come with me while I deliver it."

He blanched, flinched, looked up and down, and while his mouth worked to formulate an answer, she picked up the tray and started out. "Come on," she urged, "You can open the kitchen door for me. It sticks."

They made their way out of the kitchen and along the hallway, past several boarded-up rooms. She knocked on the carved wooden door of Room One, waited precisely fifteen seconds, and gestured for Alexi to open it.

His mouth went slack. "Oh, well, I am not certain..."

Elbowing by him, she balanced the tray on her hip and opened it. "Good morning, Mrs. W.," she called out. "I've brought your breakfast." She bobbed a chin at Alexi. "This is..."

"Not a visitor," Mrs. W. said archly, smoothing her hands along the worn velvet of the armchair. "Surely not a visitor before the breakfast hour. Who are you then?"

Alexi stared. "I am Alexi Quinn."

"An Irishman? You don't look it."

"Irish on my father's side. My mother is Russian."

Her eyes narrowed. "Russian? And what is your business at the Lady Quail? Are you hoping to secure a room?"

"No, ma'am."

She did not appear to notice his discomfort. "That's not an easy thing during the busy summer season." She eyed him. "But you're clean-cut, not like those beatniks anyway, no mutton chops or scraggly beard."

"I...I do not believe facial hair is sanitary," Alexi started. She beamed. "Very sensible for an Irishman."

"He's helping with Lovely," Lucy put in hastily. "And he's doing delivery work." It was true on both counts, if not the complete scenario.

Mrs. W. appeared pacified. "Excellent," she said, smoothing the quilted lap robe across her knees. "We can use a reliable delivery person here. Be sure to stop in the kitchen and have Cook give you some breakfast. But there will be no drinking my establishment," she said sternly.

"I do not drink."

She offered a gracious nod. "Wise considering your ancestry."

Lucy's cheeks grew hot. She wondered exactly how Alexi would take the insult. "Will there be anything else this morning, ma'am?" she piped up.

"No, my dear. This will do for now. Thank you." She extended a beringed hand to Alexi.

He grasped it with his good hand.

"And it was lovely to meet you, Mr. Quinn. I hope you will be very happy here as part of The Lady Quail family. Our hotel has been in operation since 1851. It burned in 1879 but it was rebuilt, more glorious than ever. You are now part of that golden legacy. Times have changed, but the Lady Quail never will."

Since Alexi stood dumbly, Mrs. Winston picked up her fork and sampled a bite of scrambled eggs, mumbling about talking to Cook about letting the eggs get cold.

Lucy smiled and offered a jolly wave, leading them out into the hallway and back into the front parlor. An anxious quacking from the front yard spurred her to grab the bag of duck food from the cupboard.

"Lovely is hungry too. He expects to dine after Mrs. W. and he's much more vocal in his complaints." She went to the garden, leaving Alexi to follow or not. The air was still clinging to a semblance of cool before the summer sun blasted it away.

Lucy tried to put her words together carefully. "In answer to your earlier question, the lady you just met is the only official guest, though I have a room where I stay. Much less grand than hers. It was the maid's quarters back in the day. Manny bunks on a cot in the attic, even though I told him he has his pick of the rooms, decrepit as they are. I apologize for her remarks about Irish people. You should hear what she said about Manny when he first joined us. Absolutely mortifying."

She knew she was talking too much, but her mouth did not want to stop because she knew what was coming next. Before she launched in on another round of minutia, he stopped her with an upheld palm.

"But...who was that?" Alexi asked, standing on the cement step and away from Lovely's probing bill. Lovely seemed particularly enamored of Alexi, in between jabs at the grains Lucy had just scattered. Alexi retreated one step further away.

"Mrs. W.? Oh, she's the proprietor of the Lady Quail, like she said, though Kelby and I run things, really. She's had some, er, difficulties and she's a little confused, but it makes her feel right as rain if she believes the Lady Quail is humming along like it has for one hundred plus years. She's very happy here. She has nursing care when she needs it, and sometimes, she will sit in the garden and entertain visitors. The townsfolk are really sweet about dropping in on visiting days."

"So, you...lie to her? Pretend you are a server, and the hotel is full of guests?"

"Not lying." She hurled another handful of grain to Lovely. "I am a server and there are guests, they just don't pay to stay here."

"The hotel is in ruins."

"Not it's not," she snapped. "It needs some work, that's all."

He blinked at her. "But it's not the truth, what you encourage Mrs. W. to believe," he said. "A statement intended to deceive, even if literally true, a half-truth. That is the definition for the three-letter word l-i-e."

She wondered if he knew any words for annoying. The man was maddening, as stiff and stony as the Hope angel in a world of pliant, flesh and blood people. Yet there was no judgment in his eyes, not really, merely an honest struggle to understand. How hard it must be to be rigid as stone in a world of quivering flesh. She let out a long slow breath. "Alexi, couldn't there be something in between the truth and a lie?"

"What?"

"What, what?"

"What is between the truth and a lie?"

She massaged her temple which had begun to throb when she'd finally made herself retrieve the stack of bills from Selma at the post office. What was between a truth and a lie? "Life, I guess. We're all struggling to make ourselves think we're in control when we're not. That's a lie, right?"

His head cocked one notch to the side like Lovely's did when he was considering his food options. To deter Alexi from the barrage of questions she knew he must be formulating, she scattered the rest of the duck food and brushed off her fingers. "We, me and pretty much the whole town, keep the past alive for her so she can live happily. We tried to move her to an assisted living place once and she nearly died of grief, so we keep the pretense going. God forgives transgressions like that, I'm pretty sure."

The gray of his eyes silvered to pewter as he strove to

understand. "Why would you do all that for Mrs. W.?"

"Because," Lucy said with the tiniest wobble in her voice, "she's my mother."

***

Trooper sat under the shade of the prickle ball tree outside the church, listening, enjoying the breeze. Gummy was also relishing the cool, indicated by the lazy swish of his tail. Thursdays were the best days to hold down a patch of grass outside The Angel of Hope Church. On those days church secretary SueAnn cleaned out the refrigerator and he could usually score a paper plate full of week-old banana bread leftovers from Sunday service, Jello salad from the Bible meeting, and one time even a whole jar of homemade pickles that SueAnn deemed was taking up too much room in the old coffin-sized Admiral fridge.

Today the haul included the obligatory banana bread and some coconut raisin cookie things. Coconut was not Trooper's favorite, but one could not be too choosey. Gummy kept one eye on the food and the other in a wary lookout across the street for Mittens and General George Washington, his mortal feline foes. In the past decade, Trooper had only seen the Murphy sisters, Bee and Pearl, in town precisely once, when the church had become an emergency shelter during a power outage and cold snap that threatened to freeze out the old ladies and their cats. Gummy and Trooper were also seeking shelter and the ensuing animal drama was one for the record books. Ten years later, Gummy still kept a droopy eye peeled for his nemeses.

Occasionally the scrub jays would knock loose a prickle ball that fell with a plop, bouncing off Trooper's ball cap, and inciting a bark of outrage from Gummy, but that was a small price to pay. The action going on inside The Angel of Hope was better than any doings on the TV in the hardware store window, better even than the excitement of watching Evel

Knievel bust a gut trying to jump Snake River Canyon on his rocket cycle or whatever cockamamie contraption that was. Pastor Paul hied around every square inch of the minuscule church, squatting more than he'd probably ever done in his baseball days, muttering.

"Where could it have gone?" he said for the sixth time so far, leaning in the church doorway, wiping the sweat from the back of his neck.

Trooper folded his hands across his belly, uncorking the remark he'd been preparing for the past hour. "Heard you lost your head, Pastor."

Paul blinked, shot a look out the open door at Trooper. "What? Oh, yes, a joke."

Pastor must be really rattled. He hadn't even noticed that Trooper had donned his Dodgers cap before he parked himself under the tree. Alvin Wong screeched his Gremlin to a halt at the curb, scraping a layer of rubber off the tires. Ironic, since his Mountain Holler office was only two blocks away. No concern about the energy crisis for this newspaperman. Gummy readied a bark but changed his mind when he saw Alvin Wong. Alvin bustled up; camera slung around his neck. "I just heard," he panted, thick black hair bristling, adding to his frenzied aura. "What do you make of it, Trooper?"

"Make of what?"

"How can you ask 'what'? A disappearing head? A treasure map in the angel?" His expression was pure glee. "It's too incredible."

Trooper wriggled his back on the rough bark of the tree, snitching a piece of banana bread from his plate. He squinted up at the reporter, editor, janitor, and delivery man for the Mountain Holler and gave into his sinful and insatiable desire for mischief. "Well now, this could be that big story you've been waiting for."

Alvin's dark eyes sparkled. "So, it's true then? The Angel's head has been stolen and Lucy Winston uncovered a treasure map inside the statue? You can confirm?"

Even Trooper was impressed at the workings of Alvin's mind. It was known to everybody and their brother that Alvin had been working on a fictional thriller for some twenty-five years. His journalistic efforts were always made more interesting by the varnish of make believe he applied to each and every story. Nixon's people couldn't spin a story better than Alvin Wong.

"Juicy, huh?" Trooper said, with a waggle of his brows.

"Oh now, Alvin," Pastor Paul said, scuffling down the steps, palms outstretched. "Don't get your engines fired up. The head is misplaced, that's all. Rolled away somewhere and SueAnn and I are gonna find it."

"Rolled away? I don't think so, Pastor. Good try." The reporter was busily scribbling on a notepad. "What about the treasure map?"

The pastor sighed. "There isn't a treasure map, just some dusty papers."

Alvin was undeterred. "What kind of papers?"

"Dunno. Lucy hasn't told me yet. Might be an old laundry list for all that I know."

"So, it could just as easily be a treasure map," Alvin said triumphantly, dotting the period so forcefully he broke the tip of his pencil. "Where's Lucy?"

"At the Lady Quail, I think, but..." Pastor Paul did not finish his sentence before Alvin was hightailing it towards the hotel, camera banging around his neck. "Awww nuts. Now he's off and running with one of his wild stories. Gonna be plastered over the Holler in no time." Paul looked at Trooper as if seeing him for the first time. "You don't think that's gonna cause trouble, do you?"

"Sure, it will. Who doesn't love a good treasure hunt?"

Paul glowered. "You gonna help me look for the head or did you only come here to sponge food?"

"I'll help," Trooper said, stuffing a wad of banana bread in his mouth and giving a corner to Gummy.

Paul pointed a finger. "Keep that beast outside. I haven't forgotten that he peed on a box of bulletins last month."

"I'll keep him outside, but really, you can use all the help you can get."

"That head is around here somewhere and I'm going to find it if it takes me from here until the Second Coming."

"If you figure it will take that long, I'd better have another snack." He extracted a cookie from his pocket and shoved it in his mouth, earning another irate glare from the pastor.

Paul swiped at a trickle of sweat on his forehead. "And if you're gonna come into the house of the Lord, at least have the decency to take off that infernal Dodger's hat." Paul stomped back inside.

Trooper chuckled, left his hat in the comforting circle of shade, and followed the grumbling pastor inside.

***

An hour later, as Paul stood blinking against the shadows, Selma Trunk poked her head inside the church next, looking down her nose through the half-glasses at the mess. Though she'd celebrated a sixty-fifth birthday announced at church the prior month, Paul thought the woman could easily pass for eighty. She didn't "make an effort" as Libby would say. A sudden scent of lavender invaded his memory, the fragrance his wife used to wear when he'd had the sense to notice, when he'd take her arm and escort her to the movies and she would wear pink, always pink. How he burned to take her there again when she received the healing he nightly prayed for on his creaking knees. But perhaps it wouldn't be granted and how would he bear it and still shepherd his quirky flock through their own torments?

Paul cleared the thoughts away. Selma fisted hands on hips, her faded postmistress uniform was as starched as ever, black hose peeked out of Birkenstocks.

"Alvin Wong said those papers Lucy's discovered belonged to Thomas Lyman."

Paul was struck dumb for a moment. "Well, what do you know?" Thomas Lyman had grown up with Paul, an adopted brother of sorts, though they were not actually related.

Trooper chuckled. "Lyman? Well, how in the Sam Hill did Alvin put all that together so quickly?"

"He's been stuck to Lucy like a shadow." She shrugged a spindly shoulder. "Plus, he's got a nose for a story. That whole series he did about the hit man from Des Moines stirred things up, remember?"

"Fella was a life insurance salesman, not a hit man," Trooper said.

"Made for some good reading," Selma said, peering down her nose at them both.

Paul could not argue with that.

"You grew up with Lyman, didn't you, Padre?" Trooper said.

"Yes. He was a mischievous guy, always playing the joker card. Can't figure why he'd put a set of old papers in the angel, though. Wasn't the church-going type once he turned eighteen, for all my mother's pleading."

"Maybe he didn't put them in there, maybe someone else did." Her look grew thoughtful. "Lyman was always hunting around these parts for gold, as I recall. A natural-born prospector. You don't suppose he went and found the Mother Lode and hid himself a map to remember where he stashed it, do you?"

Paul shivered. "No, no I don't, and please don't speculate

within earshot of Alvin. He runs after stories like a bear after pot roast."

Selma lifted a skinny shoulder. "I'm not a gossip," she said.

Paul would not have been completely surprised if a bolt of lightning didn't incinerate her on the spot.

"Still looking for the missing head?"

"Yes," Paul said finally, "but we're gonna find it, don't you worry. There's a perfectly logical explanation about where it's got to."

She did not appear the least bit worried. The smear of mustard on her lip indicated she'd been enjoying her traditional lunch always carried in the pocket of her postmistress skirt, a cold hot dog wrapped in foil.

"Anyhoo, all Alvin's talk brought to mind this letter," she said.

"What letter?" Paul said, forcing his gaze from wandering the pews.

"This one." She held up a plastic bag with a brown envelope inside. "I inherited this job from mum, you know, and she never lost a letter in all her sixty years as postmistress. She claimed she never lost anything, but I have a box full of replacement eyeglasses so that was her pride talking."

"Uh huh," Paul prodded.

"So, this is a letter from Lyman to his girl."

Paul searched his memory. "Thomas knew lots of girls, from what I recall." He'd charmed his way into many hearts and backseats, Paul had no doubt.

"Agnes Needles," Selma said. "He wrote her before he shipped off to war in 1941, leaving mum with instructions that it was to be delivered to her upon word of his death or he would call for it personally when he got home, only it landed in the dead letter file because Agnes apparently saw his departure as fortuitous and left town. That was just before he was blown up at Pearl Harbor." She paused for breath.

Paul winced, dazed at the flood of information and her casual reference to Thomas's death. "Uh huh. My mother took it very hard. I was only a young teen at the time."

Trooper sighed. "Cowardly attack, that was. Men didn't even have a chance."

"Thomas might have had one of those premonitions and hidden a clue to his treasure before he joined up, mightn't he?"

Paul frowned. "That seems farfetched."

She consulted her watch. "Well, I don't have any more time for dilly-dallying. Can you give this letter to Lucy? Maybe it will help with the treasure hunt. I'll put the postage due in the special collection to refund box in case Lyman's people ever show up to claim it." She whirled on her heel and headed for the door.

"Thank you, Selma," Paul called after her, "but there's really no treasure hunt going on in Honey Creek." And certainly, his erstwhile brother would not have been in the thick of it. Would he?

But Paul remembered Thomas's yen for a joke, the irrepressible mischievousness that vexed his mother, Ann. She'd spent many an hour on bended knee asking the Lord to shepherd the boy she'd taken in for her deceased friend.

The door closed behind her and Trooper grinned. "I'll betcha Selma's got her theory spread all over town by sunset."

Paul could not hold back a groan. "The words of a gossip are like choice morsels; they go down to the inmost parts," he recited.

"And this gossip is the tastiest of all. Nothing more delicious than treasure." Trooper smiled broadly. "Town's gonna eat it up."

"Aww nuts," the pastor said.

Chapter Five

Alexi abandoned his packet of instant oatmeal the next morning. Since the grocery options in Honey Creek were limited, he had used tweezers to extricate all eleven raisins from the contents, so he didn't much mind abandoning the food. He bypassed the front-page news about the oil crisis and the first Venezuelan woman to win the Miss Universe Pageant. The Mountain Holler was surprisingly unnewslike, in tone and structure. Alexi surmised journalistic rules might be different in the odd town where he'd landed.

'*Is Honey Creek hiding a treasure trove?*' the headline blared. *Local resident Lucy Winston has reportedly discovered old documents hidden in the head of the Angel of Hope's statue which crashed to the floor during Wednesday night's earthquake.*

Alexi blinked. He'd run away so fast after the earthquake he'd missed that astonishing development.

"*I don't know what the Angel papers say yet,*" *Lucy Winston told this reporter after recovering the mysterious documents from the plastery bowels.* "*I haven't had time to look at them.*" *Ms. Winston's coy remarks notwithstanding, the papers could very well lead to the long-vanished treasure of Thomas Lyman. Lyman, a part-time theater owner and full-time prospector who resided in Honey Creek from 1925 to 1941, was raised by Pastor Paul Stuckley's mother, Ann.*

According to unnamed sources, Lyman was reported to have left behind the fruits from his mining efforts before he enlisted in the army during WWII and was subsequently killed in the attack on Pearl Harbor. Further, a letter from Lyman to his girlfriend Agnes Needles, indicates he may have secreted the treasure in the town of Honey Creek, though Lyman's treasure was never found. Is it possible that Winston's documents, wrestled from their secret nook, will reveal a windfall unknown in Honey Creek history? Stay tuned to the Mountain Holler for further developments."

Alexi stopped and reread the article again. Unknown treasure? Unnamed sources? The byline read Alvin Wong, editor-in-chief for the Mountain Holler. Alvin Wong was also the owner, Alexi knew, as he was the man who signed Alexi's paycheck. Additionally, he was also noted as the lead photographer and delivery supervisor.

Alexi shook his head. He had not known about Lucy's discovery pulled from the plastery bowels, as Alvin put it, but then again, he had been more interested in trying to understand the charade with her mother. Was the whole town part of the plan to convince Mrs. Winston that the hotel was still a thriving business? It was a lie, so plain and simple, that he could not understand how she could see it otherwise.

A little bit.

The three words popped up in his memory, his answer to his mother's latest query about his music when he had last phoned her.

"Have you been able to play, Alexi?" The hope throbbed in her voice, even after everything, intense like a perfectly played minor chord.

He'd yearned more than anything to keep that hope alive. "A little bit," he'd said in answer to her question. It was a lie. The first one he had ever told to his knowledge. Or was it? Hadn't he stood over the piano, running his crippled hands over the keys that would no longer respond to his coaxing? Hadn't he slammed his fist down, releasing a tortured sound that echoed the grief inside him? So, it was not a lie...totally. And yet, it was not the truth, not in the way his mother meant, not really.

So, what was in between a truth and a lie?

Life, according to Lucy. The messy work of people trying to be maestro to their own music.

He did not understand that. The inescapable truth was he could not play his beloved piano and modern medicine could not restore his gift. The lie he'd uttered was to keep that glimmer of hope alive in the mother who'd sacrificed everything for his music. Truth and lies could not co-exist, yet here he was wrestling with both.

He wandered to the piano jammed in the corner. Denny was the best piano tuner he'd ever met. It had fascinated Alexi to watch Denny toiling over each tuning pin, each minute turn of the wrench coaxing each note into perfection. He'd hired him to service his beloved instrument in his New York apartment two weeks before the car jumped the curb and pinned him to the graffitied brick wall. Denny had visited him in the hospital after the accident and again months later when Alexi sat alone in his apartment sorting through his bills with burning eyes, his hand still splinted. It was during that visit that Denny told him about Honey Creek and The Mountain Holler. At the time he'd thought he would never visit such a backward-sounding place. Now here he was, extracting raisins from his oatmeal and edging alongside a piano to get from the bed to the kitchen.

Though this specimen was a cheap instrument, rust on the pins and strings, the soundboard cracked, he knew it would be as impeccably tuned as was humanly possible.

With his ruined hand, he reached out with the fingers frozen in a forever claw, laying them gently over the keys.

He played a c chord. Yes, perfectly tuned. It made his heart ache with need.

A little bit.

How he yearned to make truth of the lie he'd told his mother, the single chord igniting a burning craving in his belly. Why? Why could he not force the tendons to stretch, the frozen muscles to spring to life? Could decades of toil, of talent be so easily erased?

A knock at the door jerked him away from the piano. He stood frozen, panting as if he'd been caught shoplifting from the corner store.

There were three subsequent knocks before he made it to the door and peeked out. He did not think there were many home invasion crimes in Honey Creek, but caution was his watchword.

Through the tattered curtain, he saw Lucy almost dancing up and down about ready to knock again. He opened the door.

She froze, knuckles suspended. "Hi," she breathed, spots of pink on her cheeks indicating her excitement if the sparkle in her green eyes was not enough.

"Hello."

"Hi," she said again with more wiggling. "Did you read the article in the paper?"

He did not think she was referring to the one about the oil crisis or Miss Universe. "Yes."

"Alvin Wong may just be right about this one."

He tried to make sense of that statement.

"It's a puzzle." Her face shone with triumph, and he felt as though he should be gleaning more meaning from her words.

"All right."

To his relief, there was more. "The papers in the angel's neck, I mean."

"I am not sure I follow."

"Thomas Lyman was quite a jokester as it turns out from what Uncle Paul remembers. Did I tell you they were raised together?"

"No."

"Yes. His mother Ann took Thomas in after Thomas's mother Bess died from a hemorrhage right after he was born. Bess would never tell who the father was, so Thomas grew up as Paul's older brother, you see?" She was slightly breathless.

"Yes, I see."

"Well anyway, Thomas was a jokester, like I said, and what we found is actually the second clue, but that stands to reason since it was only the angel crashing that brought it to light in the first place. Coincidence if you believe in that kind of thing, but personally I feel like God meant us to find it."

When she paused for breath, he leaped into the void. "Won't you please come in?"

"Uh, sure, yes, thank you." He led her in, and she perched on the edge of the wooden chair. He sat warily across the kitchen table from her as she eyed the neatly folded copy of the Mountain Holler.

"I see you've read Alvin Wong's article, such as it is."

"Yes," he said. "He seems certain Thomas Lyman left a treasure."

"And he may actually be right. Thomas wrote a letter to his girlfriend Agnes before he left for war. Selma Trunk, the postmistress gave it to me. You're not going to believe this, but in the letter, it says..."

With a sweep of her hand, she overturned his coffee.

"Sorry, sorry." She righted the mug.

"Perfectly all right." He hurried to soak up the mess with some paper towels.

"Anyway, he says right here in the letter," she said,

waving a brittle piece of paper in his direction and knocking the saltshaker to the floor.

"Sorry, so sorry."

He picked it up and fetched the hand broom to capture the sprinkle of salt from the linoleum before returning to his seat.

"I'm so excited because it says right here," she moved closer to stab her finger towards the paper.

He moved the mug out of her vicinity. "Maybe, I mean, perhaps, you could try to just move your mouth, instead of your whole body."

She laughed, a rich velvety sound and though he did not know what he had said that was funny, he was glad to hear her laugh. It was deep and full, sonorous, like a cello.

"Okay. I'm going to sit on my hands. Will you look at the letter Alexi, please?"

He carefully spread the paper out on the table trying not to cause any tears to the delicate surface. The writing scrawled across the page was bold, slanted, written with a firm hand.

My dearest Agnes,

I am shipping out on Tuesday next as you know, so I've given the postmistress money to post this letter to you after I depart if I should not return. My hope is for nothing of the kind, of course. I long to see a bit of the world, my beauty, and after we are married, we shall venture out and see it together. How can a poor lad hope to provide for his delicate flower in such a manner as she deserves? I will share a secret with you, my love. A theater manager has many idle hours at his disposal, and I have combed the hills of this rich territory in search of gold. Oh yes, I've collected my treasure and hidden it well, and I will enjoy the notion of you following my clues upon my return and securing the means to our happily married life. It will sustain me through

anything the war can dish out. If disaster strikes and I don't return, I hope you will find my treasure on your own, my darling, and live the life you deserve without me.
   As always, your devoted Tommy.
   He looked up from the paper. "This letter..."
   "Was supposed to be for Agnes Needles, but she left him without reading it." Hands jammed under her thighs Lucy wriggled. "Look at the writing across the bottom, the very bottom."
   He peered closer. "A spiritual being serving God especially as a messenger."
   She wriggled up and down, hands still pinned beneath her. "Five letters, Alexi. The answer is a-n-g-e-l."
   "Which is where you discovered the old papers."
   "So, they must contain a clue which leads to another one. Sort of a mixture of a crossword puzzle and scavenger hunt if you will." Her green eyes danced, and pink petals of color bloomed more deeply on her cheeks. Suddenly he felt breathless, too. Her enthusiasm was so very compelling, like a symphony.
   "That means..." he started uncertainly.
   "That if we follow the clues, we can find Thomas Lyman's treasure. Surely it will be enough to repair the angel and get her squared away in church again."
   "That would be…unlikely."
   "I know."
   "That a treasure would remain undiscovered, or undisturbed for so many years."
   She nodded. "I know."
   "You would perhaps be setting yourself up for disappointment."
   "I know."
   "And yet you persist?"
   "Yes," she burst out.

"Why?"

"Because miracles happen in Honey Creek, Alexi, and it's been a long while since we had one so we're due."

Miracles, from the Latin *mirari*, to wonder. A surprising and welcome event that is not explicable by natural or scientific laws and is therefore considered to be the work of a divine agency.

"Haven't you ever seen a miracle, Alexi?"

"A miracle?" He thought perhaps miracles might be like unicorns and Martian men, fanciful ideas for those with imaginations. He did not believe, nor did he imagine often. "I do not think so."

Her frown only lasted a moment and then she dazzled him with another smile that seemed almost incandescent. "Doesn't matter. I have a feeling we're going to see one big time."

He thought such a fanciful outcome was unlikely, but he did not wish to say anything that would dim the sparkle in her eyes and turn the corners of her mouth down. He took a different tack. "And you came to me because..."

"Because, Alexi Quinn, there is no one in this town more qualified to help me solve the clues to a decades-old puzzle than you." She sat back triumphantly, her chair clunking into the side of the bookshelf and knocking a copy of The Illustrated Theory of Music onto the floor.

While he retrieved it, he searched for something to say.

No one more qualified than him? All he was qualified to do was play the piano brilliantly and now he couldn't, so he was left to cobble together some word puzzles that brought nothing beautiful to the world, only a brief respite from boredom.

"I am not sure you are correct, Lucy."

Her hands came loose, and she hopped from her chair and grabbed him by the shoulders. "Just listen, Alexi. Listen to the next clue."

He gaped at her, feeling acutely the warmth of her palms through the thin material of his shirt. "I...I am listening."

She let go of him and patted her pockets. "I can't make out all the words on the angel's head note, but the end says here in all caps A LICK FOR THE IRON PERFECT. I copied it down on this piece of paper. See?" She grabbed his hand and tucked the note inside.

He studied it carefully. "A lick for the iron perfect. What does that mean?"

"I don't know," she said with a gleeful chortle. "That's what we're going to find out. Are you ready to find the treasure and get this miracle under-weigh?"

Go on a zany treasure hunt in a town where the people upheld an elaborate facade to protect the feelings of an old lady? Where he'd been forced to have conversations with others and walk by a piano he could never hope to play? With a woman who believed in miracles and knocked over his things and lived with a duck?

No, he thought, looking into her green eyes, her enthusiasm playing a strange interlude on his senses. *I am not ready to do any such thing.*

"Yes," his mouth said. "Where do we start?"

HONEY CREEK TREASURE HUNT

Chapter Six

On Saturday afternoon, Lucy donned her apron and fixed a pitcher of iced lemonade and a plate of raisin cookies and settled her mother in a rocking chair on the shaded front porch. Lovely wasted no time in shimmying close to catch the cookie crumbs.

Alexi made his way up the sidewalk, carefully avoiding a kid speeding along on a bike with the white banana seat. Upon reaching the front porch, he gave a half bow to Lucy's mother.

"Mrs. W. this is Alexi Quinn, our new delivery man," Lucy reminded her.

"How do you do?" She extended her hand. "Have we met?"

"Yes, madam," he said.

She frowned. "Oh, I am sure I would remember such a tall, lanky young man."

"We met when I accompanied Lucy and your breakfast tray yesterday..." he began.

"No matter," Lucy said, waving Alexi into a chair and pouring him a glass of lemonade. "Alexi and I are solving a puzzle, Mrs. W., an old historic puzzle and we wondered if you might be able to help."

She took a delicate sip of lemonade. "I will certainly try."

Alexi sat stiffly in his chair, even more rigid when Lovely began to waddle around his ankles. Every few minutes he would sidle out his foot and try to ease the pesky bird away.

"What do you know about Thomas Lyman?" Lucy began.

"I haven't heard that name in a dog's age." She considered, chasing the beads of condensed moisture from the glass with a manicured finger. "Ann, Paul's mother, brought him to town when he was just baby. His mother was a dear friend of hers and she died in childbirth, as I recall." She leaned forward and stage whispered. "Thomas was born out of wedlock, you see, and Ann's friend never did name the father. Ann married Douglas Stuckley, and Paul came along a few years later and they lived as brothers, more or less."

Lucy handed her mother a cookie. "What was he like? Thomas I mean."

"Thomas," she said, "had big dreams. He was a scoundrel in some people's eyes, always on the lookout for the next get rich quick scheme, instead of paying much attention to school and studies and such. He swept floors at the theater and fixed nearly anything that was fixable during the day and combed the hills every spare moment looking for that great gold strike. I think he worked his way up to the theater manager. Daddy didn't let us go to the theater, of course. Actors were not to be trusted, he said. My husband agreed, which was one of the few things they ever did agree on."

Her eyes grew cloudy. "My husband believed diversions like wine, women, and song should be accessible to the menfolk only. I never understood it. I went along with his wishes. Never would I disobey him. I cooked and sewed and minded the house and the children." She pressed a frail hand to her mouth. "No matter how much I gave, how perfect I tried to be, there was always another woman, prettier, younger, more exciting. That's the rub of it. You can try to be many things, but one thing you can't be is a novelty."

Lucy touched her mother's shoulder, throat thick. Her cheeks burned that Alexi should hear such an admission which Lucy had been forced to listen to dozens of times. "I am sorry."

Her mother looked up, but her eyes were still far away. "I was young and pretty once, wasn't I?"

"Oh yes, Mama. Yes."

Her mother blinked slowly as if coming back from a distant place. "And he left, didn't he?"

Lucy squeezed her hand. "Yes, he did."

"Left and never even wanted to know about his children."

"No."

She sighed. "Lucy took it hard, and so did the boys. But we didn't talk about it. No, there's no sense dragging up all that shame and misery with talking."

Exactly twice Lucy had tried to bring up their father with Kelby, wanting to articulate her desire to track him down. It brought out rage in Kelby that she never witnessed in him at any other time. She'd abandoned her notion of tracking him down right then.

"Where are the children?" her mother asked suddenly as if rousing from a dream.

"Where…?"

"Lucy, Kelby, and Webber. Where are they?" She looked around the weed-filled garden.

"I'm here," she whispered, stroking her mother's bony hand. "I'm right here."

Her mother smiled, blinking. "Such a dear. Please tell the children to come by and see me, won't you? I promised Webb I would make his icebox lemon cake when he returned from the army. As many as he wants. Cake every day." She laughed, a giggle, like a young girl's.

"Yes," she managed around the hard lump in her throat. "He would like that."

Catherine Winston fell into silence, surveying the grounds of the Lady Quail and Lucy wondered what she saw, not the weed-filled mess, no certainly not that. Perhaps lovely gardens, painstakingly tended, where her children would gather to celebrate Webber's homecoming. Tears crowded her eyelids. If that was what she saw, then her mental failing was a gift, certainly, one she would not try to argue her mother out of.

She felt Alexi watching her closely and she avoided looking at him. Clearing her throat, she began again. "Did Thomas Lyman ever find any gold?"

"He often hinted as much. Your Uncle Paul used to say he was full of beans, but he had bravado, that was sure. I always admired him for living the way he saw fit." She sighed. "That's a luxury of the male species, you know. Women could not do such things. I was never to set foot into the theater or the bar, though I'd stop by now and again to peek at her."

Lucy quirked an eyebrow. "Who?"

"The angel."

Lucy gulped. "The angel? Our angel?"

"Yes, the Hope Angel. No one knows how she got there, and no one probably ever will but when Regus bought the place, he discovered her under a pile of blankets. He kept her in the attic on account of he thought hanging an angel in a bar would have a dampening effect on sales and didn't tell a soul. Not many people knew she was there, but I heard Daddy talking about it one time because he saw her when he helped Regus patch up the roof, so I snuck in one time and found her. Her head was hollowed out you know. That's where they kept the booze during the Prohibition raids."

Alexi was gripping his glass. Mind spinning, Lucy gulped some lemonade. "How did she get to be in the church?"

"No one knows for sure, but I believe it was Thomas playing one of his practical jokes."

"He moved her to the church?" Alexi's tone was incredulous.

"As far as anyone knows, she appeared there one morning. Paul was only a young teen at the time, away at scout camp I believe, so I don't think he has much memory of it. Pastor Bill was convinced it was some sort of miraculous appearance and Regus didn't correct him. I don't think too many folks in town bought into it, but they loved Pastor Bill and besides, it spiced up the place. The Pastor changed the name of the church to the Angel of Hope, and it's been that way ever since."

"Uncle Paul's going to flip when he finds out Hope used to be a saloon angel," Lucy said with a sigh.

"But it explains how Thomas Lyman knew where to hide his next clue," Alexi said, edging to the side of his chair to avoid Lovely's probing beak.

"Clue to what?" her mother said.

Lucy explained about the treasure hunt. "Thomas Lyman left clues for his girlfriend to follow to find his stash of gold."

"My stars." Her mother shook her head in astonishment. "My stars."

"Does 'a lick for the iron perfect' mean anything to you?" Lucy asked.

"Not a thing, but Thomas was a trickster, as I've said. He loved his jokes. One time he tied tiny bells to a chicken in Mr. Dooley's coop. Almost drove him crazy until he figured out where the jingling was coming from."

Alexi chuckled at that one and Lucy almost stared outright at him. It was just shy of miraculous the way the laugh softened the planes of his face. Camera ready, she thought.

Mrs. Winston touched Lucy's arm. "By the way, I was wondering if you've seen my daughter, Lucy. She's gone away to New York and I miss her so."

Lucy's breath caught. "Oh Mama," she said, through eyes suddenly brimming. "I'm right here."

There was a moment, a scant second where Lucy thought she saw recognition in her mother's eyes. She hugged her and pressed her cheek to her mother's soft neck. Stay, her heart cried. Stay.

Gentle as a breeze, her mother caressed her head. "Thank you anyway, dear. Please let me know if you hear any word from Lucy, won't you? And would you mind phoning the gardener? This yard has gone a bit to the dogs, or should I say the ducks?"

Lucy straightened and wiped a hand across her cheeks. Alexi sat patiently, eyeing her, but when she looked at him, he glanced away, pushing the white duck aside with his foot. Lovely finally took the hint and waddled off to set sail in the pond.

After Lucy got her mother resettled in her room, she rejoined Alexi on the porch.

"Quite a story, huh? About the angel?"

He nodded, his mouth crimped.

She sighed. "You want to ask."

"Ask?"

"About my family."

He considered. "Yes, I want to ask, but I am aware this might be impertinent and nosey."

"It's okay. I can forgive impertinent and nosey." She smiled at him. "Ask."

"What happened? With your father and brothers?"

"When I was seven, my father found another woman in

different town when he was there for a business conference, supposedly. He came home, packed up a suitcase and left. My brothers were five at the time. I cried, Webber stayed quiet, Kelby got angry and stayed that way. My mother lapsed into a depression that left her bedridden, so Uncle Paul and Aunt Libby took care of us as much as possible."

"Where is your other brother, Webber?"

She looked at the blue sky, an azure backdrop to the golden hills of Honey Creek. "Webber was drafted, Kelby volunteered. They both went to Vietnam." She forced out the words. "Kelby came home, but Webber didn't."

Alexi shifted on the chair. "I see."

"I'm not sure we'll ever get his body back. His platoon was ambushed while out on a recon mission and there were mass casualties." The words felt strange on her tongue as if they'd been waiting there for a very long time to be spoken. "They said, the government people who came, I mean, said that his body was not recovered. I remember Mama asked them when, when would she have her boy back home again so she could bury him. They had no answer. There's still no answer. He's over there somewhere, in some country he never wanted to go to in the first place." She shook her head. "Webber was a homebody. He didn't even like to visit the next town over unless he had to. Kelby thought it was going to be an adventure, exciting."

She turned her face to catch the faint breeze. "Now he doesn't want to leave town either."

Alexi nodded. "An understandable reaction."

"Mama really went downhill after we realized we might never get Webber back again. I think it was simply too much for her to accept, so she changed things around in her mind. She'd bake lemon cakes, waiting for him to come home. At one point the kitchen was stacked with lemon cakes, but she still kept on making them."

Very slowly, as if he was approaching a wild animal, Alexi moved his good hand and placed it on her forearm. "I am sorry."

She knew how difficult it must have been for him to make the gesture, this tightly coiled man, so unskilled with the mess of human emotion. The touch went deep into her soul and worked some comfort into it. After he moved his hand away, they sat quietly, listening to the creak of the porch, catching the faint breeze the rustled the grass in the garden.

Lucy finally noticed Trudy from the diner standing at the gate, holding a small paper bag. She took a breath and waved at the young woman.

"Ms. Meg asked me to bring over some fresh fruit. She said it won't keep and perhaps Mrs. Winston might like some. There's someone staying in the empty room above the diner, so she's got her hands full."

"Another stranger in town?"

"I haven't met him yet." Trudy grinned. "But maybe he's looking for the treasure. Everyone at the diner is talking about it. Do you think there's really a stash of gold?"

"Time will tell," Lucy said, grimly, offering Trudy a cookie which the girl declined. "Trudy, would you have time to do Mrs. Winston's nails again? She's got a chip."

"Sure." Trudy fiddled her hands inside her pockets. "I had a morning shift today, so I'm done. Classes are over too."

"Well, if you don't mind, we're happy to pay you," Lucy said.

"Nah." Trudy tossed away her heavy fringe of bangs. "I like it here at the Lady Quail."

"Don't you want to go home?" She'd been told the girl lived with her mother and three younger brothers in an apartment in a rundown area of neighboring Granite Springs.

Trudy shrugged. "No reason to go there."

"No reason?" Lucy started, but Trudy wiggled her fingers at Alexi. "Hi, Mr. Quinn. It's cool that you write crossword puzzles."

"Cool. Yes."

"Sometimes Ms. Meg doesn't have time to do the crossword in the paper delivered to the diner, so she says I can take them. I'm pretty good." A glint of pride shone in the girl's face.

"Would you happen to know what a 'lick for an iron perfect?' might be?" Lucy asked.

She pulled at her lower lip, a cluster of silver bangle bracelets winking in the sunlight. "I'm not sure," she said. "But I'll think on it."

"Thank you." Lucy wiped the table with a napkin. "The more thinkers the better on this one."

Though Alexi and Lucy wrestled over the clue until the heat grew oppressive, they could come up with no further ideas. Frustrated, she followed him to the street where he'd parked his car. On the way, Alexi stopped so abruptly, she almost plowed into him from behind. "What? Did you figure out the clue?"

"No," he said, looking at her.

"Then what is it?"

He was silent for a moment. "It occurred to me that I have sat on an honest to goodness front porch, drinking lemonade. I've never done that before. I am a porch sitter."

A wondering smile played across his lips.

"Welcome to Honey Creek, Mr. Quinn," she said.

***

Pastor Paul ignored the sweat that trickled down his temples as he delivered his Sunday morning message to the congregation of the Angel of Hope church. His flock sat on folding card chairs in the shade of the prickle ball trees, fanning themselves with the printed programs they'd try to recycle from the previous week's service. The temperature was climbing steadily even in the morning hours, but he could not see conducting services in a room with a yawning tear in the ceiling and besides, Kelby could not assure him that no more of the angel's bracing wouldn't come crashing down during the benediction.

He'd heard the buzzing of the gossip wheels churning already. The shenanigans of his unofficial brother Tomas Lyman, a possible treasure, a love letter written to Lyman's girlfriend, Agnes, the missing head.

A few of the more determined gossips had overheard Lucy telling Uncle Paul that the angel had hidden compartments meant to hide away a pint of bootleg whiskey. The Hope Angel, the patron of a seedy bar. Since she'd fallen, she'd become the stuff of legend.

And where was the elusive head? Bad enough the talk kept turning to treasure hunts and bootlegging. Now he had "head napping" theories cropping up like dandelions. He would talk to his wife Libby about it when he brought her some cool lemonade and cookies that SueAnn had already wrapped up for her. Libby was the balm to his soul, the compass needle that always pointed home.

How he missed the days before the disease when she'd sat proudly in the back row, ever alert for a new visitor to greet or a friend struggling with a bum knee or post-surgery soreness. He did not understand why God had given her lupus, this woman who was a stalwart help to so many. Surely, they would win more games as a team than he'd been able to do struggling on alone. As he told his congregation, God doesn't provide explanations for the detours.

There was nothing to be gained by asking why, only how. How could he ease the terrible flare-up that had left her bedridden for the past month? How was he to bear patiently the affliction that he would eagerly take as his own if it meant sparing her? He could think of nothing but prayer and cookies. Perhaps that might be sufficient for the day ahead.

As the sweating choir led the perspiring group in a rendition of High Hills of Glory, Roy Smithers took the offering, shooting Trooper a look of weary resignation as the man shot a packet of sun-dried apples into the offering plate. Far better than the newspaper-wrapped smelt he'd doled out the week before or the pair of brand-new shoelaces which comprised Trooper's Easter offering. Paul would take apple slices over fish any day.

He noted Trudy Prynne in the back, sitting with Meg. Alexi Quinn perched like a wary bird next to Lucy, sweating in his sport jacket. At least the man hadn't gone for a necktie. Paul noticed that Alexi craned his neck forward to see their organist, Jacqueline Bernard, her hands lapping nimbly across the keys. Though Paul did not know much about music, he suspected she played with more verve than talent, but the congregation seemed not to notice.

Jacqueline's French accent had not faded in the twenty years he had known her, and he found the verbal twirls and flourishes rough going so they communicated primarily through nods and smiles. Alexi stared, head cocked as if he were winding the music up like a thread on a spool, storing it so he could unwind and listen to it later. Paul hid a smile as he looked out on his little group with their hidden desires, desperate needs, and buried griefs. How completely different they were, and how achingly the same.

In the back row, sitting all alone, was a tall man with a droopy mustache and mutton chop sideburns. He wore bellbottom jeans and a plaid shirt. A guest, it seemed, perhaps the fellow he'd heard rented the room above the Gold Pan Diner. His heart skipped up a beat. Alexi and the man in plaid, two new visitors in the bullpen. That didn't happen every day in Honey Creek. He stood taller and made sure everyone could hear him, even those sweating in the back row.

When Paul concluded his message, he joined the congregants milling around the snack table. He'd promised himself he would not partake of the food offering since he was now forced to hitch his belt using the very last hole to contain his expanding waist. Spine steeled as he passed the thick slices of butterscotch cake, glossed with trails of white icing, he made his way to the mustachioed stranger being chatted up by Alvin Wong.

"So, you read it?" Alvin was asking. "I think it was one of my best pieces to date."

"Yeah, I read it."

Alvin beamed. "I'm sure you noticed…"

"Where's the angel's head?" the stranger interrupted.

Paul felt a tingle of concern.

"I have a theory about that," Alvin began. "I mean, who would have the most plausible motive to steal the Hope Angel's head?" He shot a furtive glance around and lowered his voice. "If you ask me…"

Paul thrust himself into the middle. "Hello, sir. My name is Paul Stuckley. I'm the pastor here. Welcome to Angel of Hope Church. We are so pleased to have you join us today."

The man extended a smooth palm, remarkably cool for the sweltering morning. "Lawrence."

"Welcome to Honey Creek, Lawrence. Whereabouts do you call home?"

"Granite Springs."

Close by. "Ah, visiting family?" There seemed no other plausible reason a person would motor from a big town like Granite Springs to Honey Creek on a ferocious Sunday morning.

"Taking care of some family business, you could say. I'm looking for Lucy Winston."

Paul waited for the man to continue, but he did not. He felt as though something was about to go down like a ninety-mile-per-hour sinker ball. "She's my niece." He did not feel the need to explain that his title was not born out by birth lines. A mere technicality in his view. "I'm happy to introduce you." He felt the uncle side of him, the one that had tended to Lucy since she was a wee one, navigating her mother's "spells", edge out in front of his pastor side. "May I ask what you'd like to see her about?"

"I want to talk to her about the treasure," he said smoothly.

Paul took a handkerchief from his pocket and mopped his bald head. "Well, Lawrence," he said. "There isn't really a treasure that we know of, it's all sort of a fun story that folks have grabbed hold of, thanks to Alvin here." He clapped Alvin on the shoulder perhaps a little too hard and went for a joke. "They need something to talk about now that the Watergate thing's all wrapped up."

"Oh, but it's more than a story, there are clues," Alvin put in eagerly. "Clues indicating there may be a stash of Lyman's gold somewhere in town."

Pastor Paul tried again for a laugh. "Alvin, let's not get everyone stirred up over a rumor."

"It's more than a rumor." Mr. Lawrence removed something from his pocket and held it in his palm. The bean-sized lump glittered like captured sunlight.

"Is that...?" Alvin breathed mouth slack with surprise.

"A gold nugget, from Thomas Lyman's horde," Lawrence said. "Now, if you please, would you mind pointing out which lady is Lucy Winston?"

Chapter Seven

Trooper swiped at his sweaty forehead and clapped the Dodger's cap back into place. Even in the shade, the heat was unbearable, and he figured God didn't mind if you wore a hat if the pastor was ditzy enough to deliver the message outside in the middle of July. He watched the kids run out of their Sunday School classroom and beeline for the snack table. Fran Trawler followed her proteges, looking winded, a hand clutched to the small of her back. A spasm again, he figured, but she'd pooh-pooh him for suggesting such a thing.

"One cookie each," she called. "That's all."

Trudy stepped behind the table and supervised, deftly handing out napkins with the specified single cookie apiece, ordering the children into line when the swarm became too unruly. Today she wore some sort of bunched gaucho pants and a canary yellow blouse with big round earrings of the same hue.

Fran heaved a sigh as she caught up. "Hi, Trudy. I didn't think you could help today. Did your mother bring you?"

"No, ma'am," Trudy said. "I came on my own. Took the bus."

"Well, I'm glad, anyway. I threw out my back trimming the honeysuckle and I can hardly stand. I've got quarts of peaches ready to make ice cream for the Fourth of July picnic and I can't lift my arms high enough to do it."

"You know it would not be a crime to buy some ice cream from the grocery to dole out," Trooper said.

She shot him the serrated look he'd anticipated. "Everyone expects my peach ice cream on Independence Day, Trooper, as you fully well know."

He fully well did, but he liked the spark in her eye, and deep down he knew he was growing on her, sure as skin on pudding.

Trudy unwrapped the plastic from a second plate of cookies while Fran supervised, eagle-eyed.

They made an odd pairing, Trudy chiming with jewelry, eyes thick with makeup, and Keds to complete the picture. And Fran in her neat slacks and blouse, hair pinned just so. Yet somehow, Fran and Trudy had begun to partner quite often over the last few months, wrangling errant Sunday school tots and marshaling cookies on the Sundays when Trudy came to church. They looked good together, he thought.

Fran might actually be enjoying the company of a youngster since she'd not had any of her own. Her husband Moe left Honey Creek and his wife some twenty years prior before Trooper dropped anchor in the sleepy town. Trooper wondered what Fran had looked like then without the disapproving pinch to her mouth and the brittle uprightness that she wore like a suit of armor. Sometimes when she laughed, he thought he might have gotten a peek.

Fran fanned herself with a napkin. "Can you keep them from devouring everything? I've got to meet with the fundraising committee."

Trudy nodded and Fran eased herself from behind the table. From underneath the brim of his cap, he watched Trudy distribute cookies and Dixie cups full of apple juice to the three-year-old twin girls whose names he could never remember and the line of grade school boys who pushed and shoved each other in good fun.

When the line thinned and he was sure Fran was out of viewing distance, he strolled to the table. "Got any left for an old guy?"

She grinned and handed him the biggest cookie.

"Appreciate it. How'd you like the service?"

"It was okay."

"Really?"

She laughed. "Well, it's super hot and honestly, I think the pastor could have cut fifteen minutes out easy and still made his point. And why does he always talk about baseball? That's got to be the most boring sport on the planet."

Now it was Trooper's turn to chuckle. "He gets all worked up, don't he?"

She ate a cookie. "He sure does."

"You into sports?"

"I wanted to run track in the worst way."

"Why didn't you?"

Her mouth twisted. "My mother said it wasn't appropriate for a lady." She rolled her eyes. "I told her Billie Jean King plays sports and she's a lady. Remember when she beat that Riggs guy on television and everything? I was eleven then and I remember watching it on TV with my Dad."

"Big mouth Riggs had it coming. That didn't convince your mum about running track?"

"Nah." Trudy shook her head in disgust. "Nothing would convince her, even if I won an Olympic gold medal, she'd still say I should learn to sew or play the piano instead."

He thought about his daughter Juliette, how Regina had taught her how to hammer out a simple tune on the piano and how that simple tune had made him nearly burst with pride as he watched those tiny fingers dwarfed by the big white keys. He stuffed the cookie into his mouth. "How's your school goin'? Summer school. Ninth grade, right?"

"Going into eleventh," she corrected, her smile faded, and she shrugged. "I don't fit in there."

"Why not? You're as smart as any, probably smarter."

She looked away. "I just don't."

A motorcycle pulled to the curb. The kid on it stared in her direction, engine idling, no helmet. He was late teens, by the looks of him, bushy of hair tousled in that painstaking way boys used when they wanted people to think they could care less about their looks. She toyed with the napkins, looking at her hands. The fingernails were bitten to the quick, he noticed. She caught her lip between her teeth.

"He waitin' on you?" Trooper asked quietly.

She flashed a quick look towards the motorcycle. "Yeah."

"From your school?"

"We're both going to be seniors. We just finished a math class together this summer."

"Not my business, but it seems like a man should come over and greet a woman proper."

He'd said the wrong thing. Probably just fallen squarely into the same camp as her mother. Trudy's cheeks flamed. "Um, yeah. I gotta go."

She hastened away, beat-up backpack slung on one shoulder. As he watched her go, he helped himself to the remaining six cookies, secreting them in his pockets.

Chin down, Trudy got onto the motorcycle behind the kid, and they roared off. Trooper allowed himself a moment to imagine what he would have said to his own daughter if she had lived long enough to straddle the line between girl and woman. But she would forever be frozen in time, five years old, round-cheeked, innocent, too young to know real grief, too young to grasp how he'd failed.

Was that a blessing or a curse? He was not sure. Never

would be.

Stolen cookies sequestered neatly in his pocket, he ambled away.

***

Lucy squeezed herself into the chair next to Alexi, hugging a corner of the shade. Alexi must have been hot in his slacks, button-up shirt, and wide necktie but he did not appear to be uncomfortable, physically anyway. He sat, ramrod straight in the seat, a cookie resting on a napkin in his palm.

"Aren't you going to eat it?" she whispered.

"I avoid foods prepared in noncommercial kitchens that aren't my own."

How did the man survive in the real world? It made his porch sitting even more remarkable. She was anxious to get the meeting over with so she and Alexi could start examining the clues again. This time, she'd borrowed a magnifying glass from Selma, a passionate stamp collector, who parted with it grudgingly after making Lucy sign an 'I pledge to return your magnifying glass' note. She'd agreed to return it by sundown, so the solar clock was ticking.

"We're most certainly not having a chili cook-off," Fran was saying, eyeing the row of congregants as Lucy and Alexi Quinn joined them.

"Why not?" Meg asked. "That went great last time, and we can fit it into the Fourth of July celebration next week."

"No, it didn't go well last time," Fran said, wincing and clapping a hand to her back. "Don't you remember the entire judging panel had heartburn for the rest of the day? And besides, it's July, expected to hit triple digits all next week. No one wants chili in July."

Alvin scribbled notes with the stub of a pencil which Lucy suspected had nothing to do with fundraising. She wished she was closer to sneak a peek.

Lucy pulled her sticky shirt away from her neck to allow for air circulation. "I wish Nan was here," she murmured to Alexi. "She is so good at coming up with ideas."

"Who is Nan?" Alexi asked.

"My cousin sort of, Uncle Paul's daughter."

"There is no such thing as a 'sort of' cousin."

"There is if you have a 'sort of' uncle." Lucy could see that Alexi was not going to stop puzzling over it until she explained. "When Uncle Paul and Aunt Libby helped take care of us, I was kind of raised alongside Nan. He's my uncle and she's my cousin," Lucy said with a firm nod.

"To be precise..." he started.

"Family isn't precise It's a messy pot of boiled noodles that sticks together for no practical reason at all."

He closed his mouth with a snap, and she regretted her strong tone.

"Nan's away doing some mission work in New Mexico." She continued more gently. "She was the mind behind the ice cream social and the time we sold tickets to get on a bus and go see Jaws in Granite Springs. That one lit up the town, I'll tell you."

Alvin waved his pencil. "How about we sell clues to the treasure? I mean, folks can pay five bucks a pop to get a copy of the clue. If somebody finds the next clue, we can sell that, too. People will go wild for it."

"But Alvin," Lucy said. "I haven't figured out the clues yet and we don't even know if there is a treasure for sure, but if we find it, we're going to use the money to restore the angel."

"We can have 'em sign a disclosure that they'll return the treasure to the town coffers," Alvin continued. "It's a brilliant idea."

"The opposite of brilliant," Fran said.

"Why?" Alvin demanded.

Fran folded her arms across her chest. "This purported treasure belongs to Thomas Lyman so if it's found, we need to contact his relatives and let them have first dibs. Does anyone know who his next of kin would be?"

"I do."

Everyone turned to look at the man with the mustache and mutton chops. Uncle Paul trotted up next to him, puffing slightly. "This is Lawrence," he said. He wants to talk about Lyman's treasure."

"Not Lyman's," Lawrence said. "It belongs to Agnes Needles or did. She died in May."

"Agnes?" Lucy said, standing. "But she dumped Thomas just before he enlisted."

"They reconciled. They were secretly married as a matter of fact in late November of 1941, just before Thomas was killed at Pearl Harbor. I have the paperwork to prove it."

Lucy stared. "You do?"

"I do," he said. "Thomas and Agnes were married shortly before he was killed and for a wedding gift, he gave her this nugget." He held up a jellybean-sized object which sparkled in the light. "I believe it's only part of his stash here in Honey Creek, the one he left for her to find as a game while he was gone."

Her mind struggled to process. "But if Agnes and Thomas were married then..."

"Then whatever you find belongs to Agnes's only living relative."

"And that would be..." Fran said, eyebrows furrowed.

"Me," Lawrence said. "I am Lawrence Needles Lyman, the only child of Agnes and Thomas Lyman."

Chapter Eight

Trooper puzzled over Lawrence Needles's announcement as he returned home in the evening after treating himself to a swim in the pond and a long nap as was his practice. He caught a rerun of Happy Days on the hardware store television and bought himself a cup of coffee and a day-old treasure donut at Steffi's before she closed up for the evening. Long after the sun mellowed towards the horizon, it continued to bake Honey Creek, and the mosquitos in the glen where Trooper called home were kicking it into high gear. Gummy beelined for his favorite spot under the sprawling limbs of the oak tree because he was too old and fat to climb the steep ramp up to the treehouse like he used to. Gummy whined.

"Don't worry. I'm gonna build you your own chateau before the rainy weather comes in," he said, but his mind was someplace else, far away, overseas, in fact, to the time and place where Thomas Lyman died in the attack at Pearl Harbor. Seemed to Trooper that there were new battlefields being drawn up right here in Honey Creek since Needles arrived, claiming he was entitled to Lyman's treasure. There was something slick and cloying about Needles, like the residue that remained on your fingers after gutting a fish. It troubled Trooper.

He'd tried to wrap his mind around the changing world where notions like self-exploration and resistance to the establishment were tossed about, but darn it all if it didn't seem like the same struggles people had always wrestled with, packaged in sparkly new names. Things were hard, harder than they had to be on some folks who were just trying to get their fair slice of the pie.

Perhaps Needles was actually an honest guy looking to claim what he believed was his due. But then again, maybe he really was a shyster, setting out to con Pastor Paul. That was a notion that couldn't be stomached. Not Paul, the man who would and had shared everything with his flock. And it didn't stop there...Paul operated as if the world were his congregation. Trooper would not allow his man to be fleeced.

He sat down in the pickle barrel he'd been pleased to fish out of Honey Creek last storm season. He'd cut away the top and set it inside to make a sort of armchair, complete with a nifty foam pad that'd blown off someone's car as they tore along the highway. Pulling down his hat to shade his eyes, he crossed his fingers over his belly and settled in for a spot of thinking about assets and death and legal matters, but Gummy's whine interrupted him.

He opened one eye. "Whatsa matter? You got a nice bowl of cold water there and a mat to sleep on. You're better off than most."

Gummy turned a circle, whimpering.

Trooper opened the other eye as a shadow caught his attention from up in the treehouse, a shadow that shouldn't have been there at all.

A pale face peeked down at him, the nose spangled with freckles and streaked black with smeared eyeliner. He sat up and blinked at Trudy. A thick dog-eared book was splayed across her knee. He stayed still for a minute, thinking perhaps he was dreaming. Her face remained when he blinked harder, so he got up and stood under the tree. Many verbal options scrolled through his brain before his mouth decided on the most ridiculous one.

"Sometimes you can see clear to the American River if there's enough moonlight."

She rubbed a hand under her nose and swung her legs over the platform so he could see the pebbled soles of her Keds. "I'm sorry. I didn't have anywhere else to go. I was walking and I got so hot and tired. I saw this place."

He waited.

She sniffed. "The lease is up on our apartment and the landlord wants quieter tenants. My mom is going with my brothers to stay with her cousin, but their place is crammed, and I want to stay here."

He rubbed his chin, picturing the boy on the motorcycle. "Ah."

Her voice quavered. "It's not fair. Things have been hard since my dad got killed in Vietnam, but it's like my mom doesn't even love me anymore like she wishes she never had me."

What to say to that? Some platitude about people speaking in the heat of the moment things they didn't mean? He didn't even know Trudy's mother. The teen would sniff through that hypocrisy in a heartbeat. He remained silent, staring up at the bottom of her shoes. The left one was developing a hole in the heel.

"We...we had a fight, me and my mom and, um, I guess I got kicked out."

"Nowhere else to go?"

She shook her head. "No. I shouldn't have crashed your pad," she said, wriggling to her feet. "I'll go."

"Nah. Rest a while up there. Rolled up in the corner is a mat you can sleep on, with a blanket that's not too full of holes if you get cold. Hungry?"

"A little."

"There's a jar of pickles and couple of apples up there. Help yourself."

"Thanks, Trooper." She swallowed a sob. "But I shouldn't take all your food and your sleeping mat. It wouldn't be right."

"It's okay. I'm gonna stay down here and think."

"About what?"

About what to do with a displaced teen.

"This and that," he said. "Just this and that."

***

On Monday morning Alexi sat in front of the fan in the relative cool of The Lady Quail's sitting room. The heat in Honey Creek was relentless and he missed the climate-controlled buildings in New York. There was something to be said for ruthless consistency. A piano shrouded in a faded tarp drew his attention, whispering to him to come closer, but he ignored it. Lucy handed him a magnifying glass, distractedly giving him the lens end first.

"I had to return Selma's magnifying glass and I found this one in a drawer. It's not as good. Scratches."

He carefully rubbed the prints away with the handkerchief he always kept in his pocket and peered at the yellowed papers through the maze of scratches.

Lucy chewed on her thumbnail. "Could it be true that Agnes and Thomas really were married secretly?"

He considered the question. "Do you suspect Mr. Needles is lying about their union? Or his parentage?"

"Yes."

"It's possible he is telling the truth."

"No, that can't be."

"Why not?"

"Because..." She flapped her hands. "Because it would be the perfect story otherwise."

He was not at all sure what she meant, but he figured

she'd get around to the explaining part without delay. He was correct.

Her expression went a bit fuzzy, and she gazed at a spot in the air above his head. "I mean, wouldn't it be like a fairy tale story if Thomas's treasure was found, and we could convince the rightful owner to use it to repair the church and the angel? That's the way a story is supposed to go, isn't it?"

"No," he said.

"No?" Her voice bristled with offense. "Why not?"

"Because this is not fiction and real-life stories do not go that way."

She stared at him, with eyes so green they could have been cut emeralds. "Alexi, what happened to you?"

He felt something in his stomach drop because she had asked, and he was a very poor liar, and he wouldn't want to deceive her anyway and the silence was stretching between them taut as piano wire. "I was a concert pianist. And now I am not."

"Your life story cannot be written in ten words." She scraped a chair close and turned those irises on him like searchlights. "Tell me more."

"It is…uncomfortable."

She nodded. "Messy, I know, like my story. Tell me anyway."

"Which part?"

"Start with your parents."

The fan whirred and clanked, moving the warm air around as he cleared his throat and smoothed his palms on his thighs. "My mother is Russian, an accomplished pianist. She met my father while playing for an orchestra in Berlin. Father was Irish, a carpenter, called to assist during an emergency when a careless timpani player damaged my mother's piano bench. My father said that crash was his invitation to meet the woman he was meant to marry."

"How romantic."

He did not see how timpani damage could be romantic. He waited.

She waved a hand. "Now the next part."

He stumbled on. "We lived in Europe until my father emigrated to the U.S. in search of a better education for me and my twin brother. We did not…thrive in public school and my parents did not feel welcomed to intervene, you might say, so my mother began to teach me at home, academics, manners, chess and she taught us, from my earliest memory, to play the piano. We played piano every waking moment and when we outgrew her tutelage, she got a job at a distillery to pay for outside lessons."

"So, you were very good?"

"Brilliant. I was a child prodigy, I debuted internationally at age twelve and won the Chopin Competition in Warsaw the day after my seventeenth birthday. I performed with the Berlin and New York Philharmonics where I was criticized for a lack of musical "conversation" with the audience. I have never understood this. My performance was perfect."

She smiled. "Did your brother stick with it, too? Is he a prodigy also?"

Alexi paused. "He died as a child."

Her mouth pinched in sadness, irises taking on the sheen of grief at his words. He marveled at it. This woman before him entertained grief for a boy she had never known, not even heard of until the moment before. It was extraordinary, he thought and for a second, he desperately yearned to feel like that, to twine together around the emotions of another, to join in the "messy" as he believed Lucy would say. The silence lingered and he filled the awkward void with words. "Mother did not think she could even have children, but she became pregnant with me and Nikolai at age forty. Nikolai died of a blood infection when he was seven and my father six months later of a brain aneurysm."

A little sigh escaped her.

And on he went, caught in the current of that small sound. "That is when the fear took hold of my mother. Without my father and brother, she felt adrift, far from her homeland. America became unwelcoming to her mind, you might say, hostile. We stayed in our studio apartment, only going out when we had to, to play, to practice, to buy food. We did crossword puzzles together and when they became too easy, I created some myself to keep us amused."

He took a breath, amazed at the avalanche of words. "But I did not really need a diversion. The piano was all I wanted. Mother cloistered me in music, and I built my world within the walls of the music staff." He was surprised at his own language, the poetry of it. "And I am caged by them too." The realization stopped him cold. Caged by his greatest love.

"Because now... you can't play." She grazed her fingers very gently over his crumpled hand. Her touch felt warm, soft as her sigh.

A lump formed in his throat and he swallowed hard. "Correct, I cannot. On my way home from a rehearsal, an automobile jumped a curb, pinned me to the door of a cigar shop, and crushed fifteen bones in my hand including the metacarpals which connect the fingers to the carpal bones of the wrist." The drone of the words seemed only a faint echo, a quiet resonating of the crashing dissonance of his life. "I tried everything to get the function to return, everything."

She kept her hand on his, urging him to continue.

"When I was inside the cage, I did not mind because I had my music. Now I am outside, looking in." He glanced from the piano to the slender strand of hair that fell across her forehead. "It is much worse, to be outside without my music. It is frightening here."

"Oh, Alexi." She held his hand harder and it caused his heart to pound like a timpani drum. A flicker of panic cascaded down his spine.

"Mother is not well. She had a stroke. I pay for her care. Very good care and I call her every couple of days."

Lucy nodded.

"I write crossword puzzles now," he blurted.

"I know."

"Denny is a very good piano tuner. He worked on many of the instruments I played. He knew...he understood that I required a job after my injury, a place to live since everything I earned must go to caring for Mother. He told me about Honey Creek, how they needed a crossword puzzle writer, I...I am not equipped to do anything else, so I left New York and came here. Just temporarily."

"Do you miss New York?"

"Yes. People paid no attention to me there. I could get lost in the noise." His mind drifted back to the bustle, rumbling traffic, the smell of hot pretzels from the corner vendor, the sound of his piano, his music.

Again, the sense of familiarity washed over him as if he'd seen her face, somewhere, sometime. He wanted to ask about her life, but he could not find any more words and her hand was still patting his softly and he did not want to move and sever the connection. What was the word that would capture what he was feeling at that moment? He longed to jot it down into neat boxes of across and down letters, to define it, to understand it.

"Do you have any other family?"

"My Aunt Mimi, my mother's sister. Mother lives with her in the care home. I gave them all the money from my playing before I left to come here." He paused. "My mother thinks I will play again."

"Do you, Alexi?" He could see his face mirrored in her

eyes. "Do you think so?"

A wave of longing surged over him again, he could almost taste the music, rich and sweet that trickled from his fingers like thick honey. Sometimes he would awaken from a dream of playing, full, satiated as if he'd finished the most delectable meal until wakefulness stirred the hunger to life again.

"No," he said, the word burned in his throat and across his tongue. "No, Lucy, I will never play again."

Chapter Nine

Paul found the untouched plate of six cookies in the kitchen a smidge before eight p.m. that evening. Libby was feeling unusually poorly, exhausted, achy. Her list of symptoms seemed to grow and change over the years since her diagnosis, but what preyed upon his soul most keenly was that her smiles had become rarer, the big toothy grin that took over most of her small face and never failed to bring a smile to his own. What could he do besides offer up fervent prayers? He felt more and more the edges of exhaustion creeping closer. Like now, when the church was crumbling, and Libby was pining, and he held the tender fears, pains, and petitions entrusted to him by his flock. There were times, very small moments, when he wondered if God had chosen wrongly in making him a pastor.

He fiddled with the cookie wrapping. Oatmeal raisin with walnuts, his wife's favorite kind, a preference of which the congregation was well aware, but Libby had lost her appetite of late. What would paint the grin back on her face if only for a short while? Peach ice cream. Aside from cookies, that's what was needed. He did not know how a woman prone to sour spells such as Fran Trawler could produce the most divine ice cream, but that was one of God's mysteries, so he left it to Him. Perhaps if Libby was not up to the Fourth of July festivities, they could sit together with a procured pint of Fran's finest and watch the fireworks from their porch. He wished their daughter Nan would be there to enjoy it too, but she was serving in Mexico until the end of the month. Peach ice cream for the short term and Nan home in a few weeks. Surely that would go a long way towards cheering up Libby.

The aroma of the cookies escaped from their plastic shroud made his mouth water. The church ladies had been feeding him and Libby relentlessly since her diagnosis. Casseroles, cookies, pot roasts. He wondered why it was such a hardwired need to comfort others with food. These cookie specimens were Ida's, and he knew she always added a pinch of freshly grated nutmeg. His resolve to keep his calories in check vanished under the onslaught. Cookies were cookies and it had to be a near on sin to toss them in the dust bin, so he tiptoed with the plate across the worn linoleum.

Sprawling in his ragged recliner, he eased off his shoes with a sigh of pleasure. His big toe was paining him again, not a surprise after the hike up the wooded trail for his Sunday visit to the Murphy sisters. They were too laid up with the challenges of being eighty-six and eighty-eight years old to attend church. He took church to them and their two cats, delivering his conversational version of his sermon while sipping sweet tea which coated his throat like rubber, though he'd never say so, and eating the three hard molasses cookies they anxiously laid out for him which had cost him two fillings over the years. He'd learned to gum each bite before he got down to the crunching.

The road to their house was simply too punched out with potholes and crumbling turns to challenge his stuttering Pacer with the journey, and with the energy crunch in full swing. Creaking the footrest up, he settled in, picking up the sports section of the Mountain Holler which Libby used to set aside for him every day, but now he retrieved himself in the mornings when he snuck out in his pajamas. He headed right for the baseball stats, setting his watch alarm for exactly thirty minutes, just long enough to indulge in his passion, but not so long that he let his baseball addiction run rampant. The spirit of competition quite often steamrolled his sense of Christian brotherhood. God loved everyone, sinner and saint, he was sure, but he could not bring that to mind when he considered the Dodgers. Thirty minutes was all he allowed himself.

Smoothing the pages, he got down to business, just as a quiet knock sounded on the front door. No one ever knocked loudly for fear of waking Libby from a rest. He worried Pearl or Bee Murphy might have taken a spill. Or maybe the unusual hour indicated someone had found the missing head. He eased open the door, pulse ticking up.

"We've got news," Selma Trunk said without preamble.

"Big news," her nephew Brodie confirmed, nodding his bald pate, Adam's apple bobbing from his nervous swallowing habit. Paul felt ridiculous standing there with no shoes on, with Selma dressed in a flowered smock and her nephew in short sleeves with a wide tie, but it seemed silly to pull on his loafers now.

"Come on in."

They did, settling on his sofa. Selma helped herself to one of Ida's oatmeal cookies. Paul felt an unholy stab of resentment. Five left. "Libby asleep?" she stage whispered.

"Yes."

"Then you'll have to tell her tomorrow."

"Tell her what?"

"The big news," Brodie said.

They both sat nodding, barely contained excitement, watching him.

Paul decided to wait it out. It didn't pay to rush the pitch. He wanted grab his remaining cookies, but instead he gamely offered up the plate to Brodie.

"Thanks," Brodie said, snagging one.

"You're never going to believe what we have to tell you."

"Okay." He eyed the remaining four cookies. "You've got my undivided attention."

"It's about Thomas Lyman. You're blood kin," Selma said.

"Afraid not," Paul said. "Mother said he was an orphan, from her friend Beth in Copperopolis who died of a hemorrhage when Thomas was born. They were..." he cleared his throat, "well Beth was an unwed mother, and that kind of thing was a big deal back then."

"Yes and no," Selma said.

"Come again?"

She shook her head and wiped the cookie crumbs from her mouth with her sleeve. "Yes, it was a big deal, and no Thomas was not who you think he was. No, sir."

Again, he waited until she shimmied to the edge of the sofa. "Thomas Lyman was not a family friend."

Paul quirked an eyebrow. "I would think Mother would know."

She'd opened her mouth to commence the explaining when there was another rap on the door. The next visitor was Alvin Wong, an enormous camera clinched under his armpit.

"Hey, Pastor. There's a whole bunch of them, pouring into town. They all want a piece of the action." He looked over Paul's shoulder "Oh hi, Selma, Brodie. Have you heard?" He kept his voice to barely above a whisper out of respect for Libby.

"Heard what?" Selma whispered back.

"Want to come in?" Paul said, trying his best stab at sincerity. Alvin did, sliding directly into Paul's recliner, grabbing up a cookie, and shoving it into his mouth. Three left. Paul settled on the arm of his sofa and blew out a breath.

"So, who wants to give up their news first?"

"The RVs are rolling in," Alvin said.

Selma polished her glasses with the hem of her dress. "RVs? What for?"

Bodie swallowed. "Oh yeah. I saw one of those Silver Streaks at the gas station. Must of cost a mint and a half to fill that thing up. It's a good thirty-one-footer, by my estimation. How do they afford to fuel it these days?"

Alvin ticked off the items on his fingers. "There's five so far, two Silver Streaks, one Air Stream, and an Executive Executive."

"That Executive Executive is a beauty. White with blue trim. Even has a shower," Bodie said.

"How'd you know that?" Selma asked.

Bodie swallowed twice. "Looked in the window when they were visiting the library."

"Why?" Paul said firmly, wrangling the wild pitches. "Why are there recreational vehicles arriving in our town? Can anybody answer that question?"

Alvin blinked. "Well sure. They're members of some treasure hunter club."

Paul's pulse sped up. "A treasure hunters club? Coming to Honey Creek?"

"My reporting drew them in," he said, puffing out his chest. "They got wind of the missing head and the treasure clues and they're here to solve the mystery and find Lyman's gold nuggets." Alvin sat back. "Isn't that something?"

Paul groaned. "This is getting out of hand. There's likely not any treasure at all, just one of Thomas's practical jokes."

"But," Selma said, loud enough that both Bodie and Alvin hushed her. "But," she repeated more quietly. "If there actually is a treasure, guess who it belongs to?"

He raised a suspicious eyebrow to Selma, who was clearly not done with her moment in the sun.

"Okay," Paul said, heaving out a breath. "I'll bite. Who would this fictitious treasure belong to?"

She sat up straighter. "Well, yesterday, during my lunch break I phoned a friend of mine who's a genealogist up near Copperopolis," she said. "Bernie Anderson. He's got access to the archives, microfiche, and everything."

She said the last word as if she was breathing the secrets of the universe.

"The archives, uh huh," Paul prodding, fearing she might need more cookies to fuel the remainder of the story.

"In the archives, Bernie could look through books, microfiche, any kind of records really. It's like looking right into people's dark family trees."

Paul did not think this sounded like a good idea in any way, shape, or form. Plus, he didn't like the way Selma was sort of vibrating.

"Well, Pastor Paul, he traced your whole family line, practically all the way back to the Ark."

"Impressive," Paul said. "And what did he find?"

"A birth certificate." She sat back triumphantly.

Paul snatched up a cookie and stuffed it in his mouth to keep from snapping at her to finish the cotton-picking story already. "A birth certificate," he said around the mouthful. "I imagine there are a lot of those flapping around my family tree."

She leaned forward. "This one was very revealing."

"Whose?" Alvin was so close to the edge of his chair he nearly slid to the floor. "You're killing me, Selma. Whose birth certificate?"

"Thomas Lyman's."

"Yeah? Yeah?" Alvin clutched his camera. "Quit stalling."

"Thomas Lyman," she said gravely, "wasn't a family friend. He was born to your mother Ann and a fellow named

Gomer Lyman who was killed in some sort of accident at age seventeen." Selma's cheeks pinked. "They weren't married, sorry, pastor, Ann was only sixteen, which is why I believe she cooked up the whole friend dying of a hemorrhage story before she married your father Douglas."

The cookie lumped in Paul's throat. "Are you saying...?"

"That Thomas Lyman was your half-brother."

He tried to force the lump down, but it made him cough until Alvin rose from the recliner to whack him on the back.

"Heck of a thing, huh, Pastor?" he said. "Like an episode of the Young and the Restless. I love that show."

Paul tried to process. Thomas Lyman. His brother.

"So, you see," Bodie said, "you are Thomas Lyman's closest living relative."

Alvin's face shone. "Closest living relative," he intoned. "Unless Mr. Needles is telling the truth and can produce a marriage certificate and proof that he's Thomas's son. Then we'd have a scuffle. Is a son a closer relative than a brother?"

"Doesn't matter. Lawrence Needles is lying. I can smell a liar from fifty paces." Selma sniffed, "That lying, no good, pile of..."

Paul gulped some water and held up his palm.

She sniffed again. "Sorry, Pastor, but there's no sign of this so-called marriage certificate between Agnes and Thomas that Bernie could find and he's like a St. Bernard on a scent when his interest is percolated. Needles is lying, sure as the sun rises and he's not got one sliver of a claim to that treasure."

Fictional treasure, Paul wanted to say, but he hadn't got the wind for it. As it was, he was still trying to get the cookie crumbs down his gullet.

Alvin was wide-eyed and shaking his head. "Exactly like a soap opera. Secret brother, pretend marriage. I can't get over it. It's like that new show, the one about the oil baron,

J.R. what's his name." He snapped his fingers. "Show's called Houston."

"Dallas," Selma said.

"Yeah, that's the one," Alvin said.

Paul wanted to pooh-pooh the whole thing, to rage against the insult to his mother and her character. He and Thomas had been raised as brothers and that was what mattered anyway. He opened his mouth and then closed it again when all the strange bits of family flotsam and jetsam bubbled up in his mind. There had been the occasional odd remark, the comment of a loose-lipped cousin, the cleft of the chin so very similar in both Thomas and himself, that made things as clear now as a neon sign. It was the truth, strange and upsetting as it was, he knew it in his bones. He put away the bubbling froth of emotion to examine at a more private moment. With his Pastor Paul hat on, the Paul Stuckley identity could remain on the peg until later.

"But," he finally managed, after another slug of water. "My family history aside, Thomas Lyman," he could not bring himself to say 'my half-brother,' "hid these alleged clues over forty years ago. They would have turned up by now if there really had been any."

"Oh, come on, Pastor. The Post Office still has the original carpet from 1919. Things don't change here in Honey Creek," Selma observed.

He felt a touch of the wild in his belly as if the earth had begun to move again, the underground plates crashing against each other, sending the world titling. After a deep breath, he said, "I'm certain there is no gold treasure here in Honey Creek. How are we going to convince all these treasure hunters that all they're going to find is a big pile of dust?"

"Let them hunt," Alvin said, in the tone of Marie Antionette advising her people eat cake. "It makes for a great story." He framed the imaginary headline with his hands in the air. "People swarm Honey Creek, Modern Day Gold Rush."

Paul could not imagine anything worse than a swarm of prospectors barreling down on the town. Honey Creek had remained intact from the gold mining days, through the tumult of the Vietnam War, Watergate, and the death of Elvis Presley. He knew it could withstand a dose of gold fever, but it was getting harder and harder to hold onto their simple life. His senses spun and there was a knocking in his head.

No, not his head. The door.

Selma, Bodie, and Alvin stared at each other.

Selma crimped a lip. "Well, who could that be at this hour?"

Alvin's eyes went wide as silver dollars. "Maybe someone's found the treasure."

"Good, then we can get this whole thing over with," Paul muttered as he got up and flung open the door.

Chapter Ten

Trooper held the Dodger's cap between his fingers, figuring he ought to try not to aggravate the preacher too much on his off-duty hours. Besides, he didn't know Libby's baseball affiliation and he wouldn't want to upset her for the world. "Evenin' Pastor." He eyed the three people clustered in the living room. "Am I interrupting a prayer meeting or something?"

The pastor looked a bit pinch-faced, but he waved Trooper in, offering him his pick of two cookies, Gummy oozed in too, sprawling on the hardwood near a plant stand brimming over with a silk fern. Trooper took a cookie and sat with it between his fingers because there was already a new toothbrush, a little tube of toothpaste, and three Sunday School snickerdoodles cluttering up his pockets.

"We were just telling pastor that he's Thomas Lyman's half-brother," Selma said.

"You don't say?" Trooper let the info settle for a moment. That explained the pastor's glazed look. His mother must have told him a bit of a fib. Trooper could see how a thing like that could ambush a man in his own living room.

The pastor shot him a weary glance. "And I have been told there are treasure hunters streaming into town in RVs."

"Yes," Alvin corrected. "Six of them, plus some in cars and two motorcycles."

"Seven. Saw a Winnebago bang into the street sign on

my way over here. Hardly scratched the camper but the sign's twisted up like a pretzel."

The pastor waved a hand. "What brings you here, Trooper? Did you have news to share also? Have the Dodgers pulled into first place in the league, and you've arrived to taunt me?"

Trooper noted the rough tone. He decided a little oil was in order. "No Padre. I have a situation to tend to, and I don't rightly know how to go about it. Since you're on God's good side, I figured you might know what to do."

"What situation?"

"There's a girl in my tree."

The pastor blinked. "A girl?"

"Yep. Climbed up there on account of her family moved away without her and she got nowhere to go, though I suspect that is only part of the story. Can't just let her stay up there 'cuz it's no place for a girl hanging out in the woods with an old grizzly bear like me. You know her, Trudy Prynne."

Paul sighed. "I had a feeling things weren't good at home with the amount of time she's been spending in Honey Creek. Is there any way she can be induced to call her family and patch things up?"

"Don't think so, but you got a way with people so maybe you can talk to her. She said if she doesn't find a place to stay soon, she's running away to San Francisco."

"That's no place for a girl," Alvin said.

"Neither is my tree."

"Trudy's a good kid," Selma said. "We got to figure something out for her."

Paul stared. "Okay, got any ideas?"

"Uh, no. By 'we' I actually meant you." Selma shrugged. "I have no room to take her in, what with Mama's cookbooks and my stamp collection."

Paul frowned. "Couldn't you make some phone calls? You're on the Hospitality Team at church."

"Uh uh," Selma said. "I mean, I've got my hands full helping Lucy track down your treasure..."

"And defeating the dastardly Mr. Needles," Alvin said melodramatically.

Paul groaned. "It could be that this whole nutty treasure thing is nothing but a bag of worthless trouble."

"Where's the fun in that?" Trooper asked.

The pastor closed his eyes and fell silent. Selma finished her cookie, the crunching loud in the parlor. Trooper looked for more. Since he'd been a late entry into the cookie race there was now only one left on the plate. He stood and casually sauntered closer.

"All right," Pastor said after a sigh, his eyes opening. "I have an idea."

Trooper slapped his thigh. "There you go, I knew you'd come up with a crackerjack of a notion." He could not help but add, "Or should I say you hit upon a pot of gold?"

Pastor grabbed the plate with the remaining cookie, sweeping it to his chest like a fouled baseball. The cookie sailed off the plate but was spared from hitting the ground when Gummy gulped it out of the air in one fluid motion.

For a moment, all five sets of eyes were riveted on the dog who slid a pink tongue over his fleshy lips.

"Look at that," Trooper said. "Didn't know he had it in him."

Noticing the pink tint to Pastor Paul's cheeks, Trooper gathered his dog and headed to the door.

"Will she be okay sleeping in your treehouse for tonight?" Paul asked.

"Yessir. Plenty warm and me and Gummy can keep a lookout for raccoons from the ground."

"Do you need an extra sleeping bag or something?"

Selma asked.

"Nah. There's enough to keep Trudy comfortable in the treehouse for tonight and I'll gather up a heap of pine needles to bunk on." In truth, he hadn't slept on the ground in a dog's age. He hid his grin at her wonderment. Though he was far too old to sleep on pine needles, he enjoyed spreading around the mystique that he and Davy Crockett were two peas in a pod.

If he were going to be sleeping al fresco, he would swing by to borrow a few cushions from the patio chairs outside the Gold Pan. Meg wouldn't mind, as long as he returned them before opening. Plus, he might be able to get some gossip about Meg's temporary tenant, Lawrence Needles.

"'Night, Padre. Night all."

"Good night, Trooper," Paul said wearily.

***

"A taste for the iron perfect. What in the world could that possibly mean?" Lucy said on a sizzling Tuesday morning. "I've asked everyone from the postmistress to the street sweeper," she said.

Alexi stood with his bag from the Gold Pan Cafe, watching her poke through the materials she'd borrowed from the library about the history of irons. He regretted that he'd had no further inspiration either, though he'd puzzled over it nearly all night.

Lucy plowed a hand through her hair, bunching up the strands on one side into white-blond tangles. "Did you know the electric iron was patented in 1882 and the original model weighed a whopping fifteen pounds?" she said as she took the bag from him.

"Yes."

"Yes?" She gaped. "You knew that?"

"The invention of the electric iron coincided with the widespread electrification of houses in the late 1800s." He shrugged. "My brain can hold many parcels of information."

"I wish mine could."

He noted the way her hair shone platinum; the mussed strands illuminated by the sun streaming through the parlor. Her beauty had to be a much finer gift than his ability to hold onto useless bits of information. The light gilded her profile too and something about it awakened in him that feeling of déjà vu. "You said you were in New York City. Why?"

"Why was I there?"

"Of course."

She arranged the scrambled eggs and toast onto a plate and scooped the cut fruit into a bowl. A spoon, fork, linen napkin, and a cup of coffee perked in the Mr. Coffee maker and poured into a china cup completed the arrangement. "I worked there for a while."

"In what capacity?"

"In a way-over-my-head capacity."

He started to confront this non-answer to his question when she hefted the tray onto her shoulder.

"Thank you for bringing over the breakfast again. You must really like eating at the diner."

He did not actually like eating there as he knew he was a source of curiosity for the regulars, but the oatmeal was good and he found he enjoyed talking to Trudy, which was inexplicable since he could find nothing in common with the colorfully clad girl who talked about feelings and friendships and fashion, things he knew nothing about. But Trudy did not seem to mind when his end of the conversation lagged, and it was interesting to listen to her stream of consciousness. He wondered if the mind of all teenagers were so alive with thoughts, like a cascade of arpeggio notes.

Lately, Mr. Needles had made a morning appearance, chatting with the regulars and even buying a round of coffee for them all. Alexi did not partake. He could not explain the sensation exactly, but he felt it would somehow wrong Lucy Winston. How could a cup of free coffee do that? And why should it pain him to do so? It was a puzzlement, as were many things relating to Lucy. He felt a burning need to set things in order where she was concerned.

"You did not answer my earlier question," he said, "about why you were in New York."

"Didn't I?"

"Not fully. It is almost as if you are being intentionally evasive."

She sighed. "Not evasive, Alexi. It's just a kink in my hose."

"A...what?"

"A hitch, a sore spot."

"Oh. A metaphor. You mean a memory that pains you to recall."

"Yes." Her eyes were soft, and she glanced at his hand. "Everyone has times they'd rather forget, right?"

He was swept back into the moment of impact, the sensation of his finger bones snapping like dry twigs under the onslaught. The weeks, months, years he'd labored to restore his hand to life. The moment he'd sat down on the piano bench for the last time and faced the fact that he would never play again. "Yes," he said after a swallow. The ding of a brass bell sounded loud as a gong.

Lucy jumped visibly. "Was that the front desk bell?" she whispered.

"Yes," he whispered back, though it seemed an odd time to whisper.

"Why would someone ring it?"

He considered. "Perhaps a prospective guest wants to check in to the Lady Quail."

"But we don't actually rent rooms."

"They probably are not privy to that fact. The sign says

you are an inn. Perhaps these clients were in the area, a blow in, as Meg would say."

She grinned. "You're gonna start talking like a Creeker?"

Was he? Was the town creeping inside his vernacular as well as his behavior? Like porch sitting or the chin bobbing morning greeting at the diner? "Probably not, I do not tend to use hyphenated words nor contractions often." He thought for another moment before adding, "And I do not routinely discuss the weather."

After a five-second look which he suspected could be exasperation except that her mouth was smiling, he followed her to the lobby. There was a short, strapping woman with close-cropped hair standing on the guest side of the granite-topped desk. Behind her was a line of four other people in various shapes and sizes, peeking around her doughy shoulders.

"I need a room for two," the woman said. "My name is Pat Steele. S-t-e-e-l-e."

Lucy gaped. "Uh, well, we don't have any rooms for rent, right now."

Pat snapped to attention so fast her chins wobbled. "Booked so soon? But the second clue's only just been printed."

"Printed?" Lucy echoed weakly.

The woman slapped down the latest edition of the Mountain Holler. "Clue number one, spiritual being serving God especially as a messenger. The angel, of course, but we've heard that you up and lost her head. Can you confirm that rumor?"

"Well, actually I..."

Pat waved her off. "Never mind. We intend to find the head in case it contains further clues, but it will not distract us from forward progress on this treasure hunt regardless. Clue number two, 'a taste for the iron perfect.'"

Lucy snatched up the paper, mouth gathered into an angry pucker. "Alvin printed that?"

The lady grabbed it back and hunched over, voice low. "Me and my hubby figure it's got something to do with the blacksmithy. You know, iron?" She waggled an eyebrow, the man behind straining to hear.

"But we don't have a blacksmithy," Lucy whispered back.

"Every gold rush town worth its salt had a blacksmithy," she said. "Lyman knew that and it's his little joke, see?" She spoke so softly both Lucy and Alexi bent nearly in half to hear her. "The building's been converted to a different use by now, of course, and I'm going to find it and the next clue, too."

"But..." Lucy started again.

She jerked a thumb behind her. "All these people are from the Treasure Hunters Club, division seven. We're friends and all..." Her eyes narrowed to slits. "But when it comes to finding the loot, we'll turn on each other like crabs in a bucket." She straightened and called out to the line. "Gal here says there are no rooms for rent. No vacancies. We've got competition horning in for this treasure, so you all better get cracking."

The people in the queue immediately about-faced and tramped out the doors in a noisy pack just as Trudy was entering, baggy coveralls dwarfing her slight frame. A black beret was cocked on her head. She stepped to the side and allowed them to pass before she turned to Lucy. "More treasure hunters? There were a bunch in the diner the moment we opened, but they've cleared out." She fisted a hand on her hips, the first finger glinting with what he'd been told was a 'mood ring.' The idea of a gemstone that revealed a person's feelings was fascinating to Alexi. He thought if everyone wore them, he would have a much easier time deciphering the strangely shifting cascade of human emotion.

"They eat slow, leave a mess, and they don't tip well," Trudy said.

Alexi said, "Alvin has ill-advisedly published the next clue."

"The one about the iron perfect?"

He nodded.

"Well, Miss Fran doesn't think it's that ill-advised. She's hoping they stay for the Fourth of July celebration. She figures they'll buy all kinds of souvenirs. I'm helping her make extra batches of peach ice cream to sell at the parade." She looked at her Keds. "She's letting me stay with her for a while until I can figure something else out. Pastor Paul arranged it."

Lucy finally snapped out of her reverie. "Really?"

Trudy ducked her head, a flush staining her cheeks. "Yeah. I, uh, I can't go home right now."

Lucy patted her shoulder. "It's okay. It's real nice that you're going to stay with Fran. She could use some company."

Alexi did not see how it was nice to be thrown out by your mother when you had a year of high school to go, as he'd heard Meg whisper to the regulars when Trudy had gone to fetch more napkins. Trudy nodded, the string of beads around her neck catching the light.

"I'm on my first break. Miss Meg doesn't like me to hang out at the diner with my nose in a book. She says it's unhealthy, so I thought I'd come over and paint Mrs. Winston's nails," Trudy said. "I found this color polish I forgot I had, and I thought she'd like it." She wiggled a bottle filled with shimmering paint. "Gingersnap bronze."

Alexi did not think the color was cookie-like in the least, but he got the sense it wasn't the thing to say.

"She'll love it," Lucy said. "Thank you, Trudy. I'll be up in a minute with her breakfast."

Trudy nodded and headed for the stairs, stopping with her sneaker on the first step. "I was thinking maybe you got the word wrong."

"What's that?" Lucy was still peering out the front window at the departing treasure hunters as they climbed into their vehicles.

"Oh, never mind. Probably dumb." The curtain of hair was half concealing her eyes. "I'll get the manicure going."

"What word?" Alexi asked.

She looked at him from under her fringe of bangs. "Perfect. You know the clue about the iron perfect."

He intended to stay quiet and allow the girl to find her way to the words, but Lucy was not one to wait.

"Yes, a lick for the iron perfect," she pressed. "Did you have a thought about that?"

"Aww, it's probably stupid, like I said."

Lucy shook her head. "We'll take any thoughts at the moment. I'd love to hear it. Please."

Trudy thumbed the clasp on her overalls and sucked in a breath. "I really like history and I sort of didn't return my book from last semester. I figured they wouldn't notice if one was missing. We stopped before World War II and I wanted to know how it all turned out, you know? Anyway, I remembered that Benito Mussolini had this weird nickname because he spased out trying to smash the Italian mafia."

Alexi was struggling to translate 'spased out' when Lucy jumped in again.

"What was the nickname?" she said, lips open in an eager smile that made Alexi want to smile too.

Excitement thrilled through him like a chord. "Six letter word for a chief officer, magistrate, or regional governor in certain countries."

"Six letters?" Lucy's nose wrinkled as she pondered. "Sounds like perfect?" She snapped her fingers. "Oh, man. The clue isn't 'the iron perfect, it's…"

"The Iron Prefect," he and Trudy said at exactly the same moment.

Chapter Eleven

Fran stood holding the bushel basket as Trooper handed down the peaches from his perch on the top of the stepladder. The aroma of ripe fruit perfumed the air. There could be no sweeter scent, Fran was sure, but it made her stomach quiver just the same. The fragrance was indelibly connected to memories of Julys long past when she and Moe gathered in the peach crop. They'd sucked greedily at the luscious fruits, the juices sticky on their fingers before returning to their tidy home, the one she still lived in, where she would make pies like her Nana Jo had taught her.

The pies were marvels or perhaps it was because she and her husband were young, and life spread out before them like the wide Honey Creek sky. Pie and dreams and youth and promises. She didn't understand why being with Moe had made her somehow feel attractive, pretty even, though she had never thought of herself so until she met him. Fran was plain, her mother had informed her from an early age, with features a little too strong, a waist a bit too thick, and no particular supply to wit or talent to offset the deficits. But Moe's laughter ignited hers, his happy-go-lucky attitude added a tincture of joy to her personality that she'd never known before. Moe made her different, better, lovelier. When he pulled her to him with that gleam in his eye, she knew he believed she was desirable and she could believe it too, her, a plain woman so far removed from the tousle-haired, mini-skirted lovelies of the day. And wasn't that what every woman craved in the deepest part of her soul, to be desirable to the man she loved? But with each miscarriage, the blue sky clouded, and her dreams narrowed, and her youth moved an inch further into the past. She had become obsessed with her grief, holding the memory of each lost baby so close that they hardened inside her like a gnarled peach pit, her face pinched and creased into the same stone. Sometimes her own reflection in the mirror stopped her cold. Who was that old woman staring back at her? Moe could not understand. Perhaps it was not in his nature to try. He was a boat built for calm lakes, not the tempest that had overtaken her with each silent loss. She pushed him away and he, being the cooperative sort, had let her. Their connection weakened until it faltered and died altogether. Still, she resented him for not fighting to keep their marriage alive, and most of all, for finding happiness with another woman.

The thunk of an overripe peach broke her reverie as the juice dripped through the bottom of the basket into her hands. "That one's a dud, Trooper."

"The mature ones are best," he said, waggling his eyebrows at her. "I like my peaches to have a few miles on them."

"Oh, for goodness sake you scoundrel, just pick the last few. I'm melting." Sweat ran down her temples, dampening her hair into wiry whorls. He climbed down the ladder and they sat on the porch in the shade, the basket of peaches between them. She fetched him a glass of lemonade, the least she could do since he'd gone up on the ladder for her and what did it matter to add a tuna sandwich on the side and a bowl of water for the ridiculous walrus of a dog?

He stood as she approached which set her to waving the plate at him. "Oh, sit down, Trooper. No chivalry needed.

Here's some lunch."

He set to it and she felt that tiny stroke of satisfaction that came with the act of feeding someone, the same small vibration she'd gotten from opening a jar of homemade blueberry jam to spread on Trudy's toast that morning. She wrinkled her nose when Trooper tucked his paper napkin in his shirt front and took a bite. Chivalry indeed.

"So, how's it going with your houseguest?" he said around a mouthful of tuna.

"Tolerable. I set some ground rules right from the gate. None of those miniskirts or halter tops in my house. No smoking and no drugs of any kind and no keeping company with any boys."

"Regular prison warden."

She ignored the jibe and took a bite of her own sandwich. "And she's to help me as much as I need, in exchange for room and board. Actually, I showed her how to peel the peaches and sprinkle them with lemon juice and she already finished two quarts before she left for the diner this morning."

"Good kid."

"Hard worker." Fran fingered the bread. "I wonder about a mother who moved away and left her alone."

"Trudy's choice to stay, wasn't it?"

"That's what she says, but it seems like a mother could have persuaded her in a different direction. A girl that age is vulnerable, especially after losing her father to that stink hole of a jungle."

"Stink hole of a war," Trooper added. Something passed across his face, a flicker, no more.

"What?"

He ate another bite. "Nothing. Just thinking it'd be hard for a kid to leave her friends, even if some are better left behind."

She cocked her head at him. "What does that mean, Trooper? Speak plainly. When you try to be secretive it makes you look like you've got a case of indigestion. What do you know?"

He laughed at that one, but she kept a straight face. "Nothing. You're right. She's vulnerable with no father around and such. All's I meant." He took another enormous bite. "Good tuna."

An RV rumbled by the magnetic map on the back publicly proclaiming their travels. Next, a Chevy Blazer clattered past, followed by a couple jammed together on a motorcycle.

"What in the world?" Fran asked.

The motorcycle couple pulled off to the curb. "Excuse me," the gap-toothed man behind the handlebars said. "Looking for an antique shop around here called the Rusty Muffler."

"That's not an antique shop..." Fran began.

Trooper cut her off. "Two blocks, make a left."

The man nodded and fired off a salute which Trooper returned with a lazy wave of his sandwich.

"The Rusty Muffler is no more an antique shop than the public library," she snapped. "It's a scrap heap, plain and simple and it's a sin for Gabe to go around pretending he's anything but a junkyard owner."

"One man's junk is another man's treasure."

Another vehicle approached this time a sky-blue Fiat. Trooper sat up straighter. The owner rolled down the window, the stranger who'd showed up at church waving around a gold nugget, Lawrence Needles, shirt open three buttons deep.

"Looking for a place called the Rusty Muffler," Mr. Needles said.

Trooper heaved himself from the chair and clomped

down the steps. Fran followed. "Afternoon. Might I ask why you're lookin' for such an establishment?"

His eyes were covered by dark sunglasses. "Just looking."

Trooper raised an eyebrow. "You and the parade of people that passed by here? What's so interesting? All y'all just lookin'?"

He remained silent, but his mouth pinched at the corners.

"Maybe you saw the next clue in the Mountain Holler?" Trooper said. "Fixin' to find yourself Lyman's treasure?"

"The treasure belongs to Agnes," he said. "And I'm her kin. What's right is right."

"True enough." Trooper nodded, gaze drifting. Fran had known Trooper long enough to take note when he laid on the 'good ole boy' persona a little too thick. He was up to something.

Trooper shoved the toothpick from his sandwich into the crook of his mouth, completing the homespun hick disguise. "Finding the accommodations over at the diner to your liking? Got some mighty fine burgers, Meg does."

Needles lifted a shoulder. "Small towns are all the same." His lids narrowed a bit. "Everybody knows everybody, and they all pretend to be happy homespun folk."

"Maybe we are happy homespun folk."

"Just like the Waltons? I don't think so."

Fran knew Trooper made it a point to visit the hardware store where Tony always had a TV running during the Waltons show. "Waltons got their troubles too, don't they? 'Member that one episode in particular when Mary Ellen finds out her hubby ain't dead in Pearl Harbor after all? He's got one of them assumed names. Lying like a rug about his real identity."

Fran suppressed a gasp at Trooper's audacity.

"I don't have much time for television," Needles said.

"About the Rusty Muffler..."

Trooper's gaze drifted over the car. "Nice wheels. What did you say was your business exactly, Mr. Needles?"

"I didn't. Are you going to give me directions or not?"

Trooper took out the toothpick. "Oh, sure thing. You go up a block, turn right, and drive about ten miles east and you'll find it sure as shooting."

Needles motored off without a word.

Fran bit her lip to contain the smile. "You sent him in the wrong direction. You lied."

Trooper shrugged. "I'm doing him a favor. A drive in the country will do him good."

"What's all that about the Waltons?"

"Just talk."

She frowned. "You think he's a phony, don't you?"

"One hundred percent, but I been wrong before."

She stared up the road. "Still though, how did today's clue send everybody hightailing it to the Muffler?"

"Only one way to find out." He crooked his arm. "Shall we take a stroll?"

She shooed him away. "Please. Neither you nor your fat dog would make it on foot in this heat. We'll take my car. The dog can stay here in the backyard."

Trooper smiled, and she had a fleeting thought that it had been his plan for her to drive them all along.

***

Lucy pushed through the door of the Honey Creek Library. The lanky librarian, Phil Zimmerman stabbed a pencil in her direction, setting the metal chain around his neck jingling. His straggly hair was captured in a neat ponytail. "The Rusty Muffler."

"Beg your pardon?" Lucy said.

He peered through the lenses of his granny glasses. "According to the town records which no one has cared a fig about for nearly a century, the Rusty Muffler now occupies the land upon which the blacksmithy stood in 1885. That's what you want to know, isn't it?"

Her mouth fell open. "No, but why did you think so?"

"Why did I think so?" He stood so fast the rolling chair rocketed out from underneath him. "Because the horde of visitors swarming into this town has made it their point to beeline right to the library, the core of the town, the backbone of the civilized world, and what do they want? Education? Enlightenment? Social justice?"

Lucy screwed up her face. "I'm judging by your tone the answer is no."

"Of course, it's no." He slapped a palm on the desk between a potted ficus and his rubber stamp. "All they want is treasure after reading the drivel printed by Wong about some clue or another."

She bit her lip. "About the iron perfect?"

"That's the one. They've decided the filthy gold must be in what used to be the blacksmithy, so they'd swarmed like mosquitos, messing up my books, using the bathroom and depleting all the paper towels, and not even donating one cent, not ONE cent, mind you, to the cause." He gripped the glass pickle jar with the Save the Whales sticker on the front. "It's another demonstration of the greed that's eaten away at the core of this great nation. Self-serving capitalist pigs, all of them." When he wound down, he polished his glasses on the hem of his striped shirt. "Anyway," he said, "The Rusty Muffler is the location of the blacksmithy if you wanted to know that."

"Interesting, but I've come to do research. Alexi Quinn will meet me here in a minute after he turns in his next crossword puzzle at the Holler."

"Oh." Phil retrieved his chair and resumed his seat. "Research," Phil said. "Sorry. What can I help you with?"

"I want to know about Mussolini."

He blinked. "The Italian dictator?"

"That's the guy. Do you know a lot about him?"

"I've done my fair share of reading. He was the Prime Minister of Italy and he pretended to be democratic minded until 1925 when he dropped the charade and set up a legal dictatorship. Many would say..."

She cut him off. Phil was certainly the right man for the job. "Yes, that Mussolini. Do you know what his nickname was?"

"Il Duce, it's Latin for leader."

"Another one. The Iron..." she let the words trail off.

Phil's smile nearly split his face in half, and she thought he was going to leap out of his chair again but instead he perched on the edge.

"Wait just a minute. The clue isn't 'perfect' it's prefect. They got it wrong." He chortled and pumped a fist into the air. "A typo. All those treasure idiots got it completely wrong over a typo." He spun a circle in his chair. "That is so rich with irony. The tiniest vowel in the wrong place will defeat all those money grubbers."

"I'm not sure about defeat, but it might slow them down for a while. Will you help me, Mr. Zimmerman?" she asked as she dropped a dime into the Save the Whales jar.

He clasped the pickle jar to his side and beamed her a look of deep satisfaction. "Lucy Winston, it would be my honor."

Chapter Twelve

"Though the waters thereof roar and be troubled, though the mountains shake with the swelling thereof...." Paul lost the end yet again as he plodded through his lunchtime prayer walk. Thoughts of Thomas kept intruding like those troubled waters. He tried to put his finger on the feelings roiling in his gut. Sadness that he'd missed out on knowing his biological sibling intimately? Anger at his mother for keeping the truth from him? Irritation with the straitjacket society that made her believe she had to? He wondered if his soft-spoken father had known the truth. Had his mother trusted her spouse with the secret? Sweat poured down his face since it was heading towards noon.

"Though the waters thereof roar and be troubled..."

But again, he lost the verse, this time to the rumble of engine noise. Wiping his forehead with a faded handkerchief he considered the odd tableau in front of him. The Rusty Muffler with its 'Old, used, and rare antiques' sign beckoned customers through a sprawling set of iron gates, marbled with rust and speckled with bird droppings. Rarely had Paul seen more than one car parked in front of the place and maybe a couple of bicycles from the kids who pinched the occasional hubcap or two.

Now, an assortment of vehicles from motorcycles to RVs crammed in alongside the road. Even Fran Trawler's sensible Volkswagen was parked in the scant shade of an elm tree. Shouts and chatter came from the yard.

"What in the tarnation?" He pushed past the gate where Gabe had erected piles of artfully arranged hubcaps. The metal discs burned in the sun enough to make Paul's eyes water as he took in the milling visitors.

Gabe stood next to the hubcap sculpture, his tanned skin not even the least bit sweaty, his mutton chops shadowing his slim face. "Afternoon, pastor," he said, tipping the dented brim of his hat.

"Afternoon, Gabe. Business is booming, I see."

He lifted a shoulder. "Isn't that something? They're all interested in the blacksmithy that used to be here all them years ago on account of the next clue in the Holler. Didn't think anyone even read that rag, 'cept the sports section."

Another clue. His stomach dropped.

Gabe sipped something from a metal cup. "I figured I'd let 'em look around before I started the tour up."

"What tour?"

Gabe grinned. "The five-dollar tour that's going to take them to the historical spots on this very property."

Paul hid a smile. "What exactly are the historical spots, Gabe?"

"Got a respectable pile of old horseshoes behind the junker cars. Some real nicely preserved specimens. And you can still see the metal innards of a wrecked carriage just past the old pond. They're gonna go wild for that."

Another couple strolled in and Gabe offered a friendly wave. "You here lookin' for a clue in the old blacksmithy?"

They bobbed their heads in unison, squinting in the glare of the hubcap pile.

"All right then. You make yourselves at home. The historic tour gonna start up in a half hour or so."

Paul wondered why he'd not caught sight of Lucy who seemed most determined of all to find Lyman's treasure with her peculiar new friend Alexi Quinn. A shadow fell across Paul's eyes and he saw Mr. Needles striding over. Needles looked down at him through mirrored sunglasses which reflected Paul as if he'd been bloated and twisted by a funhouse mirror. He resolved to lay off the cookies for the foreseeable future. "Hello, Mr. Needles. Are you looking for the next clue?"

"Call me Lawrence. I would have been here sooner, but I got some bad directions." His mouth pinched as he glanced around. "Don't see how a junkyard is much help though."

"Oh, you'll be wild for the blacksmithy tour, sir." Gabe beamed. "Starts up in..."

"A half hour or so, yes I heard." He jutted his chin. "How about a private tour?"

Gabe's eyes glittered. "When?"

"Right now. Just for me, before you show all these other people."

Paul could see Gabe winding up for the delivery.

"Hmmm." He rubbed the fuzz on his chin. "That don't seem sporting, to give you the low down before all these other kind folks. I promised 'em, you see. A verbal agreement if you will."

Needles took a leather wallet from his back pocket. "I'd make it worth your while. You're charging five for the tour? I'll pay eight."

Gabe frowned as he considered. "Well, see. I have a touch of the nerve damage on account of that Agent Orange stuff our boys dropped in 'Nam to kill the foliage. It pains me something terrible if I walk too much. I don't know if it's gonna be worth my discomfort to do a private tour, see."

Needles worked his lips a minute. "Nine."

"Hmmm. I don't know. Hot weather brings out the pain something fierce."

"Ten," Needles said, thrusting a bill at Gabe. "My final

offer."

Gabe nodded thoughtfully. "Ten it is, my man. Let me tell my assistant I'm starting up a private tour and I'll be right back."

Needles laid a hand on the hubcaps, pulling it back quickly, shaking off the burn. "Like a furnace. The heat here is ridiculous."

"Not a fan of Gold Country summers, Lawrence?"

"No way." He wiped a trail of sweat from his temple. "After we get this treasure business sorted out, I'm moving to New York."

"Looking to be a Yankees fan?"

Needles brightened; the transformation remarkable. "Already am. I was a vendor at the 1964 World Series when I was seventeen. Hot dogs." He fished something out of his pocket, a silver dollar. "Mickey Mantle gave me this."

Paul felt the mist parting. Baseball. The man loved baseball. He could not be a villain after all. Paul felt guilty for having ever thought it. He grinned. "A Yankees man. Let's see. Mantle hit a walk-off home run in game three as I recall."

A broad grin crept across Needle's face. "Yes, sir. And I was there to see it. The crowd went wild, absolutely deafening. Best moment of my life, even though we lost the series."

"Well now, Lawrence. I would appreciate a chance to sit you down on my front porch with a glass of lemonade and talk about the greatest sport on earth. I'm for the Giant's, of course, but respect for the game, that's the important thing, isn't it?"

"Maybe it is."

"Excellent. Perhaps you will come by this evening then?" He figured there would be a cellophane-wrapped plate of cookies he could offer, and he'd have only one, to be neighborly.

"Perhaps I will."

"Perfect."

Needles shot him a look. "This friendly treatment. Is it because you want to get a look at that marriage license?"

"No, we're naturally friendly here in Honey Creek, especially to fans of the One True Sport." Paul tried to think how the thing he wanted to bring up could be managed with tact. After another two minutes in the blazing sun, he decided to go with a good country hardball. "But I would be much obliged for a look at that marriage license."

Needles stared. "Because you believe I'm a liar?"

"No, sir, but I've just recently been informed that Thomas Lyman is my half-brother."

Needles gaped. "Really? How did that suddenly come to light?"

Paul sighed. "The other thing about Honey Creek is that people feel responsible for their neighbors. I have lots of neighbors."

"Nosey."

"I prefer to think of it as dedicated to my wellbeing."

"Uh huh."

"So, I'm naturally curious about Thomas's marriage to Agnes, you see." An idea struck him. "Seems like we're both connected to Thomas. That makes you..." Paul struggled to climb the twisted branches of the family tree, "my nephew," he suggested.

Lawrence frowned, then nodded slowly as if it was a new thought for him as well. "Didn't know I had any family. Agnes's brother died as an infant. No cousins to speak of."

"Selma at the Post Office has asked her friend who's a genealogist of sorts, to sniff out the family tree." Paul paused. "He, uh, didn't find any mention of Agnes and Thomas getting hitched."

"I have the proof, don't you worry." Whatever softening had taken place in Lawrence's tone dropped away. "The treasure belongs to me and I'm not going to be cheated out of it."

Paul searched the angry face before him but found no inkling of resemblance there of mischievous Thomas. Paul felt a sudden stirring up in his gut, not for treasure or family heritage, but for his brother. The last thing, the only thing he could do for his dead sibling, was to make sure Thomas's treasure would not go to a liar. Paul vowed silently he would see to that. But surely Lawrence was who he said he was? Paul knew he was a victim of a deep-seated naïveté which the ups and downs of life had not steamed out of him. He believed there was good in people. All people, even Dodger's fans, and darn blasted if he could shake the notion.

People are evil, he reminded himself, as Isaiah clearly spelled out. *"For the vile person will speak villainy, and his heart will work iniquity..."* Yet he had a hard time seeing the villain in the people he came across. His blessing and his curse, as Libby always said. The Cold War, skyrocketing inflation, the Lufthansa Heist, nothing seemed to rattle his outlook.

So perhaps Lawrence Needles did fit squarely into the villain camp, but a man who carried Mickey Mantle's silver dollar in his pocket?

Trooper and Fran appeared around the pile of hubcaps.

Mr. Needles glared at Trooper. "Your directions were terrible."

"Were they now?" Trooper tapped his head. "I apologize. Get mixed up in the old noodle once in a while. Old war injury."

"There's a lot of that going around." Mr. Needles stalked away to find the shade offered by a wobbly tower of loose bricks.

"What is this I hear about that idiot Gabe offering tours?" Fran said.

"Not such an idiot, methinks." Paul chuckled. "He got Needles here to pay ten dollars for the tour of the grounds of the historic blacksmithy."

Fran rolled her eyes. "Honestly. Is there no shame anymore?"

Trooper slapped his knee. "Gabe never misses a trick."

"How's Trudy settling in?" Paul said.

"Fine," Fran said. "We're starting to churn ice cream this afternoon."

"It was a fine thing you did, agreeing to let her stay with you."

Paul noted the rosy flush that crept over Fran's cheeks, making her look altogether younger. "No trouble, so far. We passed Lucy and Alexi on the way over here."

"I was wondering about that. Why isn't Lucy sorting through this mess with the rest of them?'

"She and Alexi were headed on some sort of secret mission," Trooper said in a gravely sotto voce. "Got some intel from the hippie bookworm."

By which Trooper meant Librarian Phil Zimmerman.

"Intel? What about?" Paul asked.

"It's a secret," Trooper said with an elaborate wink.

Paul looked around at the folks poking through piles of broken tiles and discarded keys, while others jotted notes on tiny paper pads. He wondered what exactly they were going to get for their five-dollar investment. And what about Mr. Needles's ten-dollar contribution?

Paul realized he had lost sight of Mr. Needles who was no longer standing in the scanty brick shade.

"Where's he off to?" Trooper said, pointing to Mr. Needles who was getting into a sky-blue Fiat.

Paul wondered at that moment if he'd overheard their

conversation about Lucy, Alexi, and the librarian. Exactly how good was the man's hearing anyway?

After saying goodbye to Trooper and Fran, Paul decided to turn his feet back toward town to see if he could spot his niece. Before he exited the gates, a voice rang out through the junkyard like a smartly struck bell.

"There's her head!"

He snapped around so quickly he got dizzy. Her head? There could be only one infamous head in the tiny town of Honey Creek. He pressed his way through the treasure hunters to see if the elusive head had got around to making an appearance.

HONEY CREEK TREASURE HUNT

Chapter Thirteen

"It's the angel's head all right," a woman shouted. "The mutt's got it."

Trooper blinked to be sure his eyes weren't mutinying. Gummy stood between two piles of rubber tires looking pleased as peas, with a big hunk of the angel's head clamped between his jaws. His furry sides heaved. A ribbon of slobber dripped from tongue to angel to ground. "He busted out of your yard, Fran, and dug himself up the head somewhere. Followed us all the way here to show off."

Trooper wasn't sure which detail he was more impressed by, that the dog had found the head, or walked the six blocks in the blazing sun to unveil it to the world.

Fran gave a little start. "It's really the Hope angel's head?"

Pastor Paul muttered something under his breath that Trooper figured might not have been exactly verbatim from the Holy Book.

"Come here, Gummy," Trooper called.

The dog meandered a couple of steps before sinking to the ground in the shade of an overturned wheelbarrow, prize still clenched in his teeth.

A bearded man with a notebook peered close. "Actually, it's only half of her head, the front part. What's that called?"

"Oh wait, I know this one," Gabe said, emerging from the shack which served as his office. "It was in the crossword yesterday." He snapped his fingers to trigger his memory. "Nine letter word, starts with a vowel."

The woman who had shouted out the head sighting in the first place nodded. "Oh yeah, yeah. It's the part of the skull around the eye socket. Found a copy of the Holler at the gas station bathroom this morning. Started with a vowel, didn't it? An 'e'?"

"No, no," Gabe said, stroking at the fuzz on his chin. "Seems to me it was an 'o.'"

"What difference does it make?" Fran's cheeks were flushed red. "Is it the angel's head or not?"

"Well..." the pastor began.

"Occipital," Gabe pronounced with a snap of his fingers. "That's the ticket. Dog's got the occipital part."

Fran rolled her eyes so hard Trooper thought they looked like cherries in a slot machine. Gabe was right though. The dog was clutching only a large fragment of the whole in his jaws.

The pastor bent to look. "It's Hope's head, for certain. Wonder where in the world Gummy got hold of it?"

Trooper shrugged. "Hard to say. Could have been anywhere by the looks of him." Gummy was speckled with dirt, with bits of branch stuck in his black fur.

Paul reached out for the head. Gummy growled around the edges of the plaster. The pastor backed away.

"With all your sins, Gums, you shouldn't be snarling at the padre," Trooper chided. He went to the crooked stand Gabe had set up to razzle-dazzle the treasure hunters with genuine gold country water in white paper cups and filled one. He took it to the dog, crouching down against a twinge in his hamstring, and held it for the lapping tongue. When Gummy let go of the head to drink the water, Trooper scooped the prize out of reach and handed it to the pastor.

Gummy shot him a look of betrayal but slurped the water

anyway.

"Don't worry," Trooper said, voice low. "That was a good trick you did there, sniffing out that head. Gonna fix you up a hot dog tonight with mustard, just the way you like it. I'll toss in a bun even."

The pastor examined the edges of the plaster occipital bone and the others pressed close to get a look until the notebook man said, "Never mind about it. Clue's already been taken out of that old head, remember? We need to get on to the iron perfect. How's about starting our tour before any more competition arrives?"

"I've got a..." Gabe looked around, discovering that his private client had flown the coop. "Well, right now is fine by me. That will be five dollars per person, folks."

Trooper found himself at the periphery of the throng, Gummy oozed to full length in the dirt on his right, and Fran and Pastor Paul stood on his left, staring at the head as if it was the missing Watergate tapes.

"So where do you figure she's been all this time?" Trooper said.

"And where's her other side?" Pastor added mouth pinched. The man looked like he'd been punched in the gut. "There's only half a head there."

"Hey, I'm sorry about the wreckage, Padre," Trooper muttered. "Gummy might have been a tad exuberant with the exhumation."

Paul shoved his hands in his pockets and darned if Trooper didn't see the sheen of tears.

"I guess I figured we'd get her head stuck on again and put her back in her place. Now..." He shrugged. "Well, I guess she's beyond help."

Fran patted him awkwardly on the shoulder. "It will work out. I'm donating all my proceeds from the Fourth of July ice cream sale to the church restoration." She paused.

"We can wait until next year for some new choir robes."

"That's a very sweet gesture, Fran," Paul said. "But I know it's not cheap to feed and tend to a teenager. You'll need the extra funds for that."

Fran waved the comment away. "She hardly eats anything anyway. Nothing but a bite of toast in the morning and a mouthful of meatloaf for dinner."

"Still, there's water and electricity and such," he said. "Your ice cream funds can go to help with that good deed you're doing for Trudy." His mouth pinched even more. "It will cost thousands just for the bracing, Kelby says. As for remaking a statue...How much does it cost to restore an angel?"

No one had an answer to that.

***

Trooper's mouth watered as the wieners sizzled on the metal grill he'd fashioned out of a bent-up fender he'd found in Honey Creek in the winter. Normally he was content with church handouts, the fish he caught in his secret fishing hole and the odd, stale donut, but he'd sprung for the meat, on account of Gummy deserved it and everybody knew that dogs enjoyed the meal more if they had someone to savor it with.

No one from the salvage yard gave a Fig Newton for the angel's half head, so Trooper had carried it along after saying goodbye to Fran. It would make a nice catch-all for his fishing lures if he could convince Gummy not to chew it any further.

He rolled the hot dogs with a pointed stick, even toasted the buns, which had set him back an extra thirty-five cents. Gummy eyed the proceedings from his spot at the base of the tree, the evening breeze whiffling through his fur and bringing the temperature down to a more tolerable degree. Gummy cocked an ear and barked two sharp barks.

It was his "we've got company" bark.

"Hey," Trudy said, appearing on the path that bisected the waist-high brown grasses. She scratched one ankle with her foot, hands shoved into the cavernous pockets of her green jumper. Her mass of frizzy hair was caught up in two thick braids behind her prominent ears, taking a decade off her age easily enough. No more than a girl, it seemed to him, though she'd balk mightily if he voiced the notion.

"Hey yourself," he said.

She climbed on the flat slab of granite where he dried laundry and fish alike, knees tucked up underneath her.

"Miss Fran said Gummy found the angel's head."

"Part of it. See for yourself." He gestured towards the head with his fork. "If we ever find the other half, we can take it over to Kelby to see if there's any hope of gettin' her a face lift." He laughed at his own joke.

"Where'd Gummy find it?"

"Question of the hour. You want a hot dog? They're just about fixed."

"Yum. I'd love one."

"Fran not feeding you properly?"

"She tries to feed me all the time, but I can't stand tuna noodle casserole."

He laughed at that one. "Looks too much like the...I mean, glop on a shingle we used to get in the army."

She took the offered hot dog. "Thanks, Mr. Trooper."

"You can drop the mister. Don't cotton to titles, not since the war."

"Vietnam?"

"Korea. Too old for 'Nam, thank God. It was enough to survive monsoons and trench foot in Inchon. Wouldn't have lasted long on Hamburger Hill."

"Daddy died in Vietnam in a helicopter crash."

He let that sit for a moment. "Right sorry to hear that."

"Yeah. He got a medal for getting himself killed, but it's in a box and Mom won't ever let me see it. She doesn't want us to talk about Daddy. Like he didn't exist or something."

Like he didn't exist. Like she'd made up all these memories about her father. Trooper sometimes felt like he'd done the same thing about his lost people.

He put another hot dog on a plastic lid which served as a plate for Gummy. The dog wolfed the bun in a moment and then set to licking the hot dog with a sandpaper tongue. Round and round he neatly swabbed the treat.

Trooper laughed. "Like BonBon." Had he actually said it aloud? He was out of practice at having company and the words had slipped from his mouth before he'd remembered.

"Another dog?"

"Nah. My daughter, Bonnie. Used to lick an ice cream like that, all over, real neat like. Made a little point at the top."

"I didn't know you had a daughter."

"Don't anymore. She's gone. Mother, too."

Trudy chewed. "That's sad. Is that why you live out here instead of a shelter or something? Because your family left you?"

Nosey, like all women, but not schooled enough to be cagey about it. He pillowed another hot dog in a bun for himself and took a bite. "I like it here near the creek. Quiet. No traffic. No roosters. What about you? Why are you here in Honey Creek?"

She studied the end of her hot dog. "Told you. My mom had to move, and I didn't want to go."

"That's what you said all right."

Her eyes narrowed. "You don't believe me?"

"Doesn't matter what I believe or don't, does it?"

Trudy wiped her mouth with the back of her hand and studied the treehouse, the campfire, the trickle of river water.

"This is great, living here. So peaceful, no people bossing you."

No people. "Plusses and minuses."

"You ever gonna move back to town?"

"Dunno. You ever gonna move back to your family?"

Her lip trembled. "They don't want me."

"Why not?"

"I...I did something. Bad. You ever do something bad?"

"Every day of my life, kiddo." And lived with the outcome every excruciating moment. The hotdog turned to lead in his mouth.

Her throat convulsed. "They won't forgive me. Ever."

"Forever is a long time. Maybe they will, after the sting of the thing dies away."

She shook her head. "It's too late."

"Never too late, unless you're dead." The hot dog formed a lump in his throat, and he put the rest down. Gummy continued to massage his meat cylinder with his tongue. "Or unless you don't ask." God forgave all things, he'd been told, if only you asked Him to. He figured that would be the kind of words the padre might use.

She fixed him with those huge eyes. He must have been her age at one time, but he sure couldn't recall that far back. One foot in childhood, the other inching into adulthood, a painful straddling.

"Did you ask?" she said.

"Ask what?"

"Ask your daughter and wife to forgive you before they left?"

"No."

Her eyes narrowed. "Why not? You just said to."

He didn't want to tell her, but she'd assume hypocrisy as did all teenagers of their elders with good darn reason. "I didn't ask in time and now I can't." She started to speak. He cut her off.

"They're dead, Trudy. My wife and daughter died together."

The words had come out louder than he'd intended, loud enough to make her flinch as they hung in the sultry air, settling slowly to the dust at his feet.

She wanted to ask how, he could see it in her expression, the nosey thing.

"You want another hot dog?" he said.

She shook her head and he busied himself throwing a few more onto the grill since he had no way to refrigerate them.

"I'm sorry about your family."

The flames licked at the meat and suddenly the fragrance was oily and thick, coating his senses, sickening his stomach. "Thanks."

"Trooper, did Ms. Fran's kids die?"

"She never had any. Why you ask?"

Trudy licked at a spot on her finger. "Just wondering. Ms. Meg said her husband left 'cause of the kids."

"I believe," he said, rolling the dogs though they did not need any fussing, "that was the better part of the trouble between them. The kids or lack thereof. Dunno much about it. Their business."

She stared into the flames. "That's the problem with grownups. No one ever wants to talk about things that matter, only bills and politics and what everybody else is doing wrong." Her eyes fired a challenge at him, one he could not meet. She was right. He cooked his hot dogs.

"Okay," she said, hopping off the rock. "I'd better get going or Ms. Fran will worry. Thanks for the hot dog."

"Sure thing." He watched her walk down the path, the waning sunlight gilding the flyaway strands of hair.

"Trudy?" he called.

"Yeah?"

"Tell Ms. Fran you liked the tuna casserole anyway, huh?"

Trudy nodded solemnly. "I did."

Satisfied, he turned back to his cooking.

Chapter Fourteen

Lucy inhaled the cloud of donut-fragranced air outside the shop. Owner Steffi's Farah Fawcett hair was twined with strings of rainbow beads that sparkled in the lights. The crow's feet around her eyes put her in a much older decade than her baggy coveralls with flower knee patches would indicate. Lucy hadn't ever been able to pin down Steffi's place in the chronology of time. Alexi stood at Lucy's side, hands folded behind his back as he was likely to do, Lucy had decided, to avoid touching anything unpleasant.

Steffi called down the steps over the roar of the engine, to the truck driver idled at the curb. "Just turn around and drive to the back lot," she hollered. "It's too steep to unload here."

"What?" the driver hollered back, a nervous-looking kid with a shock of tomato red hair.

"Turn around," Steffi shouted again this time with accompanying hand gestures. "Drive to the back. The back."

There seemed to be understanding dawning and the driver set to work on the difficult task of reversing directions on the narrow street.

"Watch out for the fire hydrant," she called, earning a thumbs up from the driver. Steffi chuckled. "Dougie's new. Just started driving for his father. He doesn't get that these are super old buildings, super steep from steps."

The buildings had survived since the 1800s, but the roads had gradually been raised up over the years to combat flooding from spring rains. Hence the entrance to Steffi's shop was a hair-raising three steps downward which Steffi took now, Lucy and Alexi following behind.

"I'll unlock the back door for Dougie. He's bringing my shipment of sprinkles."

Lucy sucked in more of the fried dough and sugar scent, mouth watering at the neat trays of sprinkled and glazed donuts. "Ummmm. Don't they look divine? Look at that one with the gooey pink frosting."

Alexi dutifully examined them. "They would be messy to eat. Do you supply forks and knives?"

She goggled. "Are you serious?"

"Nearly all the time."

Steffi returned with a green sludgy drink in one hand. "Want a wheatgrass smoothie? Fresh made. There's some left in the blender. Counteracts all the sugar in the donuts."

"I'm all right," Lucy said. "Already ate."

"You?" Steffi waved her glass at Alexi. "Dunno your name."

"Alexi Quinn and no thank you for the smoothie." They'd been acquainted long enough that Lucy noted his nostrils flare of disgust, but his tone was nothing but polite.

"Oh right. You're the crossword puzzle dude."

Alexi frowned. "Yes, I am, I mean, I am that dude."

She yanked out a rumpled copy of the Mountain Holler. "I totally loved this one, the treasure hunter's delight was a hoot. A four-letter word for the chemical element of atomic number 79. Gold. Got that one right off. But what's the answer to this clue? Fazioli's grandest accomplishment. Twelve letters. I'm stumped."

Alexi seemed to fold in on himself. "Ah, I wondered if that might be too complex. Paolo Fazioli was an Italian pianist and mechanical engineer. He designed the most exquisite grand piano in the world. It is called..."

"The Grand Fazioli," Steffi cried, scribbling in the clue with a stubby pencil.

"Yes, that is the answer." There was something far away in Alexi's gaze as he stared at his shoes.

"Alexi," Lucy said softly. "Did you play one ever?"

He closed his eyes, rocking gently back and forth as if to some silent music. "Yes, I had the privilege on two occasions. The tone..." The fingers of his good hand crept from behind his back and drummed on his leg, the other, twitched in painful tandem. "It is indescribable."

Steffi looked from Alexi to Lucy and raised one penciled eyebrow.

"Alexi is...was...a concert pianist."

"Oh. Cool." The silence lingered. "So, did you want some donuts? Cinnamon twists are real popular. Jelly filled, too. I used Ida's homemade strawberry jelly."

Lucy broke the next stretch of awkward silence. "We actually didn't come for donuts, Steffi. We need to ask you something."

A rustle from a wooden crate in the corner snapped Alexi from his reverie. "Did you hear that?"

"That's my..." Steffi started.

"We're here about ice cream," Lucy said hastily.

Steffi slugged down some wheatgrass sludge. "Dairy's bad for you, plus the dairy industry's wrecking the environment. You know how much water, feed, land it takes to raise a cow? We don't sell any ice cream, not since I bought this place from Reuben five years ago. Strictly donuts."

"It used to be called Springy's Scoopery," Lucy explained to Alexi.

Alexi tore his gaze from the box in the corner. "That is

an unusual name for an ice cream parlor."

Steffi drained her smoothie. "It's named after Reuben's ferret."

Lucy tapped her fingers on the counter. "Well, no need to go into that, right now. We're here to talk to you about Thomas Lyman's clue."

"A ferret?" A line grooved its way between Alexi's eyebrows. "As in the domesticated form of the European polecat, a mammal belonging to the same genus as the weasel, Mustela of the family Mustelidae?"

It took Steffi a second to follow the word trail. "Yes," she said with a dazzling smile. "It must be fun to write crossword puzzles." She twirled the empty smoothie glass. "That little guy in the box is Springy's daughter, also called Springy. That was part of the deal when I bought the place. Had to keep Springy's kinfolk." She put down the cup and moved from around the counter over to the box. "All the kids love her. Do you want to meet her?"

Alexi's eyebrows shot to his hairline. "There is a ferret? In that box?"

"Oh no, no thanks, Steffi," Lucy said. "I've already met Springy, and I don't think Alexi..."

"She loves people, mostly. Hardly ever bites." She opened the top of the box and hauled out a long white rodent with goggling red eyes.

Alexi vaulted onto the nearest chair.

Steffi blinked. "Don't worry. He's perfectly safe. The kids love him like I said." She walked closer, holding both ends of the long dangling rodent.

Alexi leapfrogged to the next chair.

Steffi frowned. "Don't you want to get to know my ferret?"

"The name "ferret" is derived from the Latin furittus, meaning "little thief," Alexi blurted, voice pitched high as he hopped to the next chair.

"Is that right?" Steffi said as Alexi jumped to the adjacent chair.

"A group of ferrets is commonly referred to as a "business."

Alexi's body was rigid, but his hopping skills were excellent, Lucy thought. Better than a mountain goat's.

"A business," Steffi said with a laugh. "That's cool. But you don't have to freak out."

"Ferrets release their anal gland secretions when startled or scared," he blabbered.

"Oh, is that what you're worried about? You can just hang loose. Springy's been descented, glands all gone."

Alexi had finally reached the chair closest to the door. "Ferrets are strictly prohibited as pets under Hawaiian law because they are potential carriers of rabies." After that pronouncement, Alexi leaped out the door and up the steps without even touching the checkered floor.

"But Springy's had her rabies shots," she called after him. Lucy joined her at the door to watch Alexi stride across the street after checking both ways for traffic. There was none, only a kid on roller skates, stopping in a shady spot to eat a popsicle.

"I will wait over here," he shouted. "Carry on."

"Man, that dude really knows a lot about ferrets," Steffi said, stroking Springy.

"Yes," Lucy said with a sigh, "but he's not much of an animal person."

"Yeah. Kinda high strung."

"You have no idea."

They returned to the shop. Lucy purchased two pink sprinkle donuts, though she was not at all sure Alexi would eat one, and a cup of coffee and sat down opposite Steffi and the dozing ferret. It seemed only sporting to compensate for

Alexi's inelegant departure.

"Alexi and I have been doing some research at the library about this treasure business."

She brightened. "Is Phil helping?" Her cheeks pinked. "I've been pretending to research the history of donuts so I can hang out in the library. So far, he hasn't even spoken more than 'how can I help you miss?' The cool news is I'm totally a donut savant now. Ask me anything. Hanson Gregory, an American, claimed to have invented the ring-shaped doughnut in 1847 aboard a lime-trading ship when he was 16 years old. Betcha didn't know that."

"Actually, I didn't, but I'd put money that Alexi does."

She quirked an eyebrow at the window, watching him stiffly across the street. "Hmmm. You're probably right about that."

Lucy bit into the frosted masterpiece. "Oh, so good."

"You know the term 'sprinkles' and 'jimmies' refer to the same confection? Just depends on the part of the world you're living in." She grinned. "I ran out of donut research, so I had to, like expand. Phil helped me unearth that tidbit."

Lucy went in for another bite. "Uh, well, our question is more along the lines of the ice cream business you bought. You see, Thomas Lyman left a clue to his treasure."

"A lick for the Iron Perfect," Steffi finished. "Read it in the Holler. Made no sense to me, but as I said, I don't know much about anything but donuts."

"We've found out..." Lucy said, lowering her voice. She paused noticing through a tiny window high above Steffi's shoulder that looked onto the raised sidewalk, that Alexi was bent over, peering in and waving at her. What in the world? She waved back, figuring he was practicing his social skills.

"Found out what?" Steffi said, painted eyelids raised to full stretch.

"That the clue is actually 'a lick for the Iron Prefect.'"

Alexi was hopping now and waving.

"Oooooohhhhh," Steffi breathed. "What's an Iron Prefect?"

"It's a nickname for..."

"Benito Mussolini," Lawrence Needles said as he entered. Lucy sat back in her chair. So that's what Alexi had been trying to warn her about.

"Yes," she said weakly. "The clue has to do with Mussolini."

Steffi was staring at Needles. She extended her hand. "I don't think we've met. I'm Steffi, proprietor of this awesome pad."

He shook, smiling. "You've got a great shop here."

"Thanks," she said, smoothing a lock of hair behind her ear. "Tomorrow I'm baking up fifteen dozen with red, white, and blue sprinkles for the Fourth of July Parade on Saturday. You know in Australia they serve sprinkles on toast to kids and call it fairy bread. I tried that, but it didn't go over. Donuts make people happy and that's like the best thing ever, don't you think? That's what it's all about. So, what can I get you, Mr. Needles?"

"Nothing, thanks, I had a big breakfast."

Steffi sniffed. "Surely you have room for a donut. Otherwise, you're just sort of...loitering here." She swept a hand in Lucy's direction. "I've got day-old treasure donuts for only a nickel." She raised an eyebrow. "I mean if you don't want to spring for a fresh one."

Needles surveyed the case and took a gander at Lucy's two sprinkle donuts. "You're right. I'll take a dozen of your finest and freshest."

"That's the spirit." Steffi grabbed the tongs and filled a pink box.

Needles shot a sly look at Lucy who glared right back at him.

"What do you do for a living, Mr. Needles?" Steffi asked, handing him his change.

"I'm a pet groomer."

"Really?" Lucy and Steffi both said at once. Lucy would not have pegged Needles as the animal enthusiast.

"Really."

"Say, would you like to see my ferret? Her nails are a bit on the long side. It's not her favorite thing to get them trimmed so I usually have to wear welding gloves."

"I would be happy to take a look," Needles said. "But may I ask you a question first?"

"A guy who buys a dozen donuts is totally entitled to ask a question. Fire away."

The growl of the truck engine indicated Dougie was still attempting to turn around. There was no sign of Alexi in the window and Lucy wondered if he was still standing there on the sidewalk.

"Meg at the diner said you bought this place from Reuben Patterson. His uncle served in the navy as I understand it."

She nodded.

"Did Patterson leave any boxes, files, maybe some letters here that might have to do with Mussolini? Memorabilia? Family papers? That kind of thing? Something Thomas Lyman might have had access to?"

Steffi drummed her fingers on the glass top of the donut case. "I don't know about Thomas. I think I might have heard somewhere or another that he was a part-time stock clerk for Patterson way back in the day. Might have poked around all those old things. Reuben liked to talk you know, and I, well, sort of tuned him out. He did leave a bunch of stuff when he sold me the biz, actually, boxes and whatnot. I didn't have the time or energy to sort through it."

Lucy's heart jumped like a rabbit. "Do you still have it?

The boxes?"

Steffi's eyes rolled in thought. Lucy heard what she thought was Alexi's voice calling out above the truck noise.

"Yes," Steffi said. "Pretty sure I never got around to dumping it. It's still in the basement where it's been moldering away. Knock yourself out and hunt to your heart's delight as long as it doesn't interfere with the donut business. I've got to prepare for the Fourth of July rush."

Both Lucy and Needles sprang to their feet, eyeing each other as if they were in the midst of a spaghetti Western.

"I..." Lucy started.

Her words were drowned in the groan of metal, a loud percussive pop, and a shouted expletive from the red-haired Dougie. Seconds later a torrent of water poured down the donut shop steps.

Chapter Fifteen

Trudy wrestled with the paper sack full of red, white, and blue bunting as she and Fran walked from the print shop to her car. The morning events had spread, gossip zinging around the diner like pinballs. By the end of her afternoon shift, Trudy'd got the gist. It was all like something from a Rockford Files episode. Clues, and Gummy digging up the head, and a treasure hidden somewhere in town. All they needed was a body lying around. She thought that would add to the level of excitement.

"Where do you think Gummy found it?"

Fran repositioned the stack of fliers she'd just had printed. "What?"

"The head. Where'd you think Gummy dug it up from?"

She shrugged. "I don't know, and I don't care. I've got ice cream to churn. The parade's in two days. That old chewed-up head is the last thing on my list of concerns."

That was another problem with adults. They cared only about the boring things and ignored anything that might possibly add some excitement to their lives. The heat coated her in sweat, dampened her armpits, and made her crave a dish of cold canned pears. She could have anything from the diner menu during her break except the thick-cut pork chops or the last slice of pie, but Meg couldn't abide canned pears and for some reason, Trudy couldn't stop thinking about

them.
A rivulet of water raced down the curb. It widened and twisted as it surged by them.

"Hey, Miss Fran?"

"Try not to start your sentences with 'Hey' Trudy. It's not ladylike."

"Sorry." Trudy eyed the flow rippling next to them. The cascade of water increased, lapping up nearly to reach the curb.

"Miss Fran, what's with all the water?"

"What?" Fran finally peered around the stack of fliers. "Where in the world is all this water coming from?"

That's what I just asked, Trudy wanted to say.

They rounded the corner to find a delivery truck half on the sidewalk with a broken fire hydrant wedged under the back axle. A red-haired guy kept racing around the truck, groaning as he peered under, water sheeting past his knees and funneling right down the stairs into the donut shop. He was having a hysterical conversation with himself.

"Oh, my stars," Fran said. "That idiot Dougie knocked over the hydrant. The boy could hardly find his way to Freshman English without falling over a trash can. He should never have been issued a driver's license."

Trudy put her bunting down well out of the flow of water. "Be right back." Fran called out to stop her, but she pretended not to hear.

"Are you okay, Dougie?"

Dougie shoved wet hands through his hair, making the strands stand up in red spikes. "Just look...look what the truck did."

Not to mention the driver. "Are you hurt?"

"No, not yet. Not until my father finds out. He's gonna clobber me. I'm still paying off the debt I owe for running into the water fountain at the park. Oh, man. This is so lame."

There didn't seem to be anything she could say that would soothe Dougie, so she slogged through the stream and met Lucy Winston at the door of the shop.

"Oh, Trudy. Thank goodness. Can you carry this?" In one hand she held an open box of chocolate eclairs and tucked under her arm, a ferret. The ferret thrashed in an irate manner, so Trudy was glad to take the eclairs. Over Lucy's shoulder, Alexi towered above the glass counter. He must be standing on a chair. He was neatly tonging donuts into a pink pastry box as the water tumbled around him. He did not look up from his task.

"Where should I take the donuts?" Trudy asked.

Needles splashed over. "It's pouring down into the basement. Everything is under a foot of water."

"I called the fire department," Steffi said, slogging from the back room holding a dripping roll of paper towels. Her mascara was starting to spread beneath her eyes into two dark crescents. "But they don't have the tool they need to turn it off. Some sort of hydrant key. They've got to get it from Mudville." She groaned. "It's like the whole Noah thing, except this store can't close down for forty days or Springy and I will starve."

"We'll figure something out." Lucy absently stroked the ferret. "First off, let's finish packing up today's donuts and you can sell them from the inn. We'll put up a sign, so people know where to find you."

"Full," Alexi called, closing the lid of the pink box. He detached a piece of tape and neatly sealed the top.

Lucy handed the squirming ferret to Needles who looked as though she'd just tossed him a hand grenade. He immediately passed the ferret to Steffi. She cuddled the long animal around her waist. Lucy forwarded another donut box to Alexi and he began to fill it. She added it to Trudy's tower of boxes.

"Can you take these to the inn? I'll be over as soon as I can. And tell my Uncle Paul to come over here with all the buckets he can find? We're going to need more help."

Trudy nodded. She was cooler now since her pants were soaked to the upper thigh. Holding the boxes above the water, she splashed up the steps.

Fran was pacing in nervous circles outside the flood zone.

"Trudy," she said. "I worried you'd fallen in and drowned." She grasped her elbow. "Come away from that water. You'll get a chill."

It was another dumb thing that grownups said. Getting a chill when the temperature was still topping ninety. But Fran's hand on her back felt good for some reason and she let it linger there.

"That water could be swimming with ferret germs. I've always said it was not hygienic to have a ferret in a place that serves food. Revolting."

"Miss Lucy said I'm to take these donuts to the inn so Steffi can sell them there."

"This is plain silly. It's two o'clock in the afternoon. Who is going to buy these donuts anyway?"

As if there was a time limit on donut cravings? Still, Fran wrangled both the bunting and the fliers so Trudy could carry the pink boxes tucked under her chin.

"And I'm to find Pastor Paul and tell him to come help out. With buckets."

"No need," Fran said, jutting her chin since she had no hands to point. "He's already here."

And he must have gotten wind of the situation too because he had arrived wearing his hip waders, along with a few men Trudy recognized from church who were also dressed for a day of bass fishing. Everyone was clutching a bucket of some sort. The first thing Pastor Paul did was slog to Dougie, the red-haired truck driver who was still babbling to himself, arms crossed over his chest as if he was trying to keep his body from coming to pieces. He put a palm on the kid's shoulder and talked to him. Trudy couldn't hear over the water, but she figured he was talking about how even the pro baseball players struck out or some such thing. Like that would help.

Dougie bowed his head, staring at his soggy uniform pants, knuckling his eyes. At least he'd stopped pacing around the truck. Maybe the baseball story really did work. Trudy felt a warm spot under her breastbone. All these people helping out or trying to anyway. Honey Creekers were nice that way.

Cradling her tower of pink boxes, she squelched behind Fran as they got into Fran's stifling car. The scent of donuts and the cold clamminess of her clothes on top of the sizzling temperature in the car turned her stomach. Without warning, nausea took hold.

"Wait," she called as Fran started the engine.

Opening the door, Trudy bent out and gagged. She felt Fran lean over and gently gather her hair away from her sweaty face a moment before she vomited on the curb.

"Sorry," Trudy said.

Fran let go of her hair and handed her a pink scented tissue retrieved from the bottom of her purse. Trudy's mother never ran out of tissues either.

Fran clucked her tongue. "See? A chill. I told you. Let's get you home and into some dry clothes." Her tone was gentle though, under the 'I told you so.'

"But the donuts... They're already melting."

"Oh, those donuts." She rolled down the window to let in a weak draft of slightly cooler air. "All right. I'll drop you at the inn and bring you a change of clothes, okay? But then you should come right home and lie down. I will fix you some tea."

Trudy didn't like tea one bit, but the thought of sliding into bed and having Miss Fran tuck up the sheets and bring her a steaming cup warmed up that spot under her breastbone again.

Fran pulled away from the curb. "All this fuss for a bunch of gooey, half-melted donuts no one is going to buy."

Still fussing, they rolled away from Steffi's donut shop. Trudy studied Fran surreptitiously as they drove. Her mouth was pinched into a tight bow, sweat, which she refused to wipe away, sparkling on her lined forehead. Fran was all edges and walls and rules and propriety. Her only two permitted emotions seemed to be righteous anger and disapproval unless she let the softness creep in, quiet as cat feet before it abruptly darted away. She tried to picture Fran as a seventeen-year-old, eating in the school lunchroom, laughing with her friends, smiling at the boys, but she couldn't. There were no pictures of Fran around, or her ex-husband Moe, whom Trudy had learned about from gossip at the diner.

Couldn't the woman see that she had everything she needed to live a great life? She had her own house and enough retirement income from teaching high school that she was free. *Free*, Trudy wanted to shout at her, and you're too tied up in your regulation book to notice. It was tragic.

If Trudy had her own place, she'd blast her Led Zepplin and Pink Floyd music as loud as she wanted and plant towering sunflowers all over the yard and adopt dogs, big fat ones with no teeth like Gummy. She'd travel to Mexico. Before her father had been blown up in Vietnam, he'd told her that's where Grandad lived. Mexico was a place where there was color and music and naps and fiestas and sweating bottles of beer.

And uptight Fran had all the freedom in the world to do

anything she wished, with no kids to suck up her time and money, but instead, she locked herself in a perfectly dusted cage and stayed there. Even her furniture was encased in plastic slipcovers to protect it from what? Fran hadn't entertained a visitor in that tomb of a living room for years, Trudy guessed.

Miss Fran was crazy.

But the fingers on her neck had been gentle, comforting, smoothing Trudy's unruly hair into a coil, away from the muck and the mess. And she knew Fran would boil the kettle and steep the tea, adding a bit of clover honey before she poured it into a pretty china cup complete with saucer.

As the blocks passed by, Fran continued to mutter about the idiocy of selling old melty donuts, fingers clenching the steering wheel.

Trudy leaned on the headrest and closed her eyes, longing for a chilled plate of canned pears.

Chapter Sixteen

Honey Creekers had to be the most stubborn, persnickety bunch of hicks that ever broke bread and walked upright, but Trooper knew that when properly motivated, they could make a man proud. When he got the skinny on the flood from Trudy and Fran as they pulled up at the inn where he'd been dispatched by Pastor Paul to see to the donut operation, he snapped into full gear.

"Fran, my pumpkin..." he said.

She shot him a look that would curdle milk. "I'm not your pumpkin."

"A man can dream, can't he?"

She sniffed. "What do you want?"

"When you're grabbing those clothes for Trudy..." He outlined his request.

"Ridiculous. What an idiotic idea."

"That's the can-do spirit, Pumpkin."

Fran rolled her eyes and drove off.

Chuckling, he hustled into the relative cool of the Lady Quail. Trudy looked a bit wan, he thought, but maybe it was her soggy condition. "Pumpkin will bring some clothes in a minute," he said.

"Why do you call her Pumpkin when she doesn't like you?" Trudy inquired.

"You didn't like liver first time you tried it right?"

"I still don't. My mother makes it and it's gross."

"Maybe you ain't tried it enough." Smiling, he wrestled open the card table he'd borrowed from the church and set it up on the wide front porch. It was a tatty rusted old thing that complained like his cousin from Iowa. Plus, the top was scarred over from years of abuse. "Fran would say it needs a cover."

He let himself into the lobby and helped himself to the blanket that was strewn over the decrepit piano. A couple of hard whacks outside and the dust came out well enough, so he draped it over the card table. Trudy found a piece of cardboard from the kitchen and inked a respectable-looking sign with a few extra flourishes while Gummy looked on.

"Miners Treat, 25 cents, profits go to Steffi's flood relief," Trooper read. "Perfect."

Trudy was dubious. "Are you sure it's worth the trouble? Who's gonna buy all these donuts and how are we going to convince people they are Miner's Treats?"

"Now Trudy," he said. "You're beginning to sound like Fran. You're far too young for such pessimism." He spotted Manny who was fiddling with the porch light that flickered off every few moments or so in spite of his best effort.

"Manny, you know what this place needs, son?"

He sighed. "A complete electrical overhaul?"

"Besides that." Before Manny could puzzle through any further maintenance issues, Trooper supplied the answer. "Piano music."

Manny scratched his ear with the hook that served as a hand. "Not too great at that with one missing."

"More gifted with your one than most with two."

"Awww, I dunno. I like to play for myself mostly."

"So, play for yourself and rope in some of these city slicker customers for Steffi. Play something cheerful, old-timey, huh? Can you do that?"

He looked doubtful. "There's some music in the bench."

"Forward, my man."

Manny shuffled back inside. Trooper heard the ominous squeak of the bench. He prayed it would not be followed by the crack and thump of the bench giving way. Instead, there was a longish pause followed by a quick up and down scale. Then Manny commenced playing some sort of tune with lots of frills and flourishes that Trooper figured probably filled the bill. He closed his eyes for a moment, impressed again that a man with a total of five fingers could play two parts on the piano with some sort of magic that Trooper could not possibly understand. And to think, most folks he knew couldn't play any kind of music using two hands and throwing their feet in for good measure.

Trudy was impressed too, peering in at Manny. "How can he do that?"

"A medic taught him, a guy who worked at the clinic where Manny got fixed up after his forearm got blown off. The medic lost his hand, too."

They listened together and he liked Trudy's dreamy smile.

"Isn't that something?" she murmured.

"Oh, it surely is," he agreed, throwing the front doors wide so the music floated out across the sizzling Honey Creek sidewalks.

Fran climbed the steps, handing clothes to Trudy and supplying Trooper with two tubs of Cool Whip and a pile of paper plates. She read the sign and fired off another colossal eye roll.

"That's a ..."

"Ridiculous notion, I know, but it's working already see?" He jabbed a thumb at the two visitors who were making their way slowly but surely towards the inn.

"I might as well stick around so I can say I told you so." She pulled on an apron.

He dialed the phone and got Meg at the diner, letting her know what to report to her customers. He followed that up with a call to Jesse's Garage and the hardware store which would have a bunch of guys pretending to look at screws while they were watching J.R. Ewing on the Dallas TV show and chewing the fat. The last call went to Selma who was better at spreading information than any technology the U.S. Government could ever cook up with the help of their fancy computers which ran on chips or dots or whatever they were.

He sat back on the porch chair and waited. Gummy laid his head on Trooper's shoe and helped.

The first wave came from the diner. "Hey, Trooper," Meg said, still wearing her apron. "Told everyone we were closing early for flood relief."

"Real bad," Trooper said. "Still ain't got the key wrench to shut it off yet. One thousand gallons a minute. Everything's ruined."

Meg purchased three half-melted donuts on sticky napkins with an extra ten cents thrown in.

"Steffi will be much obliged," Trooper said.

The slightly runny eclairs went next, to the guys from the hardware store. "Ain't it a shame," they said. "Gonna go over and pump the water out once that bloomed fire department gets here with the key." Six melted eclairs with a dollar extra.

Alvin Wong helped with his dramatic recreation about the scene at Steffi's. He sat on a porch chair, yakking to whoever would listen. "And there she was, standing on a stool, holding her rabbit, watching everything around her get swallowed up by the water."

Rabbit? Typical, but the next three customers chipped in extra for Steffi and her rabbit.

A square-built lady leading a group a half dozen strong clomped up the steps and pointed to the sign. Trooper recognized them as the Treasure Hunting club that had descended on the town to Pastor Paul's dismay. Trooper plastered on his most winning smile.

"What's a Miner's Treat?" she demanded.

He readied his hick schtick. "Oh well back in the 1800s, mining was a tough job, laboring day in and out in scorching heat and freezing cold mountain streams. When a fella made a score, he was eager for some creature comforts so there was a lady right here in Honey Creek used to fry up some dough and serve it up with sugar and cream, iffen there was a cow around. Miner's Treat, she called it. Real authentic."

The woman nodded. "But these are..." she poked at the bowl Fran had handed over after Trudy slapped a dollop of white on the top and stuck in a spoon. "Half melted donuts, with Cool Whip on top."

"Like I said, fried dough with cream. Better than gold nuggets. You're getting a real taste of the gold country legacy right there, ma'am."

She considered, plunking down her money as did her fellow treasure hunters, sitting on the sidewalk to eat.

Phil Zimmerman, the hippy librarian was next. He contributed a dollar. "Poor Steffi. She said Lucy and that Needles individual hadn't even gotten down into the cellar to look for the clues before Dougie flattened the fire hydrant."

The lady on the sidewalk stopped, mid-bite, a plop of Cool Whip dropping off her spoon onto her lap. "What? What did you say?"

Trooper tried to give Zimmerman a 'cease and desist' look, but the man gaped like a fish tossed up on the beach.

"The clue about the Iron Prefect."

Trooper could have slapped him. Book smart and common sense dumb.

"Prefect?" Now she was gaping also. "It's 'prefect' not 'perfect'?"

"Well...yes." He was far enough away that Trooper

could not even apply a sharp kick to the librarian's shin.

"That's a reference to Mussolini," the man next to her said, though he had not stopped eating during the exchange. "Oh wait, I know." He waved his spoon. "A lick...means ice cream. Mussolini outlawed ice cream remember?"

She sighed. "And here I thought all your historical babbling would never amount to anything. So, we need to find an ice cream shop?"

"There's the Triple Scoop in Mudville," Trooper started.

The man grinned. "Nice try. I bet this Steffi's Donuts used to be an ice cream shop, am I right?"

Well, what could be said to that? "Steffie's is underwater right now, mister, so no one is getting any clues out of there unless you got yourself a snorkel and fins."

"All the same," said the woman, "we'll be waiting for the waters to recede."

"Just like Noah," said the man laughing.

They dropped their paper plates in the trash can Trooper had dragged out from the kitchen and walked away, plotting, no doubt. What was to be done about the librarian's flapping gums? Nothing he figured. Can't go putting the cat back in the bag, though he'd love to choke the guy with his own ponytail.

He considered snagging a melted donut from the box but there were only two left and surely Fran would notice. Lucy and Alexi piled out of the back of Selma Trunk's station wagon each holding two pink pastry boxes.

Trooper took Lucy's and set them on the table. He drew her aside.

"Mum's the word about the t-r-e-a-s-u-r-e, though Zimmerman already spilled the beans." He jerked his head towards another bunch of treasure hunters who seemed preoccupied with their sticky treat. "But did you get any leads on the next clue before Dougie unleashed the mayhem?"

She shook her head. "Everything is under water. We salvaged some boxes but they're all completely waterlogged. Steffi is beside herself, so we told her we'd look through the mess tomorrow and I don't think Alexi likes being wet, so I need to borrow Uncle Paul's hip waders."

Trooper looked at Alexi. The man stood with one foot on the porch step, frozen, head cocked as if he had got water in his ears.

"Alexi?" Lucy said, putting a hand on his forearm. "What's wrong?"

He didn't answer, just stood there motionless.

Lucy looked at Trooper who offered a puzzled shoulder shrug. "He got some kind of paralysis going on? A palsy of some sort?"

Lucy gently took the box from his grasp and raised her palm to his cheek. The touch roused him, and his gaze swiveled slowly to meet hers.

"I was listening. That music…"

"Oh," Lucy said. "That's Manny." She paused. "He plays with one hand, you know."

Alexi did not seem to hear.

"The tone, the sound, it reminded me…" He shook his head as if to clear his ears.

"Go in and talk to Manny," she said. "You'll be amazed what he can do."

Alexi grimaced. "His rhythm is slack, the tempo's wrong, and the phrasing is significantly distorted."

Lucy sighed. "Maybe you don't need to tell him that part."

"And he has added flourishes and glissandos when surely that was not the composer's…"

"Alexi," Lucy said, sharply enough to stop him. "Manny plays the piano with one hand. He makes music and I think it's beautiful. So, does everyone here who is listening." She pointed.

Alexi's eyes swept the sidewalk at those gathered there. He seemed to realize at that moment that he had one foot on the stairs, and he reversed until he was once more settled on level ground. "At first I was not sure if I was actually hearing music or imagining it. Sometimes, occasionally, I hear music in my daydreams." He cleared his throat. "I cannot trust my senses."

Trooper laughed. "I'd say you're doing fine. Hearing music is better than listening to voices. My Uncle Stan swore he heard President Lyndon Johnson telling him to build a brick wall around the house to protect against the Reds. Had the place half walled in before my Aunt got home from the Pick and Save. Fortunately, it was not quick-drying cement."

Alexi cleared his throat. "I will go home now."

"Okay," Lucy said. "I'm sure Selma can give you a ride. She's upstairs talking to Mother."

"No need. I prefer to walk." He brushed his hands together as if to rid himself of some invisible crumbs.

"We can get together tomorrow," Lucy called. "To…" she shot a look at the Treasure Hunters, "To discuss next steps."

Alexi did not answer, nor did he turn, shoulders stiff as he walked up the sidewalk, seemingly unaware that his pant legs were still rolled clear up to his knees.

"That guy needs to take his tension down a notch," Trooper said. "He's wound tighter than Grandad's old Timex."

Lucy did not answer either, staring after Alexi, her face awash in sadness.

Trooper gentled his tone. "Losing the music was really a blow to the fella, huh?"

"I think it might have broken him," she murmured.

"Don't count him out yet," Trooper said. "Maybe he just ain't found his tempos and rhythms and flourishes quite yet."

Lucy sighed. "What's a glissando anyway?"

"It's that thing they do when they run their fingers all up and down the keyboard real fancy-like."

Lucy arched a brow at him. "How do you know that? Do you play, Trooper?"

He smiled, as something like pain and pleasure twirled along under his ribcage. "Nah," he said. "Just knew someone who did, a long, long time ago."

Chapter Seventeen

Pearl and Bee Murphy offered Paul a third cup of tea which he declined.

"So very thrilled that you could come, Pastor Paul. We have been so worried at the news in the Mountain Holler," Pearl said. "The flood. Poor Steffi and all of these strangers coming to town."

Bee nodded in silent agreement. The sisters had put on the dog, so to speak. Normally their everyday wear was baggy overalls and old leather gardening boots with faces shaded by enormous straw hats as they toiled over their astonishing garden. The narrow plot alongside their house burgeoned with everything from pole beans to pokeberries. Now they were both in faded floral dresses in honor of his visit. He wished he had the nerve to tell them he'd prefer they remain in their overalls. The formality of it reminded him of churches he'd been in as a child. Austere and artificial, somehow, and not at all a place he figured Jesus would have strolled into with the dust the road on his sandals.

"And how is your Libby, Pastor?"

"Holding her own, thank you for asking."

Pearl frowned. "Holding one's own is not the same thing as thriving."

"No," he admitted. "That it is not." They eyed him, waiting for details.

"Not got much of an appetite and some days the pain keeps her in bed." More days than not, he didn't add.

"We'll make some strengthener," Pearl said, face brightening. "That will help her appetite."

He'd sampled the 'strengthener' they'd provided when he'd been felled by the flu two seasons before and found it so high in alcohol content that it sent him, head spinning, right to the armchair for a long nap. He was thankful he'd had the good sense not to try it right before he was due to deliver a sermon.

The inside of the house was cool, tall wooden shelves crowded with old books and a staggering assortment of salt and pepper shakers that the family had collected over the years. The upstairs was boarded shut, vacant rooms too costly to heat in the winter, left to age in place like the sisters themselves. The Murphy homestead was set apart from Honey Creek both physically and psychologically.

He'd offered many times to arrange rides for Pearl and Bee to the various church teas and ice cream socials and Christmas parties, but the sisters seemed tethered to the old house, trapped by an invisible net that kept them roosting in their musty nest. There had been six daughters in the family, he knew. All had lived in or close to the house over the generations except for one who moved away and married. He often wondered about that one. The rest stayed in the old place, tending to their rough-edged father until only these two women remained. Pearl, Bee, and their two massive cats, Mittens and General George Washington.

Bee fixed her sister's tea and broke her gingersnap into four pieces, one of which Pearl tucked away in her cheek like a chipmunk. There was something special about sisterhood, he thought, an invisible bond unlike any other. It made him call to mind Thomas Lyman.

He recollected the time Thomas had cooked up a money-making scheme and marched them both door to door, offering their dubious yard tending services. Further, he recalled his compatriot leaving to fetch gardening gloves and returning hours later to collect the money, but not in time to share in any part of the work. When he'd rustled up a good head of steam about it, Thomas made it up to him by showing him a secret rock hole, a shadowed crevice between two boulders where he swore a pile of gold was waiting to be mined. Of course, not so much as a pinch of gold had ever emerged from it to his knowledge.

"It's just an old dusty pile of rocks," Paul had grumped.

"That's because you aren't looking right. Know what I spy, Pauley? Treasure," he'd said with a wink. "But most folks don't see a thing." It pained Paul he that hadn't seen a thing either, his view always fixed on the practical, never susceptible to dreaming. He was the tiller of the soil, while Thomas was the climber of mountains, eager to get a whiff of the rarefied air.

They had drifted apart when Thomas began to work at the theater, continuing his never-ending search for gold until he joined the service and headed to war.

Maybe Thomas really had finally struck it rich before he left with promises to Agnes, a woman Paul had never met. Paul hoped that he had died knowing his schemes had finally come to fruition. He imagined Thomas would enjoy immensely the drama he'd created with his clues. Socking one away in the angel's head had been pure theater, classic Thomas.

Blood brothers. *If only I'd known, Thomas...* But they'd lived as brothers anyway, hadn't they? No matter what the official title.

Pearl refilled Bea's teacup before she asked, at some unseen indicator he had not recognized. Could brothers have as close a bond as these two sisters did? He would never know, and the thought made him unaccountably melancholy. There were so many griefs and struggles in the world now, he should not reap them from the "never was" pile. Mittens darted across the room to paw at a passing beam of sunshine, earning a smile from both sisters.

"Through the telescope we've seen the RVs rolling into town," Pearl said. "Visitors," she said, pushing out the word barely above a whisper as if it was obscene.

"Now don't you worry," Paul said. "This whole treasure business will blow on by and things will get back to normal around here."

Pearl added a hefty spoonful of sugar to her teacup. "Visitors usually rile things up," she said. "We've hardly had any visitors here, except your mother Ann."

"Pearl," he said, gumming a gingersnap. "You knew my mother quite well, didn't you? She said she stayed here with you when she first moved to town."

Pearl stirred more vigorously. "Oh, yes, well, she rented a room here from us, just for a few months, is all. Father was gone by then and two of our sisters passed on, so we had room. She was tending to your, um, tending to Thomas. He was only a few years old, toddling around, so curious, Bee, do you remember how curious he was, little Thomas?"

Bee answered with a nod.

"A towhead with such a sprinkling of freckles you wouldn't believe. Anyway, it was only for a short time. She moved to town not long after that, rented a room from Miss Harper. You remember Miss Harper; God rest her soul?"

"Only a vague memory. A seamstress, wasn't she?"

"Oh indeed. The best seamstress in the county. She could quilt too, like nobody's business, couldn't she Bee?"

Paul leaned forward. "I know that Mum helped her with the shop."

"Yes, then after a while she met Douglas and they were

married, and you came along."

She beamed as if she had set all the problems in the world to rights.

"Pearl," he said gently. "I've recently come to find out that Thomas was my half-brother."

Pearl flushed red under her tanned cheeks. "Oh. I see. We wouldn't know anything about that, would we, Bee?"

She shook her head, staring at her lap.

Paul fixed her with a gentle gaze. "I think perhaps you would."

The silence spooled between them, broken only by the clink of Bee's spoon orbiting in her chipped china cup.

"We…well, might have heard a phone conversation between your mum and her mum. It was not eavesdropping, mind you, but the phone is right in the kitchen and, well, it was not a happy conversation."

No, not happy at all he figured remembering his Grandmother's starched stiff spine and dour demeanor, spouting Bible verses and bludgeoning people with them. "Because Thomas was her baby and grandmother disapproved."

They both looked at him and he read the truth there.

"Grandma disowned Mom if I don't miss my guess. She had to raise Thomas all on her own."

Pearl picked at a spot of lint from her dress. "I shouldn't like to say."

"I was happy Ann got away." Bee's tiny voice startled Paul more than a full-on shout. He looked at her, the whorls of frizzed grey hair, the lipstick slightly smudged both on her mouth and the teacup. "She got to be a mum to her baby," Bee said. "And that's worth everything."

Everything.

He held her gaze and her heart shone there for an instant. Sadness and longing gleamed in the depths, revealing a long ago wound covered over, sealed behind a shiny scar. Bee had never married, that he knew of, this unassuming sister, but something in the words made him think she knew what it was like to birth a child and have it taken away. Still waters were indeed deep and sometimes troubled.

Pearl turned the conversation to mundane issues, the collection, the heat, Fourth of July preparations, the antics of spoiled felines.

Paul finished his tea and bid his goodbyes to Pearl and Bee as the two marmalade-colored cats wound around his ankles. As he tried to detach himself, the larger General George Washington took a swipe at his ankles. He shot back, knocking into a side table, and nearly sent an ornate lamp over onto the floor, but his baseball muscles hadn't completely atrophied, and he caught it, easing it upright.

"Whew," he said, shaking a finger at the cat. "I wasn't expecting a stealth attack, General."

"You don't need to worry about the General," Pearl said. "His nails are blunt. We've got him a nice new scratching post that Doctor Doolittle recommended. He's our mobile vet."

She said it with such enormous innocence he had to ask. "His name isn't really Dr. Doolittle, is it?"

"I've no idea," she said, "but that's the name on his business card. He takes good care of Mittens and the General. Drives all over the area but he takes the time to see us. Sometimes he will stay and chat about the goings-on in Mountain Holler and have a cup of tea. What would we do without him?"

Bee offered a shrug.

The cat circled around for another assault. Paul, who could feel the barest pinprick of General George Washington's claws begin to sink through his trouser leg, eased away to the safety of the front door.

"We'll call you when the strengthener is ready."

"Thank you kindly. I'd be happy to drive up and fetch you if you'd like to attend the Fourth of July festivities tomorrow," he said. "Fran and Trudy are making peach ice cream like it's going out of style and Vern's got the fire engine all shined up. I'm told the marching band is going to make an effort as well." Last year a flute player had stumbled on a pothole and brought the first four rows of marchers tumbling to the asphalt before all was set right. He was hoping they would not repeat the spectacle.

"No thank you," Pearl said politely, as he'd figured she would. "We will enjoy the whole thing from up here."

"All right," he said, walking to the front door. "You have the church number and mine if you change your mind." A spread of old black and white photos was strewn all over the table near where he'd replaced the lamp. "A walk down memory lane?"

Pearl waved a hand. "Sorting through some old boxes and we found more pictures than we could ever imagine. They'll go into the dust bin now, I expect." She sighed. "No one to pass them along to. No one they would mean anything to anyway."

And that was the crux of it, he thought. We hold onto our past, our moments, our family trees, as if they were treasures, only to find out our carefully curated memories wind up tossed away in trash bins by the younger generations, too busy living in the present to fiddle around with the past. He was about to pass by when one image caught his eye, an old Polaroid, slightly fuzzy, showing a woman who was a shorter, rounder version of Bee and a man, a man he knew well.

He stared closer.

"That's our baby sister Regina. She moved away to Illinois. She taught piano lessons there, we heard. She was a wonderful pianist. That's her wedding picture, the only one of us who ever actually did get married and there wasn't a single one of us there to witness. A crime, really. Father didn't approve, so none of us were permitted to attend."

Paul realized his mouth was hanging open as he stared at the young bride, with the groom's arm slung around her shoulder.

"That's..." He tried again. "The man, that's..."

"Harmon Valentine. He was a salesman, appliances." She sniffed. "After Regina and their little girl Bonnie died, we don't know what became of him. Ran away like a scalded cat after the funeral."

Paul left, thinking he knew exactly what had become of Harmon Valentine. He'd turned into a man who lived in the woods with a dog, wore his Dodger's cap, and dropped fish into the offering plate.

Harmon Valentine had returned to Honey Creek, and no one had even recognized him.

Not even his own sisters-in-law.

HONEY CREEK TREASURE HUNT

Chapter Eighteen

Alexi figured the dullness of his mental acuity was due to the accumulated nights of poor sleep. Country living was supposed to be sanguine, quiet, but the endless cricket cacophony was broken only by the yodel of a coyote and a rooster which did not seem to understand when the sun had risen and when it hadn't. Because Alexi was a planner and had experienced traveling sleep issues before, he'd prepared, tape-recorded the traffic noises and bustling din of New York City which he played on a loop to drown out the Honey Creek sounds. It didn't help, and now even though it was only early afternoon, his eyelids were heavy as cement. To rouse himself, he wandered the confines of the tiny trailer coming to a stop in front of the piano.

By now he'd memorized all the dings and scratches that adorned the cheap upright. There was a nasty chip out of the fallboard. The ugly instrument perched in the corner, tracking Alexi's every move, like a giant insect.

His brain followed the trail. Insect. An air-breathing arthropod. S-p-i-d-e-r

Some types of spiders shot out tiny, irritating hairs.

Ten letters. The tiny hairs tarantulas fling to irritate predators.

Urticating.

That must be it. The presence of the piano had driven invisible barbs into him also, like urticating hairs. Irritations, reminders of what he didn't have. Taunting him with what could never be again. Illogical personification. The piano was nothing more than wood and wire and felt, so why was he assigning it living attributes? Fatigue trickled through him and since he was not skilled at sifting through feelings, he gave up trying. He approached the piano slowly, letting his good hand drift across the keys, without enough pressure to send the string striking the hammer. The smoothness, the cool of the ivory dizzied him.

"Alexi?" Lucy's voice calling from outside made him jump. His fingers struck a dissonant chord. He slammed the fallboard closed and quickly opened the door.

"Yes?" It came out somewhat breathless.

She gave him a half-smile. "Um, I came to see if you were all right."

"I am all right." Still breathless, but more composed, he tried again. "Thank you. For checking."

She let those green eyes wander over his face and glance back behind him into his trailer. "I heard music."

"Not music." He realized he did know which words to say next, so he cleared his throat. "Won't you come in? I can make coffee. We can talk about the clues."

"Sure," she said. "Meg said to tell you she didn't like the creepy-crawly crossword theme. She doesn't like spiders and she said to pass along that no sane person does either." She stepped up in the trailer and he made room for her to pass, noting that she smelled of herbal shampoo. He liked the fragrance.

"Hmmm. I should have considered the prevalence of spider phobia. I might have gone with vermin, ferrets, and the like." He suppressed a shudder thinking about the disgusting creature at Steffi's ice cream shop.

She sighed. "Maybe skip that one and go with Fourth of July fun or something. You know, firecrackers, bunting, independence, family cookouts. People love that stuff."

He precisely measured the grounds into the filter and balanced it over the glass coffee carafe while he poured exactly four cups of water into the dented kettle and set it to boil. "The Fourth of July celebration is a major event here."

"Oh, for sure. Folks are all geared up for tomorrow."

She watched while he set the egg timer for precisely four minutes, the proper time, he'd calculated, to bring four cups of water to a perfect boil.

"You really take a lot of care when you make coffee."

He frowned. "I use the proper technique. Don't you?"

She laughed. "Yeah, if you consider it good technique to dump a handful of coffee and however much water I boiled into the contraption and hoping for the best."

She had to be joking, so he returned her smile and when the water reached a boil, he poured a half cup over the grounds to activate them for a full sixty seconds and then added the rest of the water. She sniffed the cup he handed her.

"Excellent," she said. "You should be in a Melina commercial."

He sat across from her and took a sip. "I'm not good-looking enough to be on TV, but you are."

"Awww. You're sweet." Lucy pushed a section of white-blond hair behind her ear, revealing a little American flag earring.

He was sweet? For making coffee? Or saying her face was appropriate for TV?

He sipped. She sipped. Suddenly he did not feel quite as fatigued.

"I thought we could walk over to Steffi's again," Lucy said, "And help her clean up and see if any clues survived the flood."

"All right. I've completed my crossword puzzle for

submission already, so I have available time."

"What's the theme?"

"Breakfast Foods."

She laughed. "I can't wait."

"You will have to. It doesn't go to print until Wednesday."

"That was just an expression."

"Ah."

"Alexi…"

When she tipped her head just so, he could not ignore the feeling of familiarity, as though she'd been looking at him like that for most of his life. His mind drifted back to the New York apartment he'd shared with his mother, their sparse furniture arranged around the piano occupying the bull's-eye of the living room. He posted a schedule in the lobby of his practicing times, four hours per day, and supplied a bucket of earplugs which he refilled periodically for those tenants who did not wish to hear him play. He was not offended, and they were not overly bothered.

Conversely, he found them comfortably distant, caught up in their own lives and patterns as he was in his. This also did not bother him. He had no desire for any connection other than to his beloved music. Drifting through foggy days, preparing for competitions, playing with various orchestras, he watched the world go by from his window which looked down on the humanity below at the train station. Ant columns of toiling people, the billboard smiling down on them all promising the perfect supple lips with Just A Kiss lipstick.

"Alexi," she repeated, drawing him out of his reverie. "The music yesterday, Manny's music. It affected you."

"Yes, it was poorly played."

"No, it was beautifully played by a man with one hand."

He swallowed and straightened the packets of sugar in

the bowl. "Technically flawed."

"Isn't there more to music than technique?"

He suspected she did not want a discourse on music theory, so he stayed quiet.

"You could play like that," she said quietly. "One-handed, I mean."

He shuddered. "No. I never could."

"Why not? You want to play. It's written all over you. Why not play any way you can?"

"Because it would be..."

"Technically flawed," she finished with a sigh. She stood and began prowling little circles. "Perfection is a horrible thing, Alexi, don't you see?"

He did not. "Perfection is the ultimate goal."

"Yes, and that's the horrible part. The world is killing themselves to be perfect, young, fit, smart, wealthy, and the pressure of it, the striving of it, ruins the soul." Her look was plaintive, earnest as her eyes riveted to his. "Do you know what I mean?"

"No," he said honestly, though he found himself desperately wanting to. He had no idea what she was talking about. Actually, he wondered if she was feverish, in fact. There was a subtle flush to her cheeks. Perhaps he should try to coax more cooling from the ancient air conditioner. He half rose when she rounded on him.

"You miss playing the music."

He sat back down again. "Yes."

"And Manny can teach you to play like he does but you won't do it will you?"

He shook his head this time.

"Because it won't be perfect."

"Yes. It would, perhaps, not even be exceptional, though I have vastly more training than Manny, and my skills are...were...exponentially better."

Her eyes went round. "So, you would rather live every day without the one thing you love rather than play imperfect music?"

He was silent a moment. "Yes."

"That's crazy."

"That is the truth."

And now a veil of sadness crept over her glow, muting it like the damper on the strings. He was sorry, for what exactly he could not say.

"Like I said," she murmured, something mournful tugging the lines of her mouth, "perfection ruins the soul. Faces, bodies, they can't be perfect and even if you're close, you can't stay that way. Faces age, bodies sag, people mess up and get hurt. That's life. If you can't accept it, you'll be miserable every day of your life. Believe me, I saw plenty of girls in that situation."

As she turned away, the afternoon sun streaming in through the front window caught her, painting her in golden light, blurring the profile of her into something softer, angelic.

The supple mouth. For a moment he wondered what it would be like to kiss her. He had never kissed a woman, except for his mother, never really wanted to. But Lucy, Lucy played with his heart and made him think of things like kisses...

He bolted to his feet.

"I know where I have seen you before. I looked at your face for six months, on a billboard outside my apartment window. You are the Just A Kiss model, aren't you?"

"I used to be, Alexi, a long time ago." The sun shifted and shadows crept where the light had been. "A lifetime ago."

Chapter Nineteen

On Saturday night, Trooper rapped on Fran's front door and handed Trudy another basket of ripe peaches. The aroma was so fresh, the peaches so burstingly succulent, Trudy bent her nose to the fuzz of the piled high fruit and inhaled.

Fran took a second basket and Trooper ambled into the small kitchen behind them with a third. Trooper clomped down the hallway past the pristine living room with the freshly raked shag carpeting. Fran's cheeks were pink and sweaty from the pot of simmering water they kept on the stove. Even though she'd assisted with the six quarts of ice cream stowed safely in the freezer, Trudy was still amazed at how a couple of tiny pricks to the skins and a quick dunk in ice water made the peaches split open and spill their glistening innards from the fuzzy jackets. A trick that bordered on magic.

Trooper eased himself into a vinyl-cushioned chair, crossed his legs in front of him as if he was master of the house. Trudy could not imagine anyone intruding on Fran's domain in such a way, but Fran did not seem in too much of a hurry to send him packing.

"Gummy's on the porch step," Trooper said. "Needs a spell of rest before we walk back. Pulling that wagonload full of peaches in this heat tuckered us out."

"Maybe you should get a driver's license," Fran said.

"You could haul that sad sack of a dog around more easily."

"Who says I ain't got one already?"

Fran raised a suspicious eyebrow. "I can't imagine you passing any kind of test."

Trudy thought it was a mean thing to say, but Trooper laughed.

"You'd be surprised what kind of tests I've passed, Pumpkin."

"Since you're making yourself at home in my kitchen, you might as well help yourself to coffee and don't call me Pumpkin."

Trudy pierced the first half dozen peaches with a knife and eased them into the boiling water. "Have Lucy and Alexi found the next clue?"

"Don't think so," Trooper said. "They were helping Steffi bail, mostly. Going to stop in and check on them now. Wanna come along?"

Trudy shot a look at Fran. "Well, I should stay and help with this next batch. It has to get into the freezer right quick to be ripened by the parade at noon tomorrow," she said, so Fran would know she had been listening.

Fran lifted a shoulder. "You've worked hard, Trudy. Go take a break with Trooper and ask Steffi if she needs anything, for herself, not the weasel. I don't do favors for weasels." She quirked a brow. "Except you, Trooper. You get coffee in exchange for hauling peaches."

He laughed and it was as if a mask fell away and carried the wrinkles with it. It surprised Trudy to know that under the beard and scraggly brows he was probably not much older than her Uncle Milo, her father's older brother. With that thought came the piercing longing, the excruciating, impossible desire to be daddy's little girl again, the one that collected garden snails in a yellow bucket and went fishing with her father and Uncle Milo. They watched her dig holes in the muddy riverbank and let her drink pop from the bottle and get as dirty as she pleased. But Uncle Milo had drifted away after her father's death in Vietnam, along with every other joy in Trudy's life.

She missed the mud, the fun, the unfettered thrill of a life outside the massive codex of rules and punishments that her mother insisted upon. It seemed to Trudy that her mother was allergic to happiness of any kind and she didn't want anyone else to get a whiff of it either.

Trudy wanted to be strong, like Billie Jean King who humiliated Bobby Riggs right there on national television, but she knew she was not because of the desperate way she craved to belong somewhere, anywhere, with someone. Anyone? Her gut tightened. Was she so desperate that anyone would do? She'd heard her mother talk about "those kinds of girls." Words like "loose," "tramp," "trashy" rose in her memory. The thought made her feel queasy and she retreated to the bedroom to get her lumpy denim hat.

Fran did not outwardly object to the hat, but she looked at it as if Trudy had clapped a dead animal on her head.

"Nice hat," Trooper said, and she returned his grin.

Gummy grudgingly got to his feet and Trooper loaded him into the red wagon. The two humans set off, toting the dog behind and soaking in the breeze that kept the temperatures just above stifling.

They found Steffi inside the donut shop which was still submerged under a good foot of water, standing on a chair that kept her feet above sea level. She held a thick manual with the pages curled at the edges and called directions to nobody, Steffi thought at first, until she saw Dougie crouched on the donut shop counter, fiddling with some sort of contraption.

Steffi waved. "Hey. If you're after treasure, you can hike out back to where the rest of them are."

"Just here to see if you need anything," Trooper said.

"If you can help Dougie get this sump pump working, that would be righteous. Either he's not mechanical or I'm reading the directions wrong, but either way, the thing's bogus so far."

Trooper emptied his pockets and handed the contents to Trudy. One crumpled dollar, sixty-seven cents, a broken pair of nail clippers, a half a dog biscuit, and a little golden heart charm strung on a dirty leather cord. She wondered if the charm belonged to his dead daughter, or if it was a trinket he'd found in his scrounging.

"Hang onto these things, will you? And don't get in the water or Fran will skin me for lettin' you."

Trudy tucked the collection into her pocket and watched as Trooper waded down the steps. Wandering out back, she found a dozen or so people fanned out, removing soggy papers from waterlogged cardboard boxes and spreading them out on the tarps that cluttered the empty parking lot.

She recognized the large lady who had tried to check into the Lady Quail and her husband. Mrs. Steele or something similar.

"This one's an inventory, recent," the woman snapped, handing the soggy wad to her husband. "Not what we're looking for."

He added her offering to a careless stack on the farthest card table. Trudy almost missed Mr. Needles who was unloading a misshapen cardboard box of his own, examining each and every item like a scientist analyzing bacteria under a microscope.

Lucy and Alexi waved at her. Alexi wore a set of yellow waders even though he did not seem to be the slightest bit wet. Trudy joined them.

"Any luck?"

"No," Lucy said cheerfully, "but at least Steffi doesn't

have to deal with all this mess herself. How's the water level inside?"

"Still pretty deep, but Trooper's going to help with the sump pump."

Alexi, she now noticed, wore rubber gloves, one of which puckered around his contorted hand.

"Hello, Mr. Needles," Trudy said. "How's the treasure hunting going?"

He offered a polite smile. "Slow."

"It was nice of you to buy everyone coffee at the diner this morning." Though he hadn't left much of a tip, she silently grumped.

He lifted a shoulder. "Thought I'd get to know some of the natives."

And pick their brains about where the treasure might be. "I heard you were a pet groomer."

He nodded.

"But you told Meg you were a mechanic."

He stared at her now, the friendly smile gone. "That was before and it's none of your business. Just like it's not my business that you snuck off into the woods behind the diner last night with your boyfriend."

Trudy's stomach dropped. He'd spoken in a low tone, quiet enough that no one overheard, but his message was clear. *Make trouble for me and I'll do the same for you.*

She was scared, but she squared up her chin anyway. "You're not my mother."

"No, but I don't think she'd like to find out what her daughter was up to." He smiled. "Or Fran Trawler. Think she'd let you stay at her place if she knew?"

Trudy shrank back.

"I got it," Mrs. Steele shouted waving a framed picture above her head. Her husband immediately shushed her, darting a look at Lucy and Needles.

She clutched the picture to her chest, but Lucy, Alexi, and Needles drew closer anyway. Trudy was still trying to steady her breathing.

"What? What did you find?" Lucy demanded.

She mimed zipping her lips and tossing the key. "I'm not saying."

"This isn't your treasure," Lucy reminded her.

"It isn't yours either," Mr. Needles said. "It belonged to Agnes and by proxy, to me."

Lucy jutted her chin. "We haven't seen any proof that you're Agnes's son."

"I'm not required to show you any." Needles held out a hand.

The woman clutched the picture tighter. "It's only an old picture. Nothing to get all excited about."

Steffi appeared on the back step. "Whatever you found is on my property, in my boxes, out back of my flooded store." She held her weasel under her arm. "So, you are jolly well going to let me have it."

Alexi shrank back a bit which Trudy suspected was due to the presence of the weasel, not the stern words.

Everyone stared. Steffi's overalls were rolled up to her thighs, her eyes were smudged with fatigue and there was a pencil shoved behind each of her ears.

"But…" the woman started.

"Look," Steffi's tone was pure steel. "I don't care if you're holding the keys to the lost treasure of the Aztecs. I've had a very bad day and I'm not in the mood to bicker. Hand it over right now, woman, or I'll let Springy come over there and sort you out."

With a look of sheer exasperation, the woman handed the picture over to Steffi.

Steffi shook the paper and peered close. "It's a newspaper clipping. Someone framed it." Her lips moved as she read the small print. "It goes on about Mussolini outlawing ice cream or some such thing. Just the sort of drivel that Thomas Lyman would have loved, I'm sure. All the trouble he's caused..." She shook her head. "Sorry to bust your bubbles, but there's no clue to any stash of gold nuggets so you can all get over it."

"The back." Trudy was sorry she'd said it when all six people beamed a look at her and went dead quiet. All she could hear was the trickle of water lapping over the step and grumbled cuss words from inside the shop. Trooper was not getting the better of the sump pump.

"Well, um," Trudy mumbled, "I mean... I can see some writing on the back of the frame, in dark ink, down in the bottom corner." Her cheeks were hot. "Could that be, you know, part of the clue?"

Steffi squinted at the writing. "Well...looks like Thomas Lyman strikes again."

"What?" Lucy breathed. "What does it say?"

Steffi surveyed the people staring back at her. "It says, *I am not higher than a baronet, not lower than an earl, yet you hold this title in my heart.*" She laughed. "All right then, you smarty pants treasure hunters. What exactly does that mean?"

Trudy watched Alexi, whose expression reminded her of a clock face, ticking along steadily until the hands were properly aligned to bong out the hour. While he didn't exactly bong, he did stand up straighter than anyone she'd ever seen.

"A four-letter word," he said. "Derived from the Middle English."

Lucy's mouth rounded in an 'o' of something that wasn't quite wonder and stopped short of triumph. It was sort of caught in between with a bit of worry mixed in. She clapped a hand over Alexi's mouth, muffling his next words.

"Lady," Mrs. Steele shouted. "It's Lady. A woman married to a man higher than a baronet and lower than an earl. It's a lady."

She grabbed her husband's sleeve and together they raced their way out of the back lot, around the side, huffing from the effort. Mr. Needles scurried away behind them leaving Lucy and Alexi, Trudy and Steffi standing frozen like statues.

It took Trudy a minute longer to get it.

"Uh oh. It's the Lady Quail isn't it?"

Lucy closed her eyes, freed Alexi's mouth, and breathed out a long slow breath. When she opened them, determination shone in her emerald green irises. "Uh oh is right. If they have any intentions of intruding…" She huffed out a breath. "They will ransack my mother's property over my cold, dead body." She slammed the papers down and stalked away. Alexi stood for one more second.

"That is a hyperbolic expression, often used jokingly," he said to Trudy as he hastened after Lucy, waders squeaking.

Trudy nodded, but she was not entirely sure Lucy was kidding. If the treasure hunters thought they were going to mess with Lucy Winston, they were in for a rude awakening.

She thought about Mr. Needles, the malice in his eyes when he'd cut her down to size. He would not be afraid of Lucy, not for a minute. A chill crept up Trudy's spine and she felt sick.

Steffi tossed the framed photo onto the nearest tarp. "Honestly. I don't give a rat's tail for this ridiculous treasure hunt, but I'd sure fork over some cash for a couple of buckets to bail with."

A well-timed clearing of the throat made Steffi jump. The librarian, Phil Zimmerman, appeared holding a black bucket in one hand and a roll of paper towels in the other.

"Hello, Steffi. I um, I thought you might need some help," he said. "Library's closed today, you know."

Steffi stood frozen. "Oh, hi, Phil. Gee, it's totally nice of you to offer to help." Steffi swiped a hand over her hair to straighten it, dislodging the pencils behind her ears.

Phill looked at her. "Hello, Trudy. Are you helping too?"

"Oh no, I'm just about to leave with Trooper, now that he's got the pump going."

"Okay," Phil said, his eyes on Steffi.

"Thanks for coming," Steffi said, her eyes on Phil.

Without breaking the spell, Trudy headed around the front to coax Trooper from the store.

Chapter Twenty

Lucy practically jogged along Main Street until Alexi laid a hand on her arm.

"Overexertion in these warm temperatures can result in heat exhaustion," he said, puffing. "Plus, I am wearing rubber waders which do not allow for air circulation."

"Oh. Sorry. I forgot about the waders. Here, sit on the bench and I'll help you get them off." She paused. "Do you have extra shoes?"

"Extra for what?"

"To put on after we take off the waders."

"I'm wearing my shoes underneath," he said. "Is that not proper wader technique?"

She laughed. "It is for you, Alexi."

Alexi sat and Lucy began tugging with all her might. He clutched the back of the bench to keep from being yanked onto the cement. Finally, the waders were removed, his shoes pried loose from inside, and they were ready to resume their walk to the inn after a moment to return the borrowed waders to her uncle.

Her mouth was set in a grim line. "I won't let them upset my mother. I've done enough of that to last a lifetime."

He kept pace with her on the sidewalk, skirting spots of shade from the faded awnings, passing briskly by the Gold Nugget Cafe where he saw Meg seated at a table, counting a pile of change.

Lucy smiled. "Vern always pays in coins. Drives Meg crazy."

They plodded on and Alexi wiped the sweat from his brow. The sun pounded like a relentless downbeat. Lucy's white-gold hair was damp in the back and beginning to curl. He tried to reconcile the two pictures of her, the image on the New York billboard, shining, ethereal, perfect, and standing before him, sweaty, irate, mussed, and somehow still as close to perfect as any woman he'd ever encountered.

"Why did you go to New York?" Out came the words before he could cage them in his mouth. He was not curious about people, not ever, yet there was an unaccustomed burning inside him to know about Lucy Winston.

She stopped in the shade of a gnarled oak. "You really want to know? It's not a pretty story."

"You will recall my life story is not either," he said. "I wanted you to tell me earlier, but you demurred."

"How about I tell you the particulars, a nutshell version, okay?"

He figured that was better than the burning curiosity, so he nodded. She tucked her arm through his, a gesture that both dumbfounded him and made him hold very still so she would not think the better of it and let go. They strolled on.

"I entered a modeling contest."

He nodded again. "I can see why. You are exquisitely formed."

She laughed. "You sure know how to flatter and puzzle a girl at the same time."

He was not sure how he had done so, but he was happy to see her smile and even more pleased with the laugh. "Because you are beautiful, you entered a contest," he said to keep the dialogue flowing. Her cheeks went the color of the inside of a seashell he'd once seen at a museum.

"A contest, yes. My cousin Nan took the picture, and by

some wild stretch of the miraculous, I actually won. The prize was a modeling contract with Faces, Incorporated in New York City and I was thrilled beyond imagining. It was going to be a new life of money and glamour and stardom. So off I went. My mother didn't want me to. She begged me to stay and help her with the inn, but I think mostly it was because she was afraid of what would happen to a guileless country girl in the big, bad, city. My brothers were preparing to ship out to Vietnam, and she was scared of losing all of us. I never thought much about how she must have felt. I didn't think much at all, at the time."

"What did happen, exactly?"

Her expression clouded. "My mother was right. It was a disaster."

"You did not succeed as a model?"

"No, the disaster was I did succeed. I hit it out of the park, as Uncle Paul would say."

"I do not understand."

"I got modeling jobs by the fistfuls, billboard ads, even a bit part in a movie. I made piles of money, lived in a tenth-floor apartment with another girl. She spent most of her time giving herself facials and throwing up to keep herself to a size zero, so I can't say we were actually close."

"That sounds unhealthy," he observed. "Continual vomiting can cause a multitude of problems including loss of vital electrolytes..."

"Yes," she said. "Like I told you before, the pursuit of perfection is a killer. Anyway, I was so busy I hardly had time for friends or anything else, but I managed to fall in love anyway."

He blinked. "You fell in love?"

"Yes, or what passes for love to a naive girl. I was only eighteen and he was a financial planner, my roommate's cousin who helped with her money. He helped me with mine too, by stealing all of it and disappearing on the night I thought he was going to propose."

"Oh."

"Yeah."

"Despicable. A villain."

"Probably more of an opportunist. He had some nice qualities and he treated me very well, other than stealing my money."

"You are surprisingly charitable."

She lifted a shoulder. "I've had some time to process it all. He didn't know me, not really, so I guess I should have figured out he wasn't really my soulmate. He didn't know about Mother and how our father left us, and she got sick with depression and how my Uncle Paul and Aunt Libby took over with me and my brothers." She held her face up to the sun. "He didn't know about Honey Creek and the Fourth of July Parade and Selma Trunk's stamp collection and the Christmas parade where we get a team of goats to pull Santa's sleigh because renting reindeer is too expensive."

"The oddities of small-town life."

"Yes, but those oddities, Alexi, they draw me home. The world can fall completely apart but the compass needle here always stays steady. I've got that compass needle in me, too. It always points me back here, to Honey Creek, to home. There's something solid here, something steady."

He filtered through the words. Steady. Solid. Home.

"Where does your compass needle point you?" she asked.

He would have said, "Where my piano is." But no longer. There was no home now. No true north. He gulped. "We were talking about you."

She laced her fingers through his. They were strong and unsweaty, her fingers. He held them with sufficient pressure that they did not fall away, but not enough, he calculated, to create discomfort. "You came home after your money was stolen."

"I did. My original plan, of course, was to pile up a ton of money and arrive triumphant in a parade of glory to restore the Lady Quail. I figured I'd live in New York and come home for visits, have enough to provide for Mom and my brothers if they needed help, fix up the church for Uncle Paul. I was going to be a hero, you see. I could almost hear the applause."

He could too, the ringing endorsement of audience goers who would pack the concert halls to hear him play. "You did not want to stay in New York and start over? You had lots of jobs, opportunities to begin again."

She let out a long slow breath. "I guess that compass needle kicked in and I missed the front porch," she said.

"Surely that was not the reason…"

She squeezed his hand. "Alexi, there is nothing like New York City, the excitement, the opportunity, the sheer energy of the place, but no matter where I went or how many jobs I booked, I could not find any front porch sitters in the whole darn city."

"And that is important, the moments spent sitting on front porches?"

"At the end of the day, those might be the only moments that really matter. I understood that more after Webber died."

"I am…er, not sure you are correct."

"Very tactful, Alexi."

He frowned. "I am not often tactful."

Her smile was brilliant as her billboard ad. "See? You've come a long way. Honey Creek is changing you."

Was it? He was still puzzling it over when she let go of his fingers as they approached the inn. Manny was standing at the wrought iron gate, looking as though he wanted to sink into the sidewalk and disappear.

"Just for a minute," Mrs. Steele was saying.

"No, ma'am. We have no vacancies. These are not public grounds. I mean, it is a hotel and all, but, well, not a regular type establishment." As if to emphasize the point, Lovely waddled over and bit him in the back of the calf. Manny winced. "See? There's an attack duck on the premises. Very hazardous. Get away now while you can."

Her husband took his wallet from his pocket. "Oh, come now, sonny. How about I make it worth your while? Five bucks for a few minutes?"

Manny shot a desperate look at Lucy.

"Dirty beaner," Mrs. Steele muttered at Manny.

Shocking, to hear such a slur. He realized his jaw was clenched on Manny's behalf. Also shocking. While he was trying to figure out how to react, Lucy spoke up.

"Thank you, Manny. I'll take care of this," she said in a clipped tone. Edging by the visitors, she guided Alexi through the gate, clicking it closed to hold back the woman, her husband, and another couple who must have heard of the find. Alexi eased back up the porch steps as Lovely shimmied closer.

"I guess perhaps you are hard of hearing. Manny made it plain, but I'll say it again," Lucy said. "This is private property. There will be no treasure hunting here."

"Awww," she began. "We aren't going to damage anything. I give you my word."

Lucy raised her chin. "I said no. If you trespass, we will call the police."

"Want to keep the treasure all to yourself, huh?" the woman said with a snort. "So much for small-town hospitality."

Lucy's cheeks went dusky. "This isn't about..."

But the visitors had turned their backs and sulked down

the sidewalk. Alexi noticed they snapped several pictures of the weedy front grounds and the ramshackle exterior. The man stopped to make notes on a folded piece of paper. They would not give up so easily he didn't think.

"We've got to quickly find whatever Thomas Lyman left here. I don't think we can hold them off for long." As Lucy marshaled Lovely back to the pond and Manny carefully latched the gate, Alexi wondered, where, exactly, had Mr. Needles gotten to?

DANA MENTINK

Chapter Twenty-One

Paul sank onto his perfect sitting spot on the fallen log, relishing the branches that blotted out some of the afternoon sun. Visitors usually assumed afternoons in Honey Creek would mellow into more friendly temperatures as the day wore on, but locals knew that four o'clock was the most ferocious hour.

He closed his eyes, listening to the tiniest gurgle of the creek which was all but dried up. Honey Creek had not escaped the years of drought unscathed. Thoughts of the upcoming Fourth of July fireworks showering down across the bone-dry acreage made his stomach muscles tense. He had begun to pray on the topic when Mr. Needles appeared, walking along the path.

"Well, hello," Paul said, after a moment of surprise. "Fancy meeting you here."

Needles shrugged. "Figured it might be cooler in the woods."

"That's my theory too." Paul gestured to the spot next to him on the old stump. The wood was worn smooth, the bark rubbed away by the repeated application of his bum. "Good thinking spot," he said.

Needles considered as he eased down next to Paul. "Do you come here much?"

"Every day. SueAnn from the church office can't find me to tell me about another committee meeting or ask me how we're going to pay for the altar flowers. It's quiet here." Needles rubbed a finger along his mustache. "This whole town is quiet."

Paul laughed. "More action here than you'd think." They both gazed down into the dry creek bed until the silence became awkward. Paul filled it with a universally accepted subject. "Who do you favor for the World Series this season?"

"Still got plenty of baseball to play yet, but it will be the Pirates, I'm thinking." He quirked an eyebrow. "That suits me, right? You all think I'm a pirate, here to steal what's rightfully yours?"

"Nothing is rightfully mine." The thoughts he'd been hashing out suddenly came into sharp focus. "If Thomas left a treasure here, he meant it to go to Agnes and I don't see why it shouldn't be passed to her kin if that's who you are."

His eyes rounded, brows quirked in a 'v' of surprise. "You kidding me?"

"No."

"Is this some sort of trick?"

"I've never been much good at tricks."

"You don't want the gold for yourself?"

"Wouldn't be for me anyway. Well, maybe I'd have bought the missus a little something. Libby could use one of those fancy gliding rocking chairs. She's hurting most of the time and it would soothe her, but otherwise, a treasure windfall would go to the church. The old building needs a new roof, and the angel is busted six ways to Sunday. At the moment, she only has half her head, which is more than most people, I suppose."

Needles stared. "I wouldn't give a fiddler's fart to any church."

"That right? You had a bad experience?"

"I don't mean to offend."

"You didn't. Many folks would say the same thing."

He shrugged. "Sorry to say it, but there isn't any church anywhere that isn't full of sinners, especially the pastor."

Paul laughed and slapped Needles on the back. "Well of course. Why else would they be in church?"

"What?"

"Jesus didn't come for the healthy. He came for sinners and the darn thing is, he can even use a busted up old sinner like me to lead a church. Don't that beat all? Talk about your bench players."

Needles opened his mouth to answer and closed it again. "So, this is a guilt thing then, right? If I find the treasure, I'd squander it selfishly whereas you'd be all magnanimous and use it on your church."

"And a rocking chair, don't forget that. That's not for the church, only for my best gal, purely for her."

Needles got up from the log and walked a few paces, letting loose puffs of dust that rose like a gold mist over the packed earth. "Agnes died too young. Cancer. All alone in that house with a bunch of birds. Six canaries. They drove the cats crazy, made an awful racket but she thought it was music."

"Wonderful," Paul said.

"What is?"

"Hearing music out of the racket. And she had you. That was good too."

"Me?" Needles watched a lizard scrabble in the dried leaves of the creek bed. "We weren't that…close."

"Close enough to hear the canaries sing."

He cocked his head. "You all are a little odd here in Honey Creek."

"Odd?"

"Yeah, like the whole world around you is all about parades, and what's growing in the garden, and shooting the breeze at the hardware store. The real world is all wrapped up in politics, the Cold War, race against race." He folded his arms. "And this town is like...like..."

"Coming home?"

"More like falling off a cliff into some weird time warp." Paul laughed again. "We won't be putting that on any postcards."

"No," Needles said, a small smile quirking his mouth. "I guess you won't. Why do you stay here? Don't you want to see the world?"

He considered. "When I played in the minors, I saw plenty of cities, small towns, big towns, people from all walks of life, I guess you could say. Never did find a place where I wanted to set down my roots except right here in Honey Creek."

"Why here?"

"Dunno. A feeling, I suppose. Where's your home, son?"

Needles didn't answer and for a while, Paul thought he might not have heard the question.

"I guess I haven't found it yet." His mouth twisted. "Don't worry. It won't be here in Honey Creek, I promise."

Paul shrugged. "Plenty of room if you change your mind. I mean, you do have kin here, even if it is a busted-up old pastor. Say, why don't you come for dinner on Saturday night? I'm sure Libby would love to meet you since we're related and all. Won't be anything fancy, 'cuz I do most of the cooking now, but I can almost produce an edible meatloaf with a side of crunchy rice. 'Al dente' is what Lucy calls it."

He brushed off the dust from his corduroy pants. "Thanks, but I think I'll be moving along pretty soon."

Paul winked. "Without your gold nuggets?"

His smile went sly. "Maybe I've already found them."

"That right?"

"Maybe."

"Well, you're still welcome for dinner anyway. Plenty of baseball left to be jawed over. We hardly got started on that subject."

With a short nod, Needles walked away.

Paul watched until he disappeared into the shadows along the path.

***

Alexi tried to ignore the disturbance brewing in the back room of the diner. He was alternately drinking his eight-ounce glass of water and the cup of coffee with one sugar which he allowed himself on account of his low energy. He was still reeling over the notion that Lucy was the model who had been smiling down on him from a billboard and who now smiled at him in person. His mind boggled at the incredulity of it all. It was as if she was meant to know him and he to know her. Wild coincidence for a man who did not believe in such things.

The clue. It pointed directly back to the Lady, there was no doubt about that, but how would they ever find another clue or the treasure for that matter? The house was centuries old, empty rooms filled with nooks and crannies, boxes of papers in the attic, closets filled with moldering coats that could conceal any number of clues in any number of pockets. It could be a lifetime project and Honey Creek was not a lifetime stop for Alexi. It was a temporary job, a short-term position until...until what? Until he got a real job in a real city. So, he was in stasis then, waiting to land in a place he could call home? No, he decided. More like sheltering in place until inspiration visited him.

He sipped more water and the sound of a woman's voice, high and angry, floated from the back room.

"How could you let this happen?"

He tuned it out. Perhaps the grounds of the inn held a

clue. The old weathervane? The dilapidated pool house? Trudy pushed into the diner, pale, holding a pitcher of water, lips tight together.

Behind her followed a woman with the same nose and wide cheekbones, an older, pinched version of the girl herself. "You have to get away from here. There's no other choice."

There were only two other diners in the restaurant. Both stared at the girl and her mother.

"You can't tell me what to do," Trudy said, chin dropped, and gaze fixed on her shoes.

"I'm your mother and I certainly can."

"I'm almost eighteen."

"Almost eighteen, huh? Such a grown-up, aren't you? Old enough to disgrace your family. How am I supposed to hold my head up in church? To tell your brothers they should behave and keep themselves pure when their sister is a tramp?"

"Don't say that," Trudy mumbled.

Mrs. Prynne hissed out a breath like a venting tea kettle. "You're a tramp, Trudy."

Tramp. Alexi turned the word over in his mind. To walk heavily and noisily. He discarded that definition.

"I'm your daughter, you shouldn't say that."

"You're not my daughter. I didn't raise a tramp."

A person who travels from place to place in search of work...Alexi jerked as he hit upon the proper context. Tramp...a five-letter word for a promiscuous woman.

Tears began to roll down Trudy's face, she did not wipe them away.

Alexi stood, uncertain, dropping his napkin.

Meg stepped closer. "Mrs. Prynne, maybe you would like to return to the back and finish talking about this? It's hardly the place..."

Mrs. Prynne's eyes went wild. "Why? Trudy wasn't shy about spreading her legs for that delinquent from school. Why should any of this remain a secret?"

Trudy's shoulders curled inward as if she'd taken a blow to the stomach. Alexi felt like he had too.

Mrs. Prynne laughed, hard and bitter. "No need to worry about her reputation. She's knocked up."

Knocked up. Alexi was not sure what that meant.

"She's going to live with my sister in Alabama until the brat comes and we'll put it up for adoption. God help whoever winds up taking it."

Adoption. He was getting an idea but surely, he must be in error. Trudy was so young, so very young.

"No," Trudy said, looking at her feet. "I'm not going."

"And what's your other choice? Is your punk of a boyfriend going to raise it? Take care of you both?"

Raise it? Take care of you both? He understood. A baby.

Trudy did not answer her mother, cheeks scarlet.

Her mother's expression took on a glint of victory. "I didn't think so. He dumped you, once he got what he wanted, didn't he? After you let him turn you into a tramp, he couldn't get away fast enough."

"I'm not a tramp." The tears dripped onto the front of her faded waitress's uniform.

"Oh yes, you are." Mrs. Prynne's eyes burned. "You are a soiled tramp, and no decent man will ever want you now."

Alexi stumbled from the booth. "Stop."

Trudy's mom glanced at him only for a moment. "This isn't your business, mister."

"This is a diner," he said loudly. "And I would like some oatmeal please," he said.

Mrs. Prynne stared at him now. Trudy lifted her gaze.

"I want oatmeal," he said, "With no raisins. Trudy knows the right way to prepare it."

Meg waved a hand. "In a minute, Alexi."

Trudy looked at him and he tried to say with his eyes what his mouth could not produce. Her face was scarlet, her mother's mouth open to speak again, to unleash more punishment, more blows.

"No," he said, voice rising to a shout. Meg gaped. Mrs. Prynne's cheeks mottled with fury. Before she could speak again, he snapped out, "I would like some oatmeal right now with no raisins. Trudy will make it. She is an excellent waitress. Excellent." His words struck silence across the diner, eyes staring as if he was an animal at the zoo, staring at him, not at Trudy.

The girl whirled and raced to the kitchen.

Mrs. Prynne shook her head. "All right then. If she's going to try to live some kind of life in this town, with you people, then she's your problem. I wash my hands of her." Mrs. Prynne slammed out of the diner.

I wash my hands of her.

A six-letter word: to refuse to acknowledge as one's own. Disown.

He did not think that six letters quite captured the pain and power of it. It was too much hurt for six letters to hold. Disowned, dead to her own mother.

Trudy got the message though, he saw her through the swinging kitchen door, face shining with tears, looking more like a small child than a pregnant woman.

Without waiting for his oatmeal, he quietly slid his money on the table and left the diner.

Chapter Twenty-Two

Lucy was surprised when Alexi pulled up outside the church in the battered station wagon. She was helping to unfurl the plastic red, white, and blue covers over the picnic tables for the morning pancake breakfast, talking with her uncle about her fruitless search of the inn. Alexi's mouth was drawn, forehead furrowed.

"Hi, Alexi."

"Hello." He picked up the other end of the tablecloth and awkwardly fluffed it out while she secured it to the table.

"I haven't found a single trace of Thomas Lyman anywhere at the Lady."

He nodded, still frowning.

"Is something wrong?"

"I was thinking about my mother and a word...a special word, but I cannot bring it to mind. It's probably due to fatigue. Honey Creek is noisy with nocturnal nature."

She hid a smile. "Ah. Maybe I can help."

"What is the word that means a mother will love her child no matter if the child proves a disappointment?" He rubbed his shriveled hand on his thigh. "Or does not realize certain ambitions for which the mother sacrificed? I know the word...I cannot recall it. Fatigue, like I said."

She took his hand. "Unconditional."

He sighed. "Of course. Thirteen letters. I should have known."

"Oh, Alexi. Your mother loves you that way, doesn't she?" Lucy hoped with all her heart that the answer would be yes.

He shrugged. "Yes, though she will always be disappointed that I lost my music." Seemingly without thinking, he lifted her hand to his mouth and brushed his lips across her knuckles, eyes closed.

She held her breath.

When he gazed at her again, his eyes still held worry, consternation. "I never considered the value of it before."

"Alexi, what's wrong? Tell me what happened."

He looked at her then and she saw moisture gleaming under his lashes. "I was at the diner," he said. "And so was Trudy and her mother." Then he shook his head, unable to speak another word.

She didn't understand what he'd seen, but she knew it grieved him deeply, not for himself, but for Trudy. Without another word, she folded him into her arms, and they grieved together about a thirteen-letter word and a troubled teenage girl.

***

Paul had picked the wild red roses from the snarl of bushes that edged the old cemetery, earning a couple of punctures for his efforts. Contrary things, roses, he'd always thought. The most beautiful blossoms and the most ferocious weaponry. It was July Fourth, his mother's birthday. She'd always been so dedicated to remembering everyone's birthdays, his, Libby's, Nan's, Lucy and her brothers. It was her personal mission to be sure no one was forgotten on their special day. But who had remembered hers before she'd married and had kids? Disowned by her family, abandoned by the man who'd left her pregnant with Thomas. She'd lived a long hard road at times, but he'd only known her for a few miles of it.

Thoughts bumbled around in his head like the bees among the roses.

Why didn't you tell me? I am your son. I deserved to know the truth.

But he already knew the answer. He deserved to know nothing. It was her story, her struggle and he did not have the right to know anything about that time in her life. Shame ran deep and she'd loved both her sons he had no doubt. Timing made one pregnancy a joy and the other a humiliating secret. A piece of paper, a marriage license, or the lack of it rendered judgment on a newborn life.

Meg's frantic phone call still rang in his ears.

"Oh Pastor, Trudy's pregnant and her mother was here, and it was the most awful scene you can imagine."

Decades after his mother, Trudy was living out that same scenario for all of Honey Creek to see, an unwed mother, practically a child herself. Had his mom felt so utterly alone? Did she experience the whispers, the judgmental eyes that followed her every move? Tracked the burgeoning of her body as it expanded with life she was in no way ready to meet? He didn't blame her for moving to Honey Creek, for concocting a lie that would spare her own reputation and keep Thomas safe from the dreaded label of bastard child. But still, it grieved him that he had not recognized Thomas as his blood brother, that he'd lost something he'd never really known he had.

And what was to be done about Trudy? He'd hoped the quiet of the cemetery might give him some direction, but so far, he had no answers.

He knelt at his mother's grave and plucked away the taller grasses that threatened to overtake the stone. The roses shone in the sun and he knew she would have thrilled to the rich burst of color. A free gift from God, she would have said. She'd collected every free thing she could, bestowing them on him with grand ceremony. A notepad she'd gotten at the bank. A scarf she'd received after collecting labels from soup cans. Two packets of chewing gum acquired for visiting a new grocery store that had opened and closed in a matter of months.

"I love you, Mama." He felt rather than heard another presence in the cemetery then, moving slowly among those quiet stones. The cool of the shady place, or perhaps it was his all-fired curiosity, made him linger when he should have respectfully left the other visitor to their own devices. Instead, he kept to the shrubby boundary of the path, strolling past the gravestones that hearkened back to the gold rush era. A soft swell of ground led him to the lower hillside where a collection of mismatched stones lay in a grove of eucalyptus trees. The sun fractured into rays between the sturdy tree trunks, blanketing the spot in blessed coolness. He froze when he saw who knelt there, next to a flat marble marker and a smaller stone placed beside it.

Trooper did not see Paul, and Gummy lay in a patch of sunlight, too sleepy to alert his owner to Paul's presence. As he watched, Trooper knelt with a groan and put both his palms flat, one on each marker, dirty overalls draping the grass, and the bottom of his boots showing a hole in the toe. He didn't speak, simply crouched there on all fours, eyes closed, expression etched in an agony that Paul realized he must have been holding onto for a very long time. An old pain, like a broken bone that healed badly, never set right, a perpetual reminder of a grievous wound.

Paul stood frozen, unsure, until he backed away, walking up the hill to find a seat on a shady bench. Pondering, he pictured the photo he'd seen at the house of the Murphy sisters. Harmon Valentine, AKA Trooper as a young groom, smiling, proud. He realized he'd stumbled onto the answer to the question born in his mind that day at the sister's house.

Why had Harmon Valentine returned to Honey Creek to live the life of a vagrant?

After a time, he heard Trooper and Gummy ambling their way out of the cemetery, along the path that would take them out the rear entrance. Though he was quite sure it was another sin of curiosity, Paul walked to examine the stones where Trooper had just visited.

Mrs. Regina Murphy Valentine, wife of Harmon Valentine.

Bonnie Murphy, beloved daughter, gone too soon. The date was the same for both of them. They had died together. An accident?

The facts assembled themselves in his mind in a flash. Twenty-five years ago, a wreck, not here in Honey Creek, but in Illinois. Paul had been a young seminary student, and not yet received his pastorship in Honey Creek, but the previous pastor, the beloved Bill Tingley, had conducted the funeral ceremony since Bea and Pearl's father insisted that the dead be buried in their hometown. A terrible shame, the wreck that killed a mother and child. And the father? Safely on a business trip, the important man, the top appliance salesman on the entire West Coast as a matter of fact. He'd fled the town as soon as the services were complete.

"And I never saw a man so broken," Pastor Bill had said. "Blamed himself for not being there. He'd not come home when he'd promised. Missed the daughter's birthday party. Duty called."

The duty of business, of money, of making a name for oneself.

But unbeknownst to everyone, Harmon Valentine had returned to Honey Creek, still broken and grieving. He lived as a homeless man, hiding behind a scraggly beard, dropping fish and dried apples into the offering dish, wearing his Dodger's hat on every occasion, tending to an ancient dog and an abandoned teen, visiting his wife and daughter's grave.

Tied to Honey Creek as tightly as he was to his grief.

"Oh, my friend," he whispered. "How could I not have seen it?"

Paul closed his eyes and let the pain of it wash over and through him. Then he said a prayer for Trooper and turned his feet on the path towards home.

HONEY CREEK TREASURE HUNT

Chapter Twenty-Three

The Fourth of July bustle was in full swing as Lucy set up chairs along the shady part of the sidewalk smack in front of the Lady Quail. It was a textbook Honey Creek melee. The all-volunteer band honked and drummed their way into some sort of messy formation as they prepared to mosey down Main Street on their way to the ending location at the empty lot. Since there was no official band director, Ralph the tuba player assumed command, sweating profusely in his long-sleeved tunic as he shouted orders. Volunteer Fire Chief Ed Tooney had shined the old firetruck to a brilliant glow, and he sounded the siren repeatedly, his grin as broad as his belly. The scout troops unfurled their banners and a collection of small American flags in preparation for their own moment in the parade spotlight.

"There's Charlie," Lucy's mother said.

Charlie and his father Mick prepared for their annual fireworks parade kick-off extravaganza which involved a half dozen illegally acquired firecrackers and a bucket of water for emergency purposes.

"The guests love the Fourth of July, don't they?" Her mother's expression went dreamy. "Mr. Winston always loves it too." She frowned. "Where is Mr. Winston? Has he gone to get more briquettes for the cookout?"

Pain stabbed at Lucy's insides. Not grief for her father, no, he had made his choice long ago and never looked back.

Rather it was the sadness of knowing her mother still longed deep down for her husband, the heart craving what the mind could not accept.

"I'm not sure," Lucy said finally, handing her mother a paper fan. "I will keep my eyes peeled for him, Mrs. Winston."

"Thank you, dear."

Ed announced in a booming voice that all parade goers must remain on the sidewalks, also for safety purposes. The townsfolk had not forgotten the year Vern's dachshund Scooter had grabbed hold of a flaming sparkler, lead a merry chase, and set an entire field on fire before he finally dropped the thing.

On any other Fourth of July, Lucy would have escorted her mother to a spot on the library steps where she could enjoy waving and visiting with the townsfolk that lined the Main Street, but she did not dare leave the Lady Quail unguarded with Needles and the treasure hunters lurking at every turn. As it was, a half dozen of the treasure club had milled around for hours talking and pointing. Great effort was required to keep her mother away from the windows so she wouldn't be disturbed by the gawkers.

Manny had even removed one whip-thin tourist who had snuck over the fence and began scouring the yard with his metal detector. Lovely got credit for the apprehension, as she'd chased after the man, causing him to fall flat near the edge of the pond. He should be grateful that Manny showed him the gate before Lovely finished his furious pecking.

Lucy sat in the chair next to her mother and used her own paper fan to ward off the heat.

"Is it time?" her mother asked, peering along the sidewalk. "Have all the guests found places to sit? Is there plenty of lemonade in the parlor for them?"

"Yes, ma'am," she said.

Her brother Kelby walked over, handed their mother a paper dish of peach ice cream, and sat next to her to eat his own.

"Fran's finest, Mrs. Winston," he said. "I would have asked for one for you too, Lucy, but, uh, Fran looked, well, I mean she was, um…"

Lucy grimaced. She'd gotten a picture of what happened from Alexi and several of the church congregation who'd shown up to help with pies to serve after the parade. The small-town gossip train was chugging along at full speed. Trudy was pregnant by her boyfriend and Fran had tossed Trudy out, heaving her bag onto the front grass and slamming the door, according to Meg. At the moment, Trudy was staying in Nan's room at Uncle Paul's house. Lucy did not think Trudy would have the nerve to attend the parade. Places exchanged, Lucy probably wouldn't either. Her heart ached at what the girl might be feeling. And Fran must have forgotten the 'love thy neighbor' command to have booted her out in such a fashion.

Lucy shot a look at her brother. Teen pregnancy was a topic that hit painfully close to home for Kelby who had both fathered and lost a child before he turned twenty. He'd never stopped searching for his son, who'd been snatched away by its mother, and she knew he never would. She suspected the sadness might have been a contributing factor in Kelby's decision to enlist. If he'd been sitting closer, she would have wrapped an arm around his shoulders.

Her mother gave Kelby a piercing look. "What are you talking about? What is the matter with Fran? Is there trouble?"

"No, no trouble." A headache was settling behind Lucy's temples. *No trouble other than people trying to burgle our property, Needles lurking who knew where, a pregnant girl with no one to turn to, a soggy donut shop, and the Hope angel still dumped on the floor of the church like a stony decapitation victim.* Trouble? They had bushels of it, but she would not cast a cloud over the festivities. Her mother seemed to accept her soothing and nibbled at her ice cream. Kelby devoured his own in heaping spoonsful.

Lucy smiled as Alexi joined them, holding out a sack for her to take. "These are donuts. Steffi is selling her red, white, and blue speckled ones today which she was able to make since Trooper repaired the sump pump."

"That was so nice of you to bring them, Alexi," she said, opening the bag and snagging one for herself. "Would you like to share?"

He shuddered. "I do not consume sticky foods."

She laughed and patted the extra chair next to her. "I saved you a seat."

He cautiously eased into it and she thought he looked a little less tired since they'd shared a hug, less "wrapped up tight" as Trooper would have said. Awkward and neurotic as he was, there was something earnest and gentle about Alexi that made Lucy want to stay close.

Alexi eyed Charlie who lit a firecracker. It danced and wobbled a circle of flame in the middle of the street, drawing oohs from the crowd.

Kelby tensed.

Alexi blinked. "Surprising. I had supposed the use of fireworks in such a dry climate was…"

"Illegal," Kelby said, his voice raspy. "Yep."

"That is logical, as they are a class of low explosive pyrotechnic devices which account for over three hundred injuries annually. Is Charlie not aware of this?"

Kelby finished the rest of his ice cream and reached for the donuts. "Oh, he knows."

Alexi quirked an eyebrow.

"And he doesn't care," Kelby finished. Now he was on

his feet. "No one does."

Lucy felt her brother's tension. How they'd loved to watch the fireworks as kids, even tried to sneakily light some themselves, but that was all before Vietnam. Cars backfiring, fireworks, a sudden unexpected touch on the shoulder were now the cause of severe stress for Kelby.

Alexi rearranged himself into the chair as he mulled her brother's pronouncement.

"You still have your fork and knife in your front pocket," she whispered.

He frowned. "I forgot that I left them there, after the...altercation."

"I heard the details," she whispered again. "Meg said you tried to help."

He cocked his head. "In retrospect, I do not think I was extremely helpful. There was screaming which I attempted to stop."

"How did you do that?"

He sighed. "I demanded oatmeal.""

She gaped. "You did?"

"Yes, it was foolish, I can see that in retrospect, but I did not know what else to say. The shouting was..." He shook his head. "I should have thought of another way."

"You tried to help."

He shrugged, looking at his shoes. "Trudy's mother was angry. Her verbal attack on Trudy...I am surmising of course, that it will leave scars." He tapped a finger on his chest. "Here."

Very slowly, Lucy reached over and took his hand, the one with the twisted tendons, the bent fingers. He flinched.

"Alexi, you are a good man."

It seemed like he would pull away, but after a moment, he merely stared at her hand cradling his.

Charlie let off another firecracker which made them both

jump. Lucy and her mother giggled. Kelby began to pace the sidewalk behind them. Alexi started in on the detrimental effects of fireworks again when Selma Trunk hurried up, balancing a dish of ice cream and two sprinkle donuts. She grinned, showing blue sprinkles caught between her front teeth. "I've got it, I've solved it." The glee was radiating out of her like a Fourth of July sparkler.

"Selma, would you mind sitting?" Lucy's mother said. "You're blocking my view of the fireworks display."

Selma scooted around to block Lucy's view instead.

Lucy was going to say something when Selma's words stopped her cold.

"Needles isn't who he says he is."

"What?" she and Alexi said at once.

"I contacted Gil Farnsworth over at the county office and there's no record of Agnes having had any children."

Lucy let that settle into her brain. "Maybe…"

"And what's more," Selma said, shoving another quarter of a donut into her mouth. "Gil called up Agnes's neighbor personally and do you know what?"

Lucy wanted to shake her. "Tell me."

"After Phil described Needles, Agnes's neighbor dropped a bomb."

Lucy was so far forward she almost tipped out of the lawn chair. "What? What bomb? What?"

Selma smiled in triumph. "This Mr. Lawrence Needles is actually a pet groomer."

"We know," Lucy huffed. "That's not a revelation."

Selma arched an offended eyebrow. "He's a pet groomer and he has one of those vehicles with Dr. Doolittle painted on the sides. Agnes owned a bunch of birds and cats. Who kept them clipped?"

"Needles?" Alexi put in.

She waved a donut. "The very man."

"How is this germane to the ancestry issue?" Alexi asked.

Selma squinched an eyebrow. "Come again?"

"Get back to the part about Agnes not having any children," Lucy snapped. "How exactly did Lawrence Needles go about impersonating her son?"

"Easy. She was a lonely old woman and Lawrence was her pet groomer. He visited her regularly. Probably talked about Thomas Lyman, her lost love, and all that rot. When that idiot Alvin Wong published the article in the Mountain Holler, Needles read it and cooked up his scheme."

"I didn't think anyone read the Mountain Holler outside of our town," Lucy's mother remarked after another bite of ice cream.

Selma snorted. "That's the delicious part. The sneaky Mr. Needles is also a pet sitter for the Murphy sisters, come to find out. Trudy said she recognized the van on its way up to Pearl and Bee's house, same one as used to come to visit Agnes in the town where she and Trudy's family lived before. Pearl Murphy is an avid crossword puzzler. She faithfully completed the puzzle every week and sometimes Needles would give her a hint or two. He must have seen the article while he was at it."

Alexi's eyes went wide. "I did not realize..."

Lucy beamed him a huge grin. "So, while Needles was helping her complete the crosswords, he learned of the treasure and the whole Thomas-Lyman-leaving-clues-for-Agnes business."

"That is bizarre," Kelby said, leaving off his pacing for a moment. "What are the chances...?"

"That such thing..." Lucy added.

"Could take place in Honey Creek?" Alexi finished.

Lucy laughed. "Well, when you put it like that," she said. "I'd say the chances are pretty darn good." She pumped a fist in triumph. "At least Mr. Needles is off our backs now."

Selma started waving across the street. "There's Pastor Paul. I'm going to go break it to him that the no-good Needles is not his relation, just an old-fashioned scammer. Any gold nuggets found in this town belong to the pastor, fair and square." Cramming in the rest of the donut, hamster-like, into her cheek, she crossed the street and headed for the church.

Lucy could not hold back a laugh. I wouldn't have seen that coming in a million years. It's like a novel or something."

Alexi raised an eyebrow. "Anagnorisis."

"God bless you," Kelby said.

"Anagnorisis. An eleven-letter word referring to the protagonist's sudden recognition of another character's true identity or nature. We have just discovered the truth about Lawrence Needles."

"Whatever you call it, it couldn't have worked out better," Kelby said. "Now all you gotta do is find the treasure, sis," Kelby said. "That should be a snap for you. You used to spend your summers reading every Nancy Drew book you could get your mitts on, I recall."

Lucy was still steeped in the wonder of it when Charlie set the match to a firecracker. The little cylinder hurtled up into the air where it was meant to explode into a colorful starburst. It would not be nearly as dramatic as the nighttime firework display, but it was the traditional signal to launch the parade.

Kelby blew out a long slow breath. Alexi, Lucy, and her mother watched the projectile zoom into the sky and then change trajectories, arcing across the street, trailing a tail of flame. The crowd watched, squinting.

Slowly, gracefully, it began to descend like a fallen angel, streaking towards the ground.

But not where they had anticipated.
Kelby let out a low breath. "Uh oh."
Lucy shot to her feet.
The excitement in her belly sharply turned to dread as the missile plummeted. It appeared to slow, spiraling as it lost velocity. With a trail of sparks, it thudded onto the warped shingle roof of the Lady Quail.

Chapter Twenty-Four

Alexi watched slack-jawed as the firecracker dropped and rolled, crackling over the dried slats of wood that likely should have been replaced a decade before. As the seconds ticked into minutes, one tiny burning ember popped loose from the roof, lingering against the blue sky.

He'd heard it said that certain moments in life played out in slow motion. The car that had jumped the curb in New York and crushed his hand had certainly not been moving in slow motion, but Alexi's memory of it spooled it out and made it last much longer. The silver flash of the front fender, two headlights staring as if they saw what the driver could not. Alexi's arm thrown up in a useless gesture as if he might ward off the vehicle, the other crushed against an unforgiving wall. The lady who sold pretzels on the street corner stood, mouth open so wide in shock he could see the wad of pink gum inside. Seconds stretched, long and indelible.

Now too, the time began to spin through his senses in warped, distended images. A gauzy curtain flapped out the open window, pure white against the cloudless blue sky. One tiny burning bit collided with that flutter of white, grabbing hold and consuming the fabric in greedy mouthfuls. The flames climbed up the curtain and into the inn as if invited in for tea. Within a minute, no more, smoke began to fill Mrs. Winston's bedroom.

"Oh no," Lucy cried. "No, no, this can't be happening." Her cry jolted him back into the proper flow of time. Lucy and Kelby bolted past him up the steps.

"Get Mother away from here," she shouted over her shoulder. Alexi was not sure she'd yelled the directive at him, but he took Mrs. Winston's arm, helped her out of the lawn chair, and guided the bewildered woman over to the care of Meg. Then he sprinted back up the porch as Manny stepped out the front door, holding tight to the wiggling Lovely.

"Caught him in the garden. I'll take him..." He looked around in confusion. "Somewhere."

"Is anyone inside?"

"Kelby and Lucy," Manny said. Alexi thought the man was going to thrust the duck into his arms, so he stepped back.

"I will go help them."

Manny nodded. "I saw that Needles guy a minute ago looking over the side fence as I caught Lovely, but I told him to get back. I'm pretty sure he left."

Alexi could already smell the smoke drifting down from the burning roof. His eyes began to water as he stepped into the front parlor. The air was acrid, and no doubt filled with particles that would wreak havoc on the alveoli in his lungs. Kelby thundered down the stairs. "I've got Mom's jewelry box and her picture album."

"I'll get her wheelchair from the back bedroom," Lucy called to him.

"No," Alexi wanted to shout. "*Get out. The first rule of fire safety is to evacuate, leaving personal items behind*," but she had already disappeared in the haze.

By now, Alexi heard the whine of the siren from the volunteer fire department and the clang of metal nozzles as they hooked up the hoses to the hydrant. Racing to the window, he watched as they began pumping a weak stream of water onto the roof. One thousand gallons per minute against the fire kindling on the desiccated roof was not an equitable match-up. He feared the inn would be the loser, and he desperately did not want Lucy to be hurt in the conflagration.

The smoke was thickening, an ominous crackling coming from the roof.

"Lucy," he shouted, coughing as he made his way along. "Lucy, we must get out," he yelled again, almost colliding with the wheelchair she appeared through the smoke. Her face was a pale streak in the dank air, scared, small, beautiful.

He took the wheelchair from her and ran it out the front door. Lucy followed closely on his heels. Trooper was halfway up the front walk, puffing, and he took the chair from Alexi.

"Get out of there, son. Whole place is as dry as Mama's pork chops."

Kelby had taken his place with the volunteers, pulling on an old turnout coat and baggy pants. "Stay back," he hollered to the people gathered on the sidewalk. "Everybody back."

It was at this moment that Alexi realized Lucy had not followed him out. Had she stopped for something? Fallen?

"Don't go back in there..." Trooper yelled to Alexi's back.

Alexi again dashed inside, catching a glimpse of Lucy racing back into the parlor. The interior was now filled with smoke and stinging tears blinded him. The heat enveloped him in an oppressive blanket.

"Come," he said, bursting into the parlor. "We have to get out."

"Mama's family letters, I have to get them." She snatched a carved wooden box from the mantel. The way they'd gotten in was so filled with smoke he could not see clearly. The easiest exit was the French doors, so he flung them open and took her wrist. He pushed her out first into the yard and was about to follow when his gaze fastened on the piano.

He saw a flash only, the gleam of wood under the old tapestry they used to cover the derelict instrument. The curve of it, the graceful lines. Shock made his whole body tense. It was not possible. His senses were confused, addled by the smoke. What were the chances that he could actually be correct?

What were the chances...that such a thing...could happen in Honey Creek?

In a state of shock, he raced to the piano, threw back the tapestry, and played a chord with his ruined hand. The tone sounded over the crackle of the flames and the yelling of the fire personnel like the song of an angel. Goosebumps prickled over his sweaty skin. The fire, the danger, the fear all fell away in the space of that one lingering note.

What were the chances?

His mind fired into high gear and he desperately calculated the width of the exit and the piano. Tight, but it could be managed, barely. In a moment, he'd thrown open the French doors and began tugging the piano for all he was worth.

Lucy appeared in the doorway. "Alexi. What are you doing? Stop that right now."

"I have got to save it," he called.

"No." She ran to him, tugging at his arm. "Leave it. It's just an old piano. We'll find a new one for Manny to play. Come with me."

Kelby appeared through the smoke. "Out of here, both of you, now."

"Leave the piano," she screamed again.

"Take her outside," Alexi demanded.

"I am not leaving you here, you musical idiot!" she shrieked.

Kelby picked up Lucy, threw her over his shoulder, and carried her, hollering, from the inn, yelling for Alexi to follow him.

Alexi did not pause to reply, yanking and pulling the piano inch by inch towards the threshold to the outside.

The thick smoke sent him into spasms of coughing, so he pulled his collar over his mouth. A litany of facts beat through his mind.

Smoke inhalation. Fifty to eighty percent of fire fatalities resulted due to smoke rather than burns.

Carbon monoxide, sulfur dioxide, hydrogen cyanide, and hydrogen sulfide, a deadly cocktail that would replace the oxygen in the room in a matter of minutes.

What was an eleven-letter word for the state or process of dying as a result of being deprived of air?

Suffocation.

Heat and near panic made him dizzy, but he tugged, lugged, and shoved the piano. At the exact moment he thought he would accomplish the thing, the piano caught on the edge of the worn rug. His efforts grew more frantic, but he only succeeded in bunching the material up until the instrument would not move an inch.

Now he threw his shoulder against the wood, his bones cracking. The room swam before his eyes. The piano remained wedged. Alexi sank to his knees, tears obliterating his vision. He lamented his scrawny frame, spindly arms. The only talent he'd ever possessed, the only part of him that was in any way remarkable was in his hands, and those were as useless now in moving the piano as they were in playing it. He pressed his forehead to the old wood as if he could somehow apologize both to the glorious instrument and

Lucy for his failure.

"You're some kind of idiot that's certain," a voice said. Alexi dashed his arm across his eyes and Trooper swam into view.

I have to save it, Alexi wanted to say but he was wracked by coughs.

Trooper grabbed hold of the end of the piano. "I mean, what kind of an imbecile would risk his life for a banged-up piano when he don't even play it anymore? Not to mention you've got Denny's already. A man needing two pianos who don't even play? That's just greedy, son. Or insane, I'm not sure which. I'm leaning towards the latter, in your case."

Alexi coughed in reply and once again began to push with his last remaining ounce of strength. Trooper lifted the edge of the piano over the carpet barrier and together they inched the instrument towards the precious, clean air.

***

The yard was a mess of firefighters, hoses, streams of water, and well-meaning Honey Creekers doing whatever they could. Through the choking smoke and the noisy haze, she sought Alexi once she realized he had not followed her unceremonious exit tossed over her brother's shoulder. Why? Why had he stayed inside for a broken piano? What possible reason could he have for doing such a reckless, useless thing except pure insanity?

Her stomach knotted tight as she searched.

"Have you seen Alexi?" she asked Manny.

"There." He jerked a finger around the side. "He and Trooper are over by the gazebo."

She bolted, nearly falling flat on an overturned lawn chair. Alexi sat on the steps of the gazebo, one hand clutching the leg of the old piano. Trooper was there shaking his head, thumbs tucked into the pockets of his overalls.

Lucy stopped so suddenly her feet skidded on the grass.

"Alexi Quinn you are crazy. Do you hear me? Certifiable."

"I already told him that," Trooper said.

"You could have died, running back into the inn."

"I told him that, too."

She looked from Trooper to Alexi. "Well, why?" she said, voice nearing a squeak. "Why did you do it?" She looked at Trooper. "Why did he do it?"

Trooper shrugged. "Don't look at me. I figured from the first time I saw him he had a screw loose." He marched away, boots squelching in the muddy ground.

She folded her arms to contain the fury. "Tell me why."

Alexi coughed several times and blinked, soot blackening his cheeks and chin. "I could not let the piano burn," he said simply.

Her brain felt stretched beyond its limits. She resisted the urge to grab his collar and shake him until his teeth rattled. "It's a thing, an old thing, made of wood and springs and ivory and nails and steel."

"Cast iron. That part is called the plate, or sometimes the harp, and it is responsible for maintaining the massive tension in the..."

"Alexi," she shouted. He jerked.

"Yes?"

"I don't want to hear one more useless fact about anything. Not pianos or ferrets or duck feet, do you understand?"

His mouth opened but she cut him off.

"No talking. Just nodding. Got me?"

He nodded.

She waggled a finger close to his nose. "You are going to tell me right this instant why you went back in there for a busted-up old piano." Tears crowded her eyes now and trickled hotly.

His lips crimped but he remained silent.

"You can talk now."

He blinked several times and coughed. "It is more than a piano."

"No, it's not." But she noticed he was not listening anymore. He was staring over her shoulder at the stained-glass picture that hung in the window. The piece was now filmy with smoke, except for one yellow piece. In spite of the sooty tarnish, the amber glass of the miner's hand was oddly clean, glowing almost by some source of illumination from inside, a flame that had not been quenched. It caught her for a moment, deflected her desire to grab Alexi by his lapels and either kiss him or throttle him.

"Could it be so?" His voice was a near whisper.

Her hands balled into fists to keep from shaking him. "What is it, Alexi? I am in the middle of yelling at you and the least you can do is pay attention."

He continued to stare. "That is an old piece of stained glass."

"Yes. My great grandfather made it. It has been hanging in the window since the inn was rebuilt after the fire. Only fell once in an earthquake about fifteen years ago but it didn't break. But that's not important now..."

He continued to stare as if he hadn't heard. "Have you ever noticed, Lucy, how the miner in the stained glass appears to point?"

She was not done being angry, so her response came out as a bark of outrage. "Point to what? Why is this relevant?"

The man was loopy. The smoke had messed with his senses. Nevertheless, she peered at the crude outline of a hand with one finger extended. Imagining a sight line in her mind, she turned out towards the side yard. "I don't see anything."

Alexi stood and put a filthy palm on each one of her shoulders, twisting her body. "There. See?"

The stained-glass miner was indeed pointing directly to the iron statue next to Lovely's pond. The old cast-iron figure was nearly grown over by a clematis vine that twined and twirled around the metal folds of the lady's dress and now the soot that rained down made it even harder to see. The woman held a little bird in her corroded hand.

I am not higher than a baronet, not lower than an earl, yet you hold this title in my heart.

The Lady Quail. Was it indeed the spot where Thomas Lyman had hidden his treasure?

Through the trance of shock and despair and sheer disbelief, she made her way to the side yard. Alexi followed, coughing every few feet. Fleshy flippers plowed across the grass as Lovely waddled alongside her. "Did you get away from Manny?" The duck deserved to be scolded, but her breast feathers were streaked with soot and it made Lucy want to cry. She kept her eyes away from the inn. Seeing the extent of the damage at that moment might break her.

Focus on the treasure.

Biting her lip, she stopped at the edge of the pond, knelt close, and examined the metal sculpture. Alexi pushed Lovely away with his foot.

Lovely persisted in poking at his pant leg and rubbing her beak onto the top of his shoe.

"Strange how much she likes you," Lucy grumbled. "She doesn't like many people." But then, Alexi was most certainly not the common man. He was most likely a lunatic, but she was so grateful he was alive, she couldn't be too mad about it.

Hands shaking with excitement, she peeled back the vines which were surprisingly weak in their hold on the Lady. Almost as if…but she pushed the thought away. Gently she tipped the statue over and peered at the bottom. Though she had never examined it before, the under part was meant to be fastened onto the upper portion, a series of rusty screw holes making her heart beat faster.

"The screws are missing," Alexi noted. "Why would that be?"

She hardly heard as she shimmied the Lady back and forth until the top came loose. With shaking hands, she turned the statue over, peering into the dark interior.

The inside was hollow and empty.

A heavy sigh escaped her. "I guess we were wrong."

Alexi pushed Lovely away. "But that must have been where Thomas hid his treasure."

"It was," a voice called over the fence.

Needles sat in his car, engine idling, a mile-wide smile brightening his face. He held up a metal box and shook it, setting it rattling like a maraca. "It's Thomas Lyman's treasure, right there in your own side yard. Gold nuggets. Approximately twenty ounces, I'd guess. Worth about four thousand dollars."

"That's Uncle Paul's," Lucy snapped, getting to her feet so fast she went dizzy. "You're not even a relative. You took advantage of Agnes."

He shrugged. "What's it matter? The treasure wasn't hers and even if it was, she didn't need it. Old lady had plenty of money and only a couple of birds and cats to spend it on. She and Thomas weren't really married anyway. I doctored the marriage license as you figured out."

Lucy searched for words big and angry enough to contain her outrage. "You're...you're despicable."

He laughed. "Despicable and rich. I can live with that. Anyway, it's been fun here in Honey Creek, but you know what they say about those rolling stones." He roared away in a cloud of exhaust that mingled with the acrid scent of smoke.

Lucy could only stare. The treasure gone, snatched from

her very own yard.

"What do they say?" Alexi asked.

She could hardly get her voice to work. "What do they say about what?"

"The Rolling Stones. He is speaking I assume about the rock group begun in Britain in 1962, successful with the youthful counterculture of the 1960s, and so on. I do not see how it pertains."

Hot tears flooded Lucy's eyes and her throat closed. The end of the treasure hunt left them with a crippled church, a dilapidated angel, and now massive damage to the Lady Quail. How would they recover? What would happen to her mother? "I..." She gasped, grief making her whole body tremble. A burning shingle slid off the roof and fell into the pond with a hiss.

"Never mind," Alexi said, taking her in his arms and folding her against his chest. "You can tell me later. And I have something to tell you later too."

Lovely circled anxiously around their feet as Lucy began to weep.

Chapter Twenty-Five

Alexi did not leave his post. After he had done his best to comfort Lucy, waiting until her shuddering sobs subsided, he took up a position at the gazebo next to the piano. He sat on a rusted patio chair rescued from the muddy grass. He waited and watched.

The firefighters had done a respectable job containing the blaze, but the roof was blackened and there was an actual hole where the rescuers had chopped through to douse the fire in the attic. Now, hours later, dark streaks marred the outside of the charming inn and the yard was a maze of troughs cut into the mud before the dry ground sucked away the water from the hoses. He did not know what had become of Lovely, but he kept a wary lookout.

Lucy and her mother had been moved in with Fran Trawler for the evening and Manny was bunking with Kelby. It was well on towards nine o'clock and Alexi still stood guard over the piano. He'd borrowed some tarps from the fire personnel and made arrangements for a hauling truck which he intended to drive personally. He wondered if Phil Zimmerman might have a book about the finer points of truck driving, but he dared not leave his post to ask. So, he sat on the rusted chair, sipping the bitter coffee that Meg had brought him, listening to the sounds of the bullfrogs which Lucy had told him were responsible for the throaty din that started up at sundown.

He tried to pick out a melody in their croaking song. The odd syncopation was in no way discernible music, but he found himself lulled by it, his foot tapping in time to the amphibian orchestra. Moths danced around the porch light and the stars began to appear as dusk gave way to evening. So engrossed was he in searching for the Milky Way that he almost didn't hear Lucy's approach. He bolted upright.

"Hello, Lucy."

She wiggled her fingers but didn't exactly look at him. He dragged another chair over and held it while she sat down. He could see by the light of the camping lantern Trooper had loaned him, that her face was tear-stained, eyes puffy.

He recalled the wild beating of her heart against his chest, her sobs muffled by his damp shirt front. Unpleasant, it should have been and was, the untidy, uncontrolled venting of her grief. But he'd been so very glad, so very grateful that he'd been the one to receive it.

He'd seen some sappy movies about a man and a woman sharing moments of intense emotion, and he'd always thought them quite undesirable. Inexplicably, Lucy's words came back to him.

Perfection ruins the soul.

Lucy was far from the perfect billboard model now, downcast, overwhelmed by grief, a twig twined in her hair that he thought it impolite to mention. Imperfect, but her soul, he fancied, was a shining, lustrous gold.

He cleared his throat. "How is your mother?"

"She's confused. She keeps asking for my father if you can imagine. Something about the trauma must have triggered it."

"And Lovely?"

"He's in Uncle Paul's backyard. They borrowed a kiddie pool from the neighbor and fenced off Aunt Libby's roses, so he's cranky but safe."

"Sensible."

Lucy rubbed a hand under her nose as her gaze locked on the ruined roof of the inn. "What am I going to do, Alexi? Our fire insurance is minimal. There's no way to pay for these repairs."

"Yes, there is."

She stared at him, the porch light making her skin marble smooth, perhaps like the Hope angel had looked like once a long time ago.

He wanted to draw out the moment. "It is a seven-letter word."

"I'm too tired for puzzles, Alexi. Please."

She looked so defeated, he took her hand in his, the fingers cold, his own shriveled grip transferring his warmth to her. "Fazioli. To be specific, his grand instrument."

She cocked her head.

"The piano." He nodded to the shrouded instrument behind them. "Your piano."

Her eyes went wide. "You are not trying to say that old relic is Fazioli's Grand Piano?"

"No, not the Grand itself, but it is a Fazioli. The tone struck me when I heard Manny play it, the deeper base, the mellower signature sound, but it took me a while to realize the truth. Your piano, this piano, is an early Fazioli, one made during his experimental phase."

It appeared she had lost the ability to speak so he added, "It is worth in the six-figure range."

A tremor went through her. "The...six-figure range?"

"Yes."

"As in six numbers after the dollar sign?"

"Yes."

"Even for a prototype?"

"Especially for a prototype. It is a one of a kind." Like

you, he wanted to add.

"Six figures?" A glaze of wonder crept over her face. "But that would replace the roof, and the staircase and redo the Lady Quail from top to bottom. We could...we could reopen. We could be a working hotel like my mother imagines we are. Six figures would do that, wouldn't it?"

He considered. "I believe it would. The Fazioli would fetch a great price, especially allowing for the inclusion of its fourth pedal. This brings the hammers closer to the strings, you see, decreasing the volume while maintaining a normal tone, functioning like…"

She put a hand on his cheek. "Alexi?"

"Yes?"

"Would it be okay if I kissed you?"

His heart hammered against his ribs. Kiss? Him? Her? Together? Lips touching? His thoughts fired in such wild disarray he could not manage anything more than a nod.

She threw her arms around his neck and kissed him on the lips, the soft light bathing them both, the bullfrog chorus drifting across the old front porch. It was almost like music. Only better.

***

The day after the fire, the town was abuzz. Everyone had a detail to add to the story and Alvin Wong scurried around with his notebook and camera, glee written all over him.

The Helping Hands committee had convened under the shade of the elm in front of the still closed church, scribbling on clipboards and jotting down notes of who was to help with meals for Mrs. Winston, visitation schedules, who had a room to offer Lucy and which stalwart folks might help tend to Lovely and keep his kiddie pool clean. Trooper lingered in the shade long enough to fill his pockets with pretzels and cheese sandwiches from the snack arrangement. He missed being under observation by Fran Trawler's sharp eye.

She'd disappeared from Honey Creek life since the Trudy bombshell was dropped. Trooper had not been present when she'd evicted the girl, tossing her bag onto the front lawn and slamming the door. He'd not witnessed her rage firsthand, but the gossip wheels had churned the news back to him in sordid detail.

"You won't stay under my roof. Not for one minute longer."

Pockets straining and a couple of pretzels in his mouth, he slunk away from the church and headed to Fran's again like he'd done every day since the blowup. Trooper had knocked on her door, which she'd ignored. Pastor Paul had visited, he knew, with no response. Even the fire hadn't drawn her from her house.

Trooper parked himself on the sidewalk. Gummy snored on the strip of grass next to him. He munched away until all of his pretzels were gone, and he heard movement from her back yard. Leaving Gummy to snooze, he walked to the gate. It was unlatched so he let himself in.

Fran was muttering to herself pacing tight circles in her yard. Her hair was straggly, hanging alongside her face, untouched by makeup, eyes deeply shadowed as if she hadn't slept in a while. Every so often she'd jam a tissue to her nose before thrusting it back into her pocket again.

It was not a scene he, nor anyone, was meant to witness, but he'd stepped too far into the yard to escape without her noticing. The sun was intense, and Trooper was sweating, but Fran did not seem to feel the heat.

She made her way to a patch of yard, arms held around her middle as if she'd got a pain there. He was about to clear his throat, to let her know he'd invaded her privacy and wait for the backlash when she suddenly grabbed a potted plant and threw it onto the immaculately kept patio. The terracotta shattered, red geraniums scattering like sprays of blood. He was so shocked he did not make a sound at first.

"Why...why should she have one?" She broke another pot, eyes burning with rage. "Why should the hussy, the tramp..." she spat the word as if it was profane.

Tears streamed down her face, and her blouse hung askew since she had not buttoned it properly. She seized another pot, dashing it to the cement as well. Then with a choking sob, she staggered to the far end of the garden and threw herself on her knees in front of three small stone crosses that he had not noticed before.

The muscles in the bottom of his stomach tightened. Breath held, he remembered what he'd heard about Fran when he first returned to Honey Creek some decades before, a bum whom nobody recognized. He was a coward, unable to shoulder his own identity, his own part in the death of the two people who meant everything to him. So, he'd drifted through life in Honey Creek, hearing all the rumors, all the gossip.

Three...the women at the diner had whispered.

Imagine losing three.

Moe walked out on her.

There was nothing to keep him, after all. Went on to another wife and they had six children.

He knew the answer to Fran's unspoken question. "*Why should Trudy, the child, have babies when I could not?*" Why would the exquisite gift of life be given in so haphazard a manner to one who did not even desire it? In Fran's mind, did not deserve it?

And what was the answer to that? Trooper puzzled as Fran cried. Why should God see fit to saddle a poor desperate teenage girl with a gift that Fran had pined for, coveted, no doubt prayed for with every atom of her being?

He could not fathom it, any more than he grasped why

he had been granted the gift of marriage and fatherhood and stripped of it in one tragic moment. It had nothing to do with desire, worth, the earning of it. Fran's tears turned into gasping gulps that left her face mottled, nose streaming. Anguish, pure and simple. Still, no words of comfort came to Trooper's mind.

All he knew was the only thing more powerful than the love for a child was the bitterness that could poison a soul from the inside out if it was allowed to.

She looked up at that moment, tears staining a face so riddled with pain she did not even register shock at seeing him. On her knees, she brushed the grass that grew under the memorials to the babies she'd never held, fingers trailing lovingly through the fringe of green.

"Why should she have a baby?" Fran whispered.

He took a deep breath and knelt next to her, knees creaking.

"I'm no expert on these things, but I think Pastor Paul would say it's an answer only God can give," was the only thing he could think of to say.

She crumpled then, crying softly. "But He didn't let me keep mine."

He swallowed. "Me neither. Kinda figured that's because I never deserved 'em in the first place, but I know you did."

Her bloodshot eyes widened, head titled slightly to the side, looking at him as though she'd never seen him before.

"You would have been a great mother, Fran. I can see it in the way you tended to Trudy."

Her gaze held his for a moment and then shame crept in. "No. I...I threw her out. Not because of what she'd done." Fran gulped. "Because she has something I wanted so badly, and I couldn't stand seeing her have it when I couldn't. That's the truth." Her lips trembled. "What kind of mother would I have been, Trooper? What kind of woman does that?"

He reached out slowly and took her hand. She jerked for a moment but let him hold on. "The kind of woman that's been hurt. And Pastor Paul would say the kind that's forgiven."

She was silent for a long moment, studying the three little crosses and clutching his hand. Slowly she got up and went to the compost bin, raising the wooden lid and drawing out the half head of the angel.

He climbed to his feet, giving himself a moment to process the shock. "You took the angel's head from the church?"

Her cheeks flooded with color. "I didn't want them to spend the money repairing the angel when they couldn't even afford decent robes, so I took it." The words started out sputtering, but now they flowed like a river where the dam has failed. "I still can't believe I actually did it. First, I buried it under the rhododendron, but Gummy dug it up part of it. I put what's left in here." He saw her throat moving as she swallowed. "I wanted to take it back to the church almost as soon as I'd done it, but it was too late." She sighed, long and slow like the sound of the winter wind, long before the promise of spring.

"I'm...I'm so ashamed. If anyone knew...if they found out..."

He moved, reached, took the angel's head, and at the same time gripped her hand again and caught her wild eyes with his own.

"I will take care of it," he said quietly. "No one will ever know."

"Why? Why would you do that? I've done something terrible, many things." A sob choked off her words. "And we're not...I mean...I treat you..."

He smiled, still gripping her hand. "Don't you worry. I

think it's time for me to take care of a few things."

"But...how?"

He gave her fingers a squeeze. "Got me a plan. I'll see to it right after I go fishing."

Chapter Twenty-Six

Alexi lay awake, listening to the sounds of the city on his cassette tape. They did not soothe him, the blood beat hard in his veins. Perhaps it was the excitement of the last few days wheeling through his body. The Fazioli had been carefully packed up after an initial appraisal and sent to New York for a thorough cleaning. Denny promised to make all due haste to the shop to tune it before it was shipped to auction. He'd need to tune it again, of course. Tuning was like living, he thought, it required constant tinkering and adjustment. Alexi was skilled at neither which perhaps explained the sleeplessness.

Honey Creek had stirred invisible parts of his soul.

He got up and roamed the confines of the trailer.

How long would he stay here? Writing crossword puzzles in a backwater town with front porches and odd people and strange unavoidable residents and croaking frogs all night? He'd saved his meager salary, but it was not enough yet. Still, he could perhaps find another place to stay since Alvin explained he could write the puzzles anywhere and mail them to the Holler. It was an enticing thought, to escape to a place where he could live anonymously, quietly. Where? Home? Not New York City anymore. Not where his mother lived with her sister.

He was unmoored, untethered. Walking to the window he gazed out into the night and thought of Lucy. So impulsive and clumsy. So beautiful and connected to people in ways he could never be. Connected to him and he to her. Nonsensical.

What was a word that could describe an illogical, inconvenient connection like that?

Love.

Four letters that made him stagger with their invisible weight. Pacing did not dissipate the feeling, though he applied himself to it for a while. He thought about taking a walk, but there were so many living things in Honey Creek, so many social navigations that tested him.

Love.

Adoration, affection, passion. Emotions he had only ever felt for his music. But that had been a passion he could control, manipulate, and measure out in precise beats and rhythms. This type of love was an altogether different animal.

He swallowed hard but inside he understood it was the truth and it dissolved a wall inside he had not known he'd built. His feet took him to Denny's piano. In a trance-like state, he imagined he was once again the pianist he had been. Forcing his bad hand onto the keyboard along with the good one, he played a few bars of a Mozart concerto. His ears told him the verdict, poor, technically flawed, he would never play again like he had before. That perfect love was gone.

"So, you would rather live every day without the one thing you love rather than play imperfect music?"

Yes, it was so when he'd said it to Lucy before, and the same now. It was the truth. He did not want imperfection. He did not want this kind of love.

He trailed his fingers along the keys, the sound dissonant, imperfect, clattering in his ears. Playing music in that way would be dishonest to his training, a lie his soul would have to whisper to force his hands to perform.

So, what was between a truth and a lie?

Life, he heard her say in that throaty joyful way of hers. Life.

And perhaps, even love.

A grin slowly spread across his face as he returned to his bed, this time turning off his city noises and throwing the window wide open to the night music of Honey Creek.

***

Lucy's cheeks hurt from smiling. Her brother Kelby strode around with each architect who came to bid on the Lady Quail project.

"My crew and I are doing the work, of course," Kelby said, "but we want to look into some improvements. Updating the electrical, adding an elevator, that kind of thing."

"While maintaining the history of the place," Lucy piped up, earning her a scathing look from her brother.

"I got this, sis. You go work on choosing the draperies with Mother."

She hid a smile. She'd make sure the design was everything she wanted it to be before they signed on any dotted lines, her brother's chauvinism aside.

So as not to make him feel self-conscious, she strolled across the street to the church, humming. It was a certified Honey Creek miracle that Alexi had dragged a treasure from the flames, a treasure she had not even known about. But she'd always thought if any place in the world could host a miracle, it would be in her very own wild and wacky hometown.

But it wasn't entirely a homegrown miracle, it had required the intervention of a stranger, an outsider, a socially awkward, maddeningly truthful Alexi Quinn. Thinking of him made her smile even wider.

"Uncle Paul..." She stopped short when she saw him,

flopped in the front row pew, hand on his chest. "What's wrong? Are you sick? Is it your heart?"

He shook his head, and she couldn't tell if the sound he made was a cry or a chuckle. "What is it?"

"I just can't feature it. In a million years, I never would be able to explain it."

Her pulse eased a fraction, satisfied that he was not having a heart attack. "Tell me what happened."

"I mean, after the piano Alexi found, I shouldn't be surprised, but I am. Slap me silly if I'm not."

She squeezed his arm. "What?"

The pressure seemed to rouse him. He got up from the pew, picked up a box she had not noticed lying at his feet, and handed it to her. "Go ahead. Look for yourself."

She peered into the box and almost dropped it. Their eyes met and he began to laugh.

"Yep. That was my reaction, too."

"How...who?"

"If you can figure that out, my dear, you're a better detective than Sherlock Holmes. It was sitting on the pew when I came in. I know I locked the door last night before I left, but it was open and there was the box, pretty as a perfect curveball."

They both stared into the box at the perfect, unchewed half of the Angel of Hope's head.

Lucy finally closed her mouth. "I've got to tell Alexi about this right away. He won't believe it."

"He's not the only one," Paul said.

She kissed him on his brow and raced from the church, borrowing a rusty bike from the side of the church where her uncle kept it in case of emergencies when Libby had the Gremlin.

She pedaled until her legs burned, up the hill and along the flat stretch of road where she'd first met Alexi in her search for Lovely. The astonishing return of the head was nearly as much of a shock as the discovery of the Fazioli.

She propped the bicycle against the bent elm and hurried to Alexi's door. For the second time, she stopped short. The sound of music crept along the drive, a piano, played hesitantly, but somehow sounding all the sweeter for it.

She crept closer, not wanting to wake herself if she was indeed in the grip of a dream.

"Denny's back," she said to herself.

But it was not Denny who opened the door, nor was it Alexi.

"Hi, Lucy." Manny grinned. "Did you know that I am a technically flawed and theoretically ill-trained piano player?"

"Pianist," Alexi said from the piano bench, his head bent to see her. He got up, carefully pushed in the bench seat, and came to the porch. "Hello, Lucy."

Lucy could do nothing but gape.

"I apologize for my remarks, Manny. Though true, I recognize now they may have been insensitive. Thank you for coming at my request and teaching me."

Lucy finally found her voice. "Teaching you?"

Manny winked at her. "Turns out a one-armed piano-playing handyman might have a few tricks to teach the master piano player after all."

"Pianist, not piano player," Alexi said.

Manny laughed and walked past Lucy. "Gotta get back to the inn and help Kelby clean out the yard for my flippered friend."

"Palmate," Lucy and Alexi both said at once. Manny shook his head and trundled off, to their combined laughter.

When her laughter petered away, she dashed away the tears. "Alexi, I am so proud of you."

He arched an eyebrow. "Proud of me for playing

something badly?"

"Oh yes. Exactly." She could resist no longer. She flung her arms around his neck and kissed him.

He kissed her back. "Maybe," he said, "we should sit on the porch in rocking chairs with lemonade to celebrate."

"Do you drink lemonade?"

"No."

"Have you ever sat in a rocking chair?"

"Not to my recollection."

She laughed again, the joy inside bubbling out until she saw a flicker of it in his face too. "Then we should do it right away, Alexi. Right away."

***

The woman at the bank in neighboring Chatwood regarded Trooper with a slight sniff, probably due to the leftover stew he'd eaten for breakfast that was heavy on the wild garlic. Or perhaps it was the overalls, though they had been washed not two days ago in the trickling water of Honey Creek and dried in the sunshine until they were as stiff as a new shoe.

"Need some money," he said.

She drew back a pace, hand sliding underneath the counter.

"From my account," he added quickly. "I ain't here to rob ya, for the love of tuna."

The penciled eyebrow raised. "You have an account?"

"'Course I do. Haven't been here in a dog's age but last I heard money don't have a shelf life, am I right?"

The eyebrows came down but the crease between them remained. She slid him a withdrawal slip, careful not to touch him. He filled it out and shoved it back across from her. When she saw the amount, her eyes widened.

"I'll need one moment," she said.

"Take all the time you like, sweetcakes."

Then he helped himself to a free cup of coffee with cream, filled one pocket with all the sugar packets, and sat down in the lobby to wait.

***

Pastor Paul felt every bit his age as he sat in the minuscule quarters that served as a church office. There was one swivel chair with a crackled wheel which he shared with SueAnn when she came in to print the programs or answer phones that generally speaking never rang until the world had gotten wind of his brother's treasure. From his window, he could see the scorched roof of the Lady Quail. The tang of smoke remained in the air, the smell refusing to dissipate on the Honey Creek breeze. Lucy's mom had been relocated to church member Ida's house but reports were she was not adjusting well. The doctor had prescribed a sedative which would not last nearly as long as the lingering trauma.

Lucy was bunking with her brother until repairs could be made to the inn or Nan returned. She'd finally explained in a way Paul could grasp, the narrow rescue of the rare piano and he knew it was providence. The old piano, more valuable than Thomas's stash of gold, had lain covered in ignominious fashion, an unappreciated treasure in plain sight would save the Lady Quail. A miracle, nothing less.

But the church, the little creaking mess of a place had still not been repaired to meet basic safety standards. The summer sunshine would not last forever and his parishioners simply could not attend services outside in the rain and cold that would inevitably come, though some of the stalwart saints would try. He glanced through the door, up at the spot where the Hope Angel should be. At the moment, she was propped up on the floor next to a supply of paper towels, her recovered half head nestled in a bag with the chewed-up half. What was to be done about that? No secret treasure to restore her, no miraculous windfall.

The weight of it drew his head down to the cluttered desk and he pressed his forehead to the pile of sample fabric swatches Fran had previously provided in an effort o push for new robes, a project which was even more out of reach than ever. Temples throbbing, he considered rifling the desk drawers in search of a stray aspirin when Jacqueline, the church organist, plowed through the door with SueAnn just behind her.

"*Je suis supris*," she said in French. Before he could get a word out, she launched into another excited avalanche of syllables.

He held up his hands. "Slower and in English. One language is all I can manage."

SueAnn crowded closer, holding a battered offering basket as if it was the Holy Grail. "She's trying to tell you what happened when we were counting the collection."

"Uh oh," he said, heart throbbing along with his head. "No more bad news, please. We collected enough to keep the lights on, right? At least that much?" There was still nowhere near enough to repair the ceiling and brace the angel properly. He could not ask Lucy to divert any of her windfall from the inn. No every penny of her treasure must go to that. The church would survive another way. He swallowed hard thinking about the parishioners who depended on the meager funds squeaked from the offering for urgent needs. What of them? What of Trudy who would need so very many things for her baby? At the moment she was still staying with him due to Fran's unfortunate reaction.

But Jacqueline was rattling away, slipping in bits of French among the English like a pitcher inserting off-speed pitches amongst the fastballs.

"*L'argent*," she said with emphasis.

"I'm sorry, I still don't understand."

SueAnn reached into the basket and shoved a stack of

bills nearly under his nose. "Just look at this."

He gaped.

"This is five thousand dollars," she said.

His mouth fell open and he might have staggered. "Where…what…where did that come from?" Had Mr. Needles reconsidered? Had he had his own reckoning of sorts?

SueAnn waved the money right in front of his nose to break the spell. He took it. "It was someone in service this morning, it had to be. I've had the basket all morning, never left my sight."

Then it could not have been Mr. Needles. But who? He held up the bills. "Who in world…?" He turned the stack of money this way and that, the crisp clean bills giving off the faintest scent of…fish. Gently he put the money back in the basket, closed his eyes, and smiled.

"Do you know who did this?" SueAnn demanded. "We have to thank them, make a plaque, put an article in the paper, something."

He thought of Trooper heckling him from under the brim of his infernal Dodger's cap. "No. This is an anonymous donation and that's how it will stay."

Both women looked at each other and then at him.

"Well, what are we going to do with all that money?" SueAnn said.

"We're gonna put Hope back where she belongs, right after we give her some surgery." He hadn't yet told them of the mysterious return of the head. He handed the money to SueAnn. "Let's deposit this right away and call Kelby. Then we'll figure out who can give Hope a new face."

He left the woman gabbling away and stepped outside, breathing in the perfect sunshine of a Honey Creek afternoon.

Author Bio: Dana's Bio: Dana Mentink is a two time American Christian Fiction Writers Carol Award winner, a Romantic Times Reviewer's Choice Award and a Holt Medallion winner. She is the Publisher's Weekly bestselling author of over forty titles in the suspense and lighthearted romance genres. She is pleased to write for Harlequin's Love Inspired Suspense, Harvest House, and Poisoned Pen Press. You can connect with Dana via her website at danamentink.com, on YouTube (Author Dana Mentink) and Instagram (dana_mentink.) Dana hosts a private Facebook reader group chock full of fun, freebies, prayers and fellowship. If you'd like to join, send her a private message on FB and she will send you an invite.

Website: www.danamentink.com
Facebook: https://www.facebook.com/dana.mentink
Twitter: @danamentink
You Tube Channel https://youtu.be/GW6d8JKY_-I
Amazon Author Page: https://www.amazon.com/Dana-Mentink/e/B001JRXHXK/ref=sr_tc_2_0?qid=1540739147&sr=8-2-ent
Instagram: dana_mentink
https://www.bookbub.com/profile/dana-mentink

www.ingramcontent.com/pod-product-compliance
Lightning Source LLC
LaVergne TN
LVHW010314070526
838199LV00065B/5561